My Son,
Your Son

Bassey Ubong

Order this book online at www.trafford.com
or email orders@trafford.com

Most Trafford titles are also available at major online book retailers.

Printed in the United States of America.

ISBN: 978-1-4669-5421-2 (sc)
ISBN: 978-1-4669-5423-6 (hc)
ISBN: 978-1-4669-5422-9 (e)

Library of Congress Control Number: 2012915218

Trafford rev. 08/25/2012

 www.trafford.com

North America & international
toll-free: 1 888 232 4444 (USA & Canada)
phone: 250 383 6864 ♦ fax: 812 355 4082

Also by Bassey Ubong

Children Books:
Butty and the Mosquito (Science Fiction)
Hippo & Other Poems (Poetry)
The Cunning Tortoise (Fables)
The Boy Who Was Wiser than the King (Fable)

Poetry:
Perils
The Hurricane Lamp

Prose:
Islands of Goodness (Novel)
The Wise Elders (Fables)

Drama:
Freeworld Square
Esemsem
By Any Means
Queen Asaari
Entangled Lives
The Gods Are Sharp Shooters!
Zero-Sum Game
Compromises
Lovelorn
Don & Flora
Usomini (BoomTown Inc.)
Season of Plots
Praise the Lord . . .
Say Yes!
My Mercedes Is Bigger than Yours

Dedicated to the memory of my father,
Elder A. B. Ubong,
my greatest source of inspiration on earth.

The author is grateful to God for life, intellect, inspiration, stamina, and wherewithal. He is also grateful to Isaac Thomas, Friday Okon, Mary, Ekwuere Utuk, Dr. Joseph Ushie, Richard Rudholm, Inyang Ubong, and Iniabasi Ubong for their various contributions. And to you, dear reader, if you find this book worth the time you have spent reading it.

*Some uncommon words and some vernacular words are explained in the glossary at the end of the book

BOOK I

Chapter 1

On her way back from the stream on a bright Saturday morning, Ekam had hit her right foot on a piece of stick buried in the ground with just a tiny portion jutting out. It was not painful, but it set in motion a trend of thought in her. Earlier, on her way to the stream, she had felt this rapid movement of her upper right eyelid, sometimes making it almost curve up and remain that way. The hitting of her right foot and the pulsating upper eyelid were positive signs. What was it that was waiting for her at home? Could some good fortune—unexpected—smile on her? Could anybody, anything, or, for that matter, God himself, suddenly change the course of her life? Ekam could not answer the questions. She, however, remained hopeful throughout the distance of about one and a half kilometers from the stream.

There was actually no doubt that something was about to happen. All through her walk to the stream, her heart had been singing. In fact, she woke up that morning with a song in her heart and on her lips. She had felt like dancing or running all the way to and from the stream. She had even prayed that the sun would come up earlier than usual so that she could pull off her dress to allow her naked frame to absorb the early-morning sunshine. Her age mates that had been to high school told her early-morning sunshine contains something they call "chemical" that is good for the skin, nay, the body generally.

Ekam's thoughts on her way home as on her way to the stream could not be interrupted by the greetings of children and peers. Even elders appeared to not be on that same road. She had walked briskly, her head tilted upward with a half smile playing on her lips.

"Perhaps she is to be married today," one woman had mused.

"*Ah*, not these days. She is too young to be married," another interjected.

"Says who? Children of today, can you contain them? Before they stop sucking their mothers' breasts, they have become mothers themselves!"

At the stream, nothing, usual or unusual, could distract her attention from reveling in her internal warmth. Even one man, who suddenly rushed into the stream holding his sagging manhood within his left palm, did not make any difference to her. After all, that was what men normally did—they would stand a little far off, wait for the attention of the women to shift away from them, throw off their clothes, and rush into the water. Women walked in, except the young and brash ones. Women tied loincloths just above their breasts while going in for a bath, surfacing shortly after with the loincloth clinging tightly to their bodies, revealing more than necessary, giving the men enough to look at, to think about, and to scratch their heads later on. She did not spare much time for those things.

Surprisingly, the music of the stream environment failed to arrest her attention. Ekam was fond of spending time to listen to the music of nature. She always believed that there was hardly anywhere else in the world other than the village stream where nature seemed to be at such ease, singing so coyly, yet so forcefully, melodies that soothe the soul. The gentle lapping of the very gentle waves of the stream on the banks, tree stumps, and human bodies combine perfectly with the chirping of birds and insects, the croaking of frogs, and the intermittent plunge of fishes to produce some kind of music that only few can appreciate. It was melody at its eternal best. Only human beings disturbed such symphony, ostensibly to fetch water, to wash clothes, and to bathe. Interestingly, the water remained perpetually clean despite the disturbing activities of human beings by way of dumping of wastes as they bathe, wash several things, and even empty their bowels.

The only thing that momentarily caught her attention that day at the stream was the scream from one girl. She had seen a snake. Snakes move very fast in water, much faster than any man could hope to swim, probably much faster than they are on land. The stream had emptied, with the real men clustering at the banks with knives and sticks at the ready. Yes, real men. For the sissies, the boys, and the pansies had scurried out of the water even before the women. The danger was declared over by the men, after the snake had crawled into the nearby bush, and activities resumed at normal tempo as if nothing had happened. After this, Ekam had taken her bath, fetched water, and dressed up.

*   *   *

Lifting a pot filled with water onto one's head could be exciting to watch for the onlooker, while it is taxing for the person carrying out the exercise. The approach could determine whether the pot reached home or was broken right there or at the hill or on the way home. Many people get a kick just watching young girls in particular struggle with pots and then see the pots fall to the ground and break into pieces, eliciting tears from the victims and catcalls from onlookers. The act of lifting a pot filled with water onto one's head is virtually like a weight lifting exercise.

The first thing is that a piece of cloth is wound in the form of a circle such that the pointed base of the waterpot fits into it. The pad of cloth is then put on the head of the carrier. From an eye survey, any adept could determine whether a prospective carrier would be able to bear the weight of the waterpot from the ground onto the head. If the person insisted that he or she would lift the burden, onlookers would allow him or her to do so. However, the wise ones would call people to assist in lifting the pot, which could be one made from clay or a dried member of the cucumber family. People who assisted in lifting pots sometimes ended up getting themselves wet, either through the deliberate action of spilling water by those helped or by accident.

When the bearer decides that he or she is strong enough to lift the pot, the process commences by proper placement of the two feet. The right hand is put into the "mouth" of the pot, holding the knoblike top. The understanding being that the potter had made the knob strong enough to carry the weight of the quantity of water the pot is designed to carry. Interestingly, even without the benefit of scientific equipment, the pots carry the expected weights. Local potters apparently function on the basis of years of experience. When the carrier is convinced that the knob would not crack, the left hand is placed under the pot for the lifting exercise. As the pot is usually wet, there is no need for use of spittle to wet the palms.

Depending on the weight of the pot, a snatch is effected, lifting the pot off the ground first onto the left knee. At this point, a wise and smart person should be able to determine whether he or she can successfully complete the exercise of putting the pot on the head.

Despite catcalls, a smart person would decide on the path of prudence by putting down the pot or calling for assistance so as to save the pot.

The next step is to lift the pot from the knee, bend the body backward slightly, shifting the left hand along the side of the pot to a point convenient enough to carry the weight as well as to allow the pot to be placed properly on the pad. When the pot is put on the head, it is shifted around till it becomes comfortable and sits on the pad. The exercise is completed when the hands are removed from the pot to see if it can stand on its own. The bearer then dusts off sand particles and laughs at those who were waiting to laugh at an unsuccessful exercise. Where the pot falls down and is broken, the jeers could be deafening.

Ekam was one of those who would not tolerate jeers and boos. Her approach was to go to the stream with a pot that she could lift without assistance. As a matter fact, she preferred carrying a metal pail that her father used for his bath. Her reason for preferring the pail was that earthen pots were rather provincial or "local." On that day, however, she did not worry about public opinion despite the fact that the container on her head was a clay pot, since it was her happy day.

On this particular morning, the girl's only problem was how to scale the hill that led to and from the stream. The hill was fairly steep and had notches made thereon through millennia of use by human feet. Some of the depressions were for tiny feet, while some were wide enough to contain the feet of an elephant. All the same, the hill was the most unappetizing part of the daily chore of going to the stream. As was the case with other children, Ekam always wondered why elders never thought of cutting the hill so that it could become flat ground or at least reduce the steepness. Rather, the hill that had certainly been there for centuries remained so—forbiddingly steep. Children grew up, used it, became adults, continued to use it, had children who used it, and then died and left it the way they met it.

"If only I could have my way, there are a lot of changes I would make in this village. If only . . . ," she had thought as she labored up the steep hill on her way home.

*　　*　　*

Ekam's family house had a long stretch of space between it and the road, the type that people say one has to eat before sweeping. She could nonetheless notice from the road that something unusual was happening. There was a motorbike standing outside. Two bicycles were also there. And a motorcar! A motorcar in her father's compound! That it was an old Peugeot 403 saloon made no difference. The car must have seen the bad roads of the area for more than one decade. The Peugeot 403 was an old warhorse. It almost lived forever. As Ekam came closer, she

7

remembered the song in her heart on her way to the stream. And of course, she had hit her right foot, and her eyelids had done a dance. She wondered whether what lay ahead had to do with those telltale signs. Probably.

"Welcome, my daughter," Ekam's uncle greeted.

"Good morning, Nte," the girl replied.

"You were very fast today. Did the stream move closer?"

"No, Nte," she replied.

"Maybe she had a hunch," was her father's response.

"A hunch about what?" Ekam thought to herself.

"Just before you arrived, I had said that if I were around when you left, I would have spat on the ground," the uncle said.

"I am sure she would have arrived before the spittle dried," a man said in a baritone voice, the person that turned out to be the owner of the car.

Ekam sized the small gathering, the waterpot still on her head. She felt slightly dizzy just looking at the men. The pot started swaying gently such that she did a little dance before she could control it.

"Go behind and put down that pot," her father ordered.

"If it drops here, you know that is an abomination. It would not be the best thing to happen today of all days," her uncle said.

Ekam went to the backyard where the kitchen was located. It was now time for the second tricky part of fetching water from the stream, which is putting the waterpot down such that both water and pot remained intact. The exercise had its own unwritten rules, which if not obeyed, led to broken pots, spilled water, tons of tears, and abuses from family members.

Spitting on her palms, Ekam slightly parted her legs, put the right hand into the mouth of the pot, and, with the left palm at the base, heaved the pot upward, then forward, and, bending her knee slightly forward, placed the pot on the left knee, pushed back her buttocks, and gently landed the pot on the soft earth. She then turned her head to the right, to the left, bent her frame forward and then backward, and, with an "*ooh*," drew a low wooden stool and sat down heavily. The trip to the stream was a success.

"One would think you have just finished breaking stones," her mother said offhandedly.

"Or cleared a virgin forest," her sister, Adiaha, added. Both were busy on some domestic chore at the backyard when Ekam arrived.

"That pot is heavy. That distance is long. And the hill!" Ekam said.

"The pot no one had carried before. The distance no one had covered before. The hill no one had climbed before," Adiaha interjected.

"*Ah*, what has brought these hard words on me this morning? Please don't spoil my day," Ekam said, turned away from the ladies, brought her legs together, and crossed her hands a little below her knees.

"That is your elder sister-o," her mother cautioned.

"I thought someone would tell me the reason for that gathering outside. I did not expect anger when I have not committed any offense."

"It is about you. Who else?" Adiaha said angrily.

"What is biting you anyway?" Ekam reacted.

"What is biting me? An ant. A bee. A bug. You are always making things happen. Don't you?"

"Mama, what have I done again?" Ekam asked her mother.

"Enough of this, the two of you. You do not need to confirm men's belief that where two or three women gather, there must be a quarrel. By the way, Ekam, you should be ready to travel."

"To?" Ekam asked, jumping up.

"Let her finish," Adiaha shouted.

"One dies when one is anxious. Where am I going?" Ekam asked.

"Where you have always wanted to," her mother answered.

"Where?"

"The city of course?" Adiaha replied with some bitterness and jealousy noticeable in her voice.

9

Ekam stepped outside the kitchen, placed her hands on her waist, stood on her toes, and started what could be regarded as a choreographer's delight. This was one girl that was good at almost anything. She sang, danced, jumped, and gyrated. One of her songs, created spontaneously in vernacular, which translated went thus:

> At last—
> Dreamer's dream
> Believer's belief
> When a dreamer believes
> The dream comes alive.
> Dear city, you have always
> Beckoned on your own
> To you I belong
> To me you belong
> Here I come;
> Open your palms wide
> And accept one of your own.

"This one—I hope you will remember that you had a mother in a village far away from the bright lights. Of course, you simply cannot remember an elder sister," Adiaha said.

"Let me get there first."

Ekam continued to sing and dance till her father's voice boomed.

"Ekam!"

"Yes, Papa."

"Bring yourself here."

"Yes, Papa."

"Whoever is your mother should come with you."

"Yes, Papa."

"While there was laughter outside at what had just been said," Ekam added.

"Whoever is Ekam's mother should go with her."

"That is a child you carried for nine months inside you," Adiaha said. To which Ekam responded with a popular primary school song:

> Some people jealous me
> Some people jealous me
> Some people jealous me
> Because of my beauty
> I will not mind them
> I will not fear them
> I will not mind them
> Because of my beauty.

"Move outside, daughter of a snake!" her mother said.

"As long as the world knows who the snake is."

The woman picked a piece of firewood. Ekam ran and appeared outside. She hid by the sidewall while her mother stood by the door. Her sister refused to appear though she positioned herself such that she could hear all that would be said.

"The two of you, bring yourselves out here," Ekam's father barked.

Ekam inched forward slightly, stood near her uncle, looked downward, and commenced map reading on the ground. Her mother gingerly sat at the edge of the bamboo chair near her husband. Clearing his throat, Ekam's uncle commenced.

"*Eh*, our visitors, I greet you all. The purpose of your visit is good. We salute you, but we cannot say we agree with you till we hear from the girl. Let the person concerned speak for herself. Each mouth, a prayer." There was silence.

"Ekam, you see this man?"

"Yes, Nte."

"How do you see him when your eyes have made a covenant with the ground? I say, do you see this man?"

Ekam kept quiet. Her heartbeat had increased so suddenly and violently that she almost ceased to breathe.

"Could this balding man be here to marry me?" she thought to herself, alarmed. Her thoughts raced. "How do I face this one? Where will my dream of marrying a handsome young man with a car go? How do I face my peers? Only a month ago, my mate, Nko married a city man who could not be more than ten years older than her. Nko should be sixteen or thereabout, not too young to marry though old enough to be a wife or mother. Here I am, face-to-face with a man who cannot claim to be younger than my father. Here—" Her thoughts were broken by her uncle's angry words.

"I am talking to you. Look, if this is how you will behave in someone's house I think we better stop before we start."

"She is only a child," Ekam's mother said meekly.

"Who asked you, woman? This is how you spoil your children. A child does something wrong; instead of correcting her, you say she is only a child. Is this head on my shoulders not that from my childhood? When rain starts as a shower, the rainmaker does not spit. When it becomes heavy, he dances around like a bee. This girl is a woman. She may know more than you do. Anyway, Ekam, as I had said, will you go with this man?"

"As what?" she asked.

"Whaat!" chorused the men.

"Did I not say it?" Ekam's uncle exclaimed. "Give way to children, what do they become? Beasts! Whoever answered more than 'yes, yes' to anything in the days of our fathers? Count yourself lucky. I would have sold you to a slave trader if this were that time. Asking elders a question in response to a question! God forbid." He swung his right hand round his head, then with the forefinger and the index finger produced a sound to emphasize his dissociation and displeasure at what had just been said by the girl.

"I agree with mama that she is only a child," said the visitor. "In any case, I think this is better. I don't like children that are dull. I can't stand children that behave like sheep. I like bright and active children."

"Well, the snail wanted mucus. See what mucus has done to it! If the victim of hernia does not complain of pain, I can't see why his neighbor should say he had a sleepless night," the uncle said and shrugged.

"*Eh*, my daughter," said Ekam's father, "this man is here to take you to his house as househelp."

"I now understand," she said, heaving a big sigh of relief.

"What were you thinking of? That you are going as a wife?" the uncle asked.

"It is possible," said Ekam's mother. "These days, men's greed is such that househelps end up as housewives."

"I think I better go home," Ekam's uncle said and stood up. The face of Ekam's father became contorted in anger. He clenched and unclenched his fists several times.

"Please sit down, Nte. I did not mean to annoy you," the woman pleaded.

"But you have! And seriously too. How much longer can I stand these insults? On elders. On men. On me. First from a child then from a woman?"

"What she said makes sense, anyway," said the visitor. "I am certainly not in that group but many men in the city bring themselves down too much in this man-woman business. In fact, my neighbor did it just over a year ago. His marriage broke down. Even a prominent man in this state did the same thing. It is unfortunately common."

"I hope your marriage will be safe," Ekam's uncle observed.

"Very. Very. It only needs self-control, a decision not to fall to temptation. Besides, this is only a child."

"*Ah*, the way they grow when they start drinking cow milk and eating tinned foods. Today my brother's daughter is bare-chested. Six months from now, you may be looking for bags to hold the big balls on her chest."

"Nte, you are talking about my daughter," Ekam's mother protested.

"No harm, no harm, I only spoke the truth."

"Did the girl agree to go with me?" the visitor asked

13

"Ekam, do you?" The uncle asked the girl who still looked confused.

"Where?"

"There she goes again!"

"Calabar. Do you know the place?" the visitor asked.

"Calabar! Do I know it?" Ekam thought to herself. "I have not been there, but I have heard of it. I have seen it in my mind's eye," she mused. She recalled that one of her friends who stays at Calabar gave her a graphic description of the *Canaan City*—the beach, the fine buildings, the lights, the life, everything. Living in Calabar had been her dream. Though others dreamt of going abroad, she was content to dream of going to Calabar.

"Ekam has never left this village," said the uncle

"*Ah ha*, Nte, she has stayed with two relations before," the mother said.

"Where?"

"In other villages."

"For how long?"

"A few weeks."

"Weeks! Look, Calabar is not Obo Atai or Afia Nsit Udua Nkọ or even Uyo for that matter. Those places are close enough even for a five-year-old to trek back to her father's house. Where she is about to visit, she must cross rivers to get back home."

"Ekam, would you go with me?" the man inquired again.

"Yes, sir."

"Good."

"Now let us discuss the terms," Ekam's uncle said. The discussions that followed floated over and above the girl's head. She did not care. She did not participate. Whether she was sold was of no consequence. What was important was that she was on her way to Calabar. Simple and full stop.

Chapter 2

One look at Ekam on the morning of her departure to Calabar left no one in doubt as to the fact that she had not slept the night before. Perhaps the one before that too. Her eyes were very red, and the lids were swollen. The situation was accentuated by the fact that she was fair-skinned. Her face looked puffed.

"One would think you have just lost a precious child," her mother said.

"I wonder what would happen if she were going to the white man's country," Adiaha added.

"She would not sleep for one whole week," the mother said.

"Perhaps more," Adiaha came in again.

Ekam made no comment. She simply carried her waterpot and left for the stream.

"This may be my last trip to the stream, one duty I dislike," she said softly to herself. "Except that it gives me the opportunity to meet my friends where my parents or teachers or pastor would not see—and hear," she conceded.

At the stream, she hurried through her bath, though she spent some time throwing water on her face. The cold water did her body some good. She felt relaxed. The sleeplessness had left her tense and nervous. Her face was a better sight by the time she left the stream. People that met her on the way home were pleasantly and warmly surprised that she greeted them. As usual, she became the topic for discussion in many homes that day. If only they knew!

*   *   *

Though Mr. Etefia, the person Ekam was to travel with to Calabar, was to arrive by ten o'clock in the morning, the anxious girl was ready as early as seven o'clock, three hours ahead of schedule. She could not eat, which was understandable.

"You should eat, for the journey is a long one," her father had said.

"Don't mind her," the uncle who had come in quite early to see her off said. Ekam was one girl he openly complained about but whom everybody knew was his favorite child. The girl was very intelligent—an old head on a young shoulder—and the uncle loved her for it.

"A man tells his wife to eat before going to bed, she refuses. We shall see who will cry during the night," the uncle further said.

"*Ah*, you should not say such a thing before a child," Ekam's mother protested.

"It was not meant for everybody's understanding. I am the son of an old man," the man replied.

The hours had dragged by. From one hour to the next, the restless girl jumped at everything that passed, man and beast alike. Etefia was not in sight. Her patience was fast running out.

"A man who is expecting somebody opens his door even for a rat," the uncle said.

"I think he should better come before I change my mind," Ekam said impatiently.

This elicited laughter, for everybody knew she would wait out the day. She would gladly go with Etefia even at dusk.

"The anger of a he-goat cannot stop its sale."

"I am not a he-goat, Nte," she retorted.

"You don't have to bleat and puff or emit the smell of a he-goat to be one," the man said.

"If only this man knew that there are times when jokes are least welcome," Ekam had thought to herself. What she needed most at that time was silence, silence so that her thoughts could wander out of Oboyo to Calabar or to any other place for that matter. She was about to start her daydream when her uncle interrupted again.

"One would think that you are about to leave hell itself."

"My village is not hell. It is home," Ekam said, paused, then observed solemnly, "but it is not Calabar either."

"Calabar was once like your village. People who were born there stayed there to make it attractive."

"That is not what our teacher told us—o. Calabar was in fact developed by visitors including the white man and workers from distant lands."

"Why did those strangers not find their way here?" the uncle inquired.

"Maybe because Oboyo is not an island. The white man first went to places close to rivers and seas," Ekam replied.

"*Hm.* This thing they call education. Did your teacher say that there are no villages which are not located close to the sea in the white man's land?"

"There must be."

"So why did they not go to where there is no water?"

"They did, but they first had to reach villages close to the sea."

"Why?"

"Because water transportation was more common in those days. The first group that came—the British—was champion of the seas. So wherever they went so as to get more lands and benefit from the land and seas, they landed on villages close to water."

"I am learning," the uncle said and nodded vigorously.

"That is why your son, Bomboy, was called Mungo Park. Mungo Park discovered River Niger."

"Talking about Mungo Park, what has my son to do with that name?"

17

"They gave him that name at school because he was always boasting about the things he did at *Ine,* out local sea."

"You mean he told you of his life at the fishing village?"

"Everything, to everybody, whether you were prepared to listen or not."

"Can you imagine that? Did he tell you why he stayed there for just one fishing season?"

"He stayed for only one year? *Sai*! We thought he was born there and had spent much of his life there."

"*Ehe.* I asked you—did he tell you why he was at Ine for just one fishing season?

"He did not."

"*Isadok* in the box makes the most noise. That is a boy who could not face a single wave on his own. We (beating his chest), yes, we, the real men, could row our boats alone, without a *fadder** from Utan Bramah, battling and conquering the waves of the great water, speaking to crocodiles and to big water snakes that are longer than the palm tree you see standing there, arriving three days later at our camp, as strong as we left. Bomboy is school Mungo Park, not the real one." The small group laughed at that.

*   *   *

The discussion was terminated by the arrival on a bicycle of Etefia. He dismounted from the rear part of the bicycle as the cyclist struggled to keep it steady. He then swaggered to the porch and casually greeted the small gathering. He offered no apologies, after all he was doing the family a favor, not the other way round.

"I think we can go," he said, more as a command than a suggestion. Ekam went into the house, brought out her few belongings that consisted of a few clothes, put in a head tie, and wound tightly with a knot at the top that served as a handle. Etefia looked at the bundle with all amount of disdain but said nothing. He directed the bicycle rider to tie the bundle by the side of the bicycle. The rider objected, saying that there was no more space to put an extra load behind.

"The girl will hold it at the front," he spat out.

Ekam looked at the bicycle. The Ibibio word for bicycle when translated would mean "metal in form of a horse," which implies that a horse, a means of transportation, is the prototype for the bicycle. Since two separate words are joined, it is common for people to regard a very old and rickety bicycle as an instrument in which the horse with its grace and beauty was no more there, leaving only the metal. This was a classic case.

"And yet this man, who can only afford to hire this metal, is looking down on what I have," Ekam thought to herself.

Nor was the state of the bicycle the only thing repulsive about the man. His luggage too. A rather dirty wooden box was carefully balanced at the back of the bicycle after the "carrier," which is attached at the rear of the bicycle. To carry extra luggage, two fresh sticks were fixed onto the carrier as "extension" so that more load could be accommodated. Lighter loads were tied by the side of the bicycle, suspended close to the wheel but not too close so that parts of the load may not enter the spokes in the wheel.

The bicycle had a rod or frame situated between the cyclist's saddle and the handle bar. The rod was used to convey human beings or to suspend luggage. Generally, male riders preferred having young ladies sit there for it gave them the opportunity to rub their bodies on the ladies sitting in front and occasionally using their hand to "adjust" the ladies if they were ostensibly blocking the rider's view. Of course, the ladies themselves were fond of relaxing on the body of an admired gent as the bicycle gracefully moved on. Numerous are the ways in which humans of the opposite gender go for intimacy, irrespective of how delicate, dangerous, or petty.

On completion of the "loading" exercise, the girl was lifted and placed on the rod by her uncle. To make her trip a little less painful, her uncle had folded a piece of cloth and tied it around the rod, a cushion of sorts. The cyclist was reminded that he had to return the cloth after the trip. Ekam then placed her tiny bundle of clothes on the handle bar, holding it with the left hand while firmly clutching the handle bar with her right hand to achieve balance. After a few good-byes, prayers, and not a few tears from Ekam's mother, the cyclist proceeded on the journey.

However, before leaving, the cyclist had checked the tires visually then gauged the pressure by pressing each between two of his fingers. He rang the bell to ensure that it was still in order, checked the air pump, the bicycle license, and the lighting system. After the thorough inspection, he shook the bicycle vigorously, apparently to confirm that the loads were well tied and that the bicycle could carry the weight. Convinced that everything was in order, he shook his head vigorously in affirmation, blew his nose with one hand, pushed back the bicycle stand, and slowly pushed man and metal forward. Though Ekam was irked by the apparent waste of time, she nevertheless admired such caution. If car and motorbike owners made such daily checks on their vehicles before leaving home, the police would not be announcing higher and higher accident figures on highways. She recalled that her father always expressed dismay whenever he heard of multiple deaths following vehicular accidents on the roads. The accidents appeared to be a result of structural failures or defects that could have been corrected had someone been as careful as the cyclist.

On leaving the compound, the cyclist pushed the bicycle a little faster, put his left leg on one pedal, and propelled the bicycle forward with a little push from his right leg, which was still on the ground. When the bicycle was a little mobile on its own, he threw the right leg deftly over the carrier and sat on the saddle. Etefia gently pushed the bicycle forward with one hand and then jumped and sat heavily, generating disequilibrium such that the bicycle swerved left and right before the cyclist brought it under control.

"I thought you were an expert in this thing," Etefia had sneered.

"An expert when mature people sit on the carrier."

"Which implies that I am not mature?"

20

"If you say so."

There was no more conversation till the bicycle, going in and out of potholes, into bushes and out, finally reached the tarred road to Uyo. Each person seemed to be lost in thought; the young woman, probably thinking of the new chapter about to be opened in her life; the cyclist, probably thinking about the poor state of the instrument that gave him daily bread as well as his distance from comfortable living, and generally, a situation in which he was evidently retrogressing while others were progressing. Etefia was probably thinking about owning a car, or at least a bicycle. He might also have thought of ways of ensuring that his children do not end up doing menial jobs as he was doing, answering everybody "sir," including those who cannot wash their heels properly, just to keep a job that merely provided food twice a day and paid for one room in a crowded house for himself and his hangers-on.

The final lap of the journey to Uyo would have passed unnoticed had the driver of a seven-ton lorry not feel that the cyclist should not just rush through the rough edge of the road and use the shoulder thereof, but should actually enter the bush and stop the bicycle till the monster in steel and wood went by. Not a few abuses were exchanged between the cyclist whom the driver told, "you will die a poor man" and the driver whom the cyclist called "houseboy" repeatedly. The abuse ended when a police van appeared but not until the two exchanged spittle, which left Ekam smeared and extremely uncomfortable. The cyclist continued to mutter to himself thereafter, insisting that he was better off as he was self-employed, owned his means of livelihood, retained his dignity and integrity, and would never be fired except by an act of God.

According to the cyclist, a driver, and generally an employee, is a perpetual servant always at the mercy of his or employer. His integrity is often assailed with impunity, and he is always afraid of his job tenure. He believed that employees were always subject to the disease called high blood pressure. The cyclist's discussion with himself left Etefia and Ekam discomfited. She found it difficult to breathe because the man had an offensive mouth odor. Etefia was discomfited because the truth was being told.

Finally, the three human beings and the metal found themselves, thanks be to God, at Uyo Motor Park along Ikot Ekpene Road, a few yards after the most important landmark in Uyo—the Uyo Circus. After Etefia paid off the cyclist, Ekam heaved a sigh of relief. She stood still for a moment to allow blood to circulate through her legs. The right leg, which was pressed against the frame, was temporally paralyzed. She kicked the leg forward twice and stood with legs slightly apart. She felt that the worst part of the journey was through. It turned out, however, that the ordeal had only begun.

Chapter 3

The bus station or garage or as it is more popularly called the "motor park" is an interesting place. Commercial transport drivers, who are regarded as dropouts by the society, are expected to own the bus station. But they don't. The lords of the motor parks are in fact touts; and some of them by deft maneuvering, political sagacity, thuggery, and sometimes, "native" means could become the leaders, holding positions in the National Union of Road Transport Workers (NURTW).

On the road, while in control of the wheels, the drivers abuse the passengers at will, deciding when and where to stop, and generally, being a nuisance. At the park, they appear meek, waiting for the touts to "load" the vehicles, collect the fares, and hand to them whatever amount they feel like after deducting "gate fee," "feeding allowance," "union fee," "government levy," and what have you.

The motor park is also one place one would not remain sad, irrespective of the weight of one's problem. The drivers and touts appear to be trained professionals in the art of jesting. They take boredom out of long wait for a car to fill up.

Etefia had sat Ekam in a Peugeot 404 wagon that had seen its better days. Given the right of choice, Ekam, nay, other passengers, would not have entered the car. The bodywork gave one the impression that paint was no longer available in the market. The frame pointed upward at both ends while the middle pointed downward. The seats had lost much of their covers. The interior and exterior were covered with layers and layers of dust. The driver was evidently a dirty man, for commercial drivers usually wash their cars at the end of every workday. Ekam has to wonder whether the car would take them to the end of their journey.

The ordeal of traveling by "public transport" had started as soon Etefia and Ekam entered the station. The touts had taken their luggage at the gate of the station. They did not even know where they were going.

"Yes, Etinan? Ikot Ekpene? Abak? Opobo? Which way? Oron? Itu? Aba? Umuahia via Ikot Ekpene?"

"Oron," Etefia had announced.

"Oh yes! Calabar via Oron. My friend, this is your man," one tout announced to another.

"Thank you very much. Yes, we are almost full. You are a lucky man. How many of you?" the tout had enthused.

"Two," Etefia said.

"*Ah*, you see! The car will move immediately." Ekam had smiled to herself. So it would be this easy. They were shown the car. As was the case with some other cars at the bus station, on the roof was a small wooden board painted green with the name of the eventual destination written in white. The traveler had no say in the choice of a car. Whichever car had the "turn" to "load" must be filled before the next. The traveler's predilection had nothing to do with it. Anyone who refused stood the risk of not traveling at all, for the touts could decide that no car would carry that passenger, to teach the person a lesson for effrontery.

There were two passengers—both of them men—in the car. One sat on the front seat while the other sat close to the door on the middle seat. The man in front looked like a schoolteacher. He had a worn handbag on his lap, wore a white short-sleeved shirt with the left pocket having two biro pens, one blue, the other red. The man at the middle seat was also fairly well dressed.

In his hand was a long umbrella, the type used by old men who had worked with some white men. He looked quite serious, apparently contemplating some very severe issue. Except that the umbrella seemed out of place at the height of the dry season, Ekam took no further notice of the man.

"When will this car be full?" Etefia asked.

"Is that a question? My brother, what is this?" The tout pointed at an inscription of the door of the front seat. The inscription read, "Driver and Seven Persons."

"You met two people in the car. Two of you joined. Seven minus four equals three, that is so, my daughter," the tout concluded, looking pointedly at Ekam with considerable satisfaction. Ekam did not say anything. The man pouted his lips.

"I hope you have passed elementary six," he sneered.

"That is not your business," Etefia cut in.

"It is."

"Why?"

"Because in our tradition, children belong to everybody. So this is my child, QED."

"And so?"

"This girl is going to Calabar, isn't she?"

"Well?"

"She is fair, and she is beautiful. Worse still, she has this fine gap between two front teeth."

"*Ehe?*"

"By the time boys and men in Calabar are through with her, she will not be able to read anything."

"So?"

"It is important for her to have a basic certificate such as the First School Leaving Certificate although it can no longer secure jobs for people these days."

"Suppose she hasn't?"

"Then you better send her back. I don't mind losing one passenger."

"You must be a Good Samaritan."

"Just a sister's keeper."

25

The discussions, arguments, brawls, screams, whistling, haggling, and so forth continued for another one hour or thereabout. Then one more passenger came in.

"Two to go," Ekam thought.

"Two chances, Oron by taxi, two chances," the tout shouted. Thirty minutes later, another passenger came.

"One to go," Ekam thought.

"One chances, Oron by taxi, one chances." The girl felt that "one chances" was not acceptable grammar. She, however, kept quiet. If that would bring one more passenger then it was acceptable. Shortly afterward, another passenger announced his presence.

"At last," she thought.

"*Aha*, at last. Bring your money," the tout declared.

Etefia paid for himself and the girl. The passengers that came after Ekam and Etefia also paid. She noticed that the tout did not ask the first two passengers to pay. Others noticed too.

"Collect money from the man by the door, mister," one passenger volunteered. The man apparently feigned anger, turned, and faced the passenger.

"What is your problem? Can't you mind your business?"

"Are you sure he is traveling?" another passenger asked.

"Look, I don't want your insults. I think I better leave this car. You people do not respect elders."

"Look at you, who do you think you are deceiving?"

The man left the car and walked into a canteen close by. The man in front turned and said to Etefia, "*Oga,** you can come to the front seat if you want."

"I thought as much. So you are one of them."

The man opened the door of the car and left. Later on, Ekam found out that the man was in fact the driver of the car.

"Two chances, Oron by taxi, two chances," the tout started again. Ekam felt like crying. Hunger was gnawing at her stomach walls. She was sweating despite the fact that all doors and the boot were open.

"When will this car take off?" she wondered. She remembered that her father had told her the journey would be a long one. It took travelers more time to warm up for a trip than to make the actual trip. She also remembered her uncle's proverb. Now she was suffering in the night, assuming that is what her uncle meant as proverbs have meanings that only the mature can understand.

"Do you people realize that I am supposed to take the four o'clock ferry to Calabar?" Etefia exploded in anger.

"Why did you not leave home early?"

"Give me my money, I want to leave," one passenger protested.

"Which money? Did you give me money? If you have given me money, come and take it."

Of course, no one could. Once the fare had been paid, there was no refund. The ticket issued, which was regarded as the contract document, clearly specified that. Passengers were always in a quandary—to pay or not to pay. If you didn't pay when the demand was made, you may lose your seat particularly if there was a sudden influx of passengers. Or an angry tout could decide that you would not travel again. If you paid and there was a problem later, the money may never be refunded. Heads or tails, the passenger lost at the bus station.

Approximately one hour later, the car was eventually full. The tout counted the money several times, wetting his fingers with spittle several times. He counted the passengers as if they normally took more or less than the seven specified. Satisfied, he went to the office. There he paid the charges and emerged again, deducted his feeding allowance and handed over the balance to the hapless driver, who did his own counting, argued briefly with the tout then swearing under his breath, pocketed the money. He opened the front door of the car, sat heavily on the driver's seat, gave out a long sigh, removed the money from his pocket, and counted it again, also wetting his fingers with spittle. On being satisfied, even if grudgingly, he carefully folded the money, slotted the pack inside the sun shield of the car and then turned the key in the ignition. No sound came. He tried again. No sound came. He went out of the car, opened the bonnet, checked the oil level, put in some water, and requested someone to give some knocks to the kick-starter. There was a sound, but the car did not start. The touts closed the boot, and after some expletives directed at the driver, pushed the car. With a jerk, the engine came to life, but with a guttural sound. The driver tried to engage a gear, and after several attempts, the second gear allowed itself to be used. The car jerked forward toward the gate. On approaching the gate, the gateman raised the metal chain to stop further movement. The driver paid the gate fee and took off.

*   *   *

Ekam had a presence of mind all through the trip from Uyo to Oron. This was because of the speed with which the driver propelled the car. She was surprised that such a car was capable of such speed. Although the speedometer was no longer part of the vehicle, it was obvious that the speed was on the high side.

The driver overtook randomly even at sharp bends. Ekam concluded that the driver was reckless. He refused to listen to entreaties for care. To drown the complaints, he sang boisterously or whistled intermittently. Ekam had her heart in her mouth all through the journey. The fear on the faces of the others was obvious too.

The Uyo-Oron Road was fairly smooth. The tarring gave the color of gray, being a blend of fairly reddish gravel and tar. This color contrasted with what a friend said obtained on some new roads. The roads were said to be black. The tarring on Uyo-Oron Road was good for driving in that there was good friction. Ekam had heard of new methods of road surfacing described as "nylon tarring" on which cars sort of float. Such tarring, she was told, was not the best for worn-out tires and driving during the rainy season. Skidding was said to be commonplace.

Despite the speed, the girl did not fail to notice a few notable places and institutions. She saw Ituk Mbang, famous for its mission hospital; Okopedi, which literally translated meant "those who hear of it must pay a visit," a popular though severely underdeveloped village; and St. Vincent's Secondary School, Oti Oron, a Roman Catholic high school and one of the few secondary schools established in the former eastern region of Nigeria.

Ekam recalled that there was a point on the road she was told drivers accelerated and then let their cars "fall" like an aircraft losing altitude. The place, near a rubber plantation at Ndon Ebom, was at the knob of a hill that slid suddenly into a slope. People were known to have involuntarily passed water there. Despite her preparedness for the event, she did not notice when the driver increased speed at the base of a hill until she felt the car was going into a pit. She let out a scream to the delight of the driver while other passengers laughed mockingly. It was obvious that Ekam was a first-time traveler on that road. There was no further incident thereafter till they reached Oron, a busy port on the estuary of the Calabar River although she did not notice a signboard on a hill with the inscription Methodist Boys High School, Oron, another church sponsored and very popular high school.

On arrival at Oron, Etefia had decided that they should eat before the next ferry, although she had no appetite for food. They had reached there just as the four o'clock ferry set sail. They had to wait for the six o'clock ferry. Etefia had taken her to a restaurant, alias "bar." Though quite a dirty place, Ekam had no alternative but to eat what was presented before her—a plate of white rice and red sauce with a piece of meat. As was the case with other customers, she had to eat the rice with the right hand firmly clutching the spoon while the left hand made war with a swarm of flies. She recalled that in the village, few people could eat in such an environment. The village may lack electricity and pipe-borne water, but the people live decent lives, observing basic rules of hygiene.

Ekam barely went through half of the plate of rice. What the dish lacked in quality, it made up for in quantity. After the meal, she wondered whether to call it food or filler. She settled for the latter. What she had just ingested only filled up space.

Food, as she knew it, implies more than filling up empty space in the stomach. Food meant satisfaction to the body, the mind, and even to the feelings. The quantity was not of much consequence. A full meal should generate satisfaction such that the eyes, the nose, the palate, the stomach, and the heart are in agreement. What happens thereafter, ordinary human beings have no control of.

Chapter 4

To Ekam's young and unexposed mind, the idea of a house on water did not go beyond the popular folktales involving "mammy water" or the water goddess that is said to own mansions inside the rivers and oceans. What she beheld when the Oron-Calabar ferry arrived was a living specimen of a house on water! The ferry was a behemoth of steel, wood, ropes, and color. This was a two-storey building shaped like a boat, floating gently and unconcernedly on the waves of the great Calabar River. She could not read the inscription on the side of the structure. She had, however, been told that there were two of such boats—MV Oron and MV Eket that ply the Oron-Calabar waterway. For those living on the "mainland" part of the state, this was the easiest, nearest, and therefore, the best route to the state capital, Calabar.

Etefia had earlier bought tickets for two. Each ticket was sold for five shillings. The boat, operated by Elder Dempster Limited, was relatively expensive to travel in, although citizens were told that the Government of the Southeastern State of Nigeria subsidized the fare.

If Ekam had gone to the wharf on arrival from Uyo, she would have had enough time to take in the scene, including the boats that were moored there or were being boarded. She could have demonstrated less diffidence that she now did, for she was a little frightened and so hesitated to board the ferry when it was time for passengers to board. Etefia shoved her roughly forward, once again showing the world that she was a first time traveler. "What a day," Ekam had thought. She had entered and stood by the side of the ferry to watch the goings-on before the departure of the great boat.

The rush to board the ferry was maddening. The way people ran in with heavy loads on their heads, backs, or hands was baffling. Some women carried baskets on their heads, suspended bags on one hand, carried babies on their backs, and still dragged one, two, or three children with the remaining hand. A number of men and boys rushed forward and backward, doing nothing. They were probably pickpockets and robbers. The presence of port security men, policemen, and army personnel meant nothing to these ruffians, Ekam had been told.

Cars were also hurrying to board the ferry. Cars! So were cattle. Human beings and cattle in the same boat! Did our forefathers not say that God should forbid one entering the same boat with a cow? Lorries too boarded! Unbelievable. Each time a car or lorry boarded, the ferry shuddered, swung to one side, and only God knew how it regained balance. Yet more entered. Ekam felt dizzy. She held firmly to a pillar in the ferry.

As the scramble continued, the ferry gave out a long and loud blast. A horn! "So boats have horns," she mused. The movements then assumed a frenzied pace with people falling over each other, loads rolling by themselves into the ferry while security personnel flogged people at random, irrespective of age, sex, and status. Touts made brisk business from those without tickets. It was simple bedlam.

From Ekam's vantage position in the ferry, she could see men drawing some chains downward. The downward movement generated an upward movement of a wooden bridge that connected the ferry to the embankment. At this point, men were jumping into the ferry from the sides. One particular young man ran all the way from the station that was slightly evident from the ferry, avoided the bridge where some people stood weeping and begging to be allowed in, threw his briefcase into the ferry, then dived and held the side of the ferry. He threw himself in thereafter, to the admiration and applause of watchers, including security men who knew he had not bought any ticket.

With clanging sounds, more horns, and puffs of smoke, the great boat slowly edged away from the embankment. Some men wound two long steel ropes and threw them in style into the ferry. *Apparently, those ropes are used to truss the boat to the concrete platform on the embankment*, Ekam thought. Slowly but surely, the journey to Calabar began amidst failing sunlight. Oron lay behind in the gathering night, with twinkles of light in houses around.

"Calabar, here I come." Ekam smiled to herself for the first time since the day began.

*   *   *

As if Etefia knew why Ekam stood where she was, he left her till the boat was well into the calm waters of the great Calabar River. It was not until Oron was completely out of sight that he went over to her and pulled gently at her dress, whereby she followed him.

She now looked at the belly of the boat and was astonished by what she saw. How much a boat could carry! Hundreds and hundreds of men, women, and children! Tons and tons of luggage, private and commercial! Cars, busses, lorries! Fowls, goats, sheep, cattle! There was a cocktail of voices, screams, cries, quarrels, laughter, backslapping, whispers, and more. Some people continued to hurry on, even within the boat. The way they brushed and pushed and shoved, one would think they were going on a walking trip or jogging of a thousand miles, when in fact, the ferry could not have been more than one quarter of a mile in length.

She also saw a flight of stairs. So it was true that this was really a storey building! Etefia took her upward. On reaching the platform, as if reading her mind, he volunteered,

"There is another floor up there. That one is called first class."

"For what?"

"Well, for whom rather. It is for very important personalities or VIPs. If you can pay, then you became a VIP at least for two and a half hours."

Ekam understood. This man who looked at her luggage with contempt once more demonstrated that he was indeed one of the poor. His luggage, his means of transportation to Uyo, the place he forced her to eat, and now, where he sat with her spoke volumes of his lowly status. There is more to a man than his looks and the way he looks at people and things. Ekam vowed there and then that on her next trip on this ferry, she would be in the first-class compartment, even if it meant using all the money on her to pay for such a facility.

The lights on the ship had by now come on. She, however, went back to the side of the ferry to see more of nature, something she always enjoyed doing at the village stream. It was indeed vastly different here, for she was on a river. In the fading light, she could still see the herbaceous plants that grew by the tiny patches of land that dot the Calabar-Oron route. She vaguely remembered her elementary science teacher talking about trees with very long roots, an adaptation to life in water. She could also see tiny boats, seriously and scandalously dwarfed by the behemoth she was in. She smiled to herself. Perhaps those people were also Calabar-bound but were so poor that they could not afford the five shillings for the ferry ride. They had to board canoes that could probably take several hours, if not a whole day, to reach Calabar. She refused to acknowledge the fact that the boats carried fishermen and women that brought the fish and crayfish she relished. That line of thought would have made her feel less important.

She was still taking in the smell of the wind and river as well as the greenery and could have continued in her reverie had her thoughts not been interrupted by a man. The man stood close to the stern directly below a hundred-watt bulb.

"Women and men, I salute you," he said again and again, paused for effect and cleared his throat. By now, those present became quiet. There were fixed smiles on most faces. Ekam was surprised that anyone could get such a motley crowd to keep quiet. *Probably this was the captain of the boat*, she thought.

"Brothers and sisters, young and old, I salute you," the man continued, "some of you have been traveling on this boat so often that one may think you do not have a place to call home. Some of you are new. That I can swear." Again he paused for effect. There was low laughter across the deck, which made Ekam uncomfortable. Was the second part meant for her? But she could not have been the only new person on board. "That I can swear," she said to herself.

"I am here with a goodwill message. I bear good news, I hate bad news. You all know that. The story I am about to tell you today happened quite recently and it is true. That I can swear. It is the story of a young man and a young woman." He paused, surveyed the crowd, and grinned.

"The young man felt he was ripe enough for marriage. He approached a damsel who was ripe enough to be plucked. They both agreed and everything was formalized. Forget about the expensive nature of today's traditional marriage. My father married my mother with ten manila, one native goat, five kegs of palm wine, one bottle of four-sided Schnapps, one bottle of local gin, five tubers of yam, one lobe of kola nut, one ear of snuff, two loincloths, one each for my mother's father and my mother mother . . ."

"Continue, continue," the crowd chorused.

"Well, all that would not amount to more than ten pounds today. But what is happening these days? Young men work for twenty years, use their life's savings to pay for a girl, I say pay for a girl! Before you can say *da*, the girl puts her fingers in her nose and says, 'We are not compatible,' which is big grammar for 'you are not good enough for me'! Will the money be returned? Ask your neighbor." There was low laughter across the deck

"The story is that after paying his dues, the boy took the girl home. After two nights, nothing happened. The girl ran home to her mother to report. 'Mother,' she said, 'what you said will happen has not happened.' Do you know what her mother told her would happen and therefore what she expected?"

"No no no!" chorused the crowd.

"She expected the man to perform, but he could not. Do you know why?" There was another chorus of no, no.

"My friend's manhood, bad boys call it John Thomas, could not dance *ajasco*.* Yes, it could not. Do you know why?" The crowd chorused another, "No."

"He had internal heat! When this internal heat is operating, you cannot perform. A man becomes a woman. A woman becomes a baby. But today, I have come with good tidings. All those problems are in past tense. I have here a wonder drug directly from a white man. I went to him, and said, 'Sir, my people are dying of internal heat and of malaria. He said (changing his accent) 'I have the solution.'

"My people, some people deceive you about malaria. They give you leaves and soap to take your bath. You wash your body and what comes out? Layers and layers of foam and dirt! I say to you, use the same leaves and soap on a goat, you will have layers and layers of foam and dirt! When did man become goat and goat become man? I only know of some men who are he-goats in the other aspect—you know what I mean. So if you refuse to take your bath twice a day and then the leaves of *dogonyaro** bring out the dirt, it is not malaria. I say it is not.

"Others say the more bitter the pill, the more it has power over malaria. It does not follow. Must you squeeze your face like a he-goat and gnash your teeth like a great grandfather before becoming well? As our people would say, before you get to eat the sweet, the bitter has killed you. What I have here is sugarcoated.

"This medicine can cure not only malaria and internal heat, but also jaundice, alias yellow fever. It can cure elephantiasis, arthritis, and weakness of any part of the body, catarrh-o, cold-o, influenza-o, name it. You don't have to use a walking stick at thirty. You don't have to run into the bush when girls are approaching because they know your secrets. You don't have to avoid meat and oil and other good foods because the doctors say so. Just take one 'tablet' of this 'capsule' daily. If you are afraid of drugs, we have an answer. Open the capsule like this, empty the contents into a small glass of local gin, *aha*, down it goes like a ball of *garri** that has been well oiled by grandma's okra soup.

"This wonder drug costs one pound overseas. But when I went to the white man, I said, 'men, you want us to develop like you?' He said, 'yea, but you people are lazy.' I said, 'men, our people are not lazy. It is malaria that has crippled them. It is disease and there are so many.' He said, 'take this for one pound.' I said, 'men, my people are poor.' He said, 'take it at ten shillings a card.' I agreed. Now verily I say to you, the first ten people that will come forward will pay five shillings for two cards. The rest will pay five shillings per card and must buy a minimum of two cards. Yes, I shall sell at a loss but I shall be a happy man if at the end of the day, we breed a healthy people. I should have gone home, satisfied that I have contributed my little quota to the development of this country!

"Now the first ten people. Yes, I can see the men, one, two, three, four, five, *ah*, too many. I don't have many cards. Besides there are other decks and other travelers. And you women—don't be ashamed to buy it for your husband. There is no need crying in the night when his manhood lies prostrate. This is the sure cure.

"One special warning, my people. When you take this drug—whichever way you take it—you will urinate a lot. The drug will drive away all the germs from your body, via your urinary track. Please do not urinate in a cassava farm. Or any farm for that matter. Avoid urinating into a stream, because plant and animal life will be in danger. And we are almost approaching famine. The reason is that anytime you urinate, gallons and gallons of toxic material will leave your system because this medicine will boot them out the way your grandmother drives away a stubborn goat from her cassava farm. Before you can say Jack Robinson, you will be as healthy as a baby even if your good health means famine for the whole village if you urinate from farm to farm.

"Yes, first ten only." There was a mild rush for the drug. The sale continued unabated for some time.

"No more please, what is left is for the lower deck. The people upstairs in first class say they are big men. What do you think are in those fat stomachs? Diseases! These capsules would clear all those things. But they are ashamed to buy the drugs from us because they say they are civilized. Civilized indeed. *Don't hide sickness.* That is my name. *Don't hide sickness.* Thank you for your attention, and may God bless us all. Even if you don't go to church. Amen."

Ekam later found out that the first few men that rushed for the drugs were part of the team.

At the exit of the drug peddler's act, rowdy discussions resumed on the deck. Of course, the topic of discussion was the peddler's oratory vis-à-vis the potency of his drug. One buyer confessed that he bought the drug out of curiosity and as a tribute to the man's salesmanship rather than his belief in the efficacy of the drug. In particular, it was doubtful that one drug had the ability to cure all the diseases listed by the peddler.

"When something is too long, it becomes soft at the middle," he concluded. Yet he had spent his hard-earned five shillings on the drug. Attention then turned to another man who had glided in and stood under the bulb.

"Women and men, girls and boys," he announced, spreading his hands sideways.

"*Hmm,*" chorused the crowd.

"Clap for yourselves," he said. The people clapped at the same time. Ekam was again baffled at the control the peddlers had on such a crowd.

"The medicine is good," someone said.

"That is my name. God bless you," he said with all amount of satisfaction.

"I am aware that most of you here know me. For those who don't, know that the name given to me by my father, bless his good soul, is *the medicine is good.* That is all I want to hear. That is all I live for." There was a low and sustained murmur in the crowd, but the salesman stopped it by raising his hand.

"My mission in life is to spread good health and the message of good living. I am not here to make any profit. Try my drugs, if they work, as they are sure to, and you meet me on the road, just call me *the medicine is good.* That is all I want." He paused and added, "You all know that I am a refined man—the way I talk, the way I walk, the way I dress, and even as I address you. While others who claim to be *mbakara** even with black skin address you as 'ladies and gentlemen,' I address you as women and men, because there is no Ibibio word for ladies, and none for gentlemen." A murmur gathered momentum at that for he made quite some sense. "So, whatever I will say, you better believe it," he said further.

"*The medicine is good,*" some youths shouted and giggled in excitement.

"Thank you, my children. Women and men, girls and boys, give me your ears. I have so far been selling to you, drugs that will do a lot of good for you inside your body. But good old disease afflicts people internally and externally. Since I have been commissioned to see to your health in and out, I present before you today, drugs that will be of interest to many, and girls in particular," he paused and surveyed the crowd, making faces at girls.

"The *meresin* is good," somebody shouted.

"That word is me-di-cine, not *meresin*. When your mates went to school, you were busy looking for snails even in the afternoon!" He paused for the laughter to die down. "Or on your way after having been forced to go to school, you used to spend time to catch grasshoppers and look at their nostrils." The crowd, including the man who was the butt of the joke, laughed some more.

"My people, let me continue. High schools are meant for education on the ways of the white man. Knowledge is supposed to be spread there. But what do we find these days—girls spread not knowledge, but lice! Yes, lice. If you have been a host to those tiny, dark, blood suckers, you will appreciate why there are so many failures in our schools today, and why the standard of education is falling."

"*The medicine is good*," chorused the crowd.

"When the poor teacher is busy teaching his life away, the children are busy scratching their lives away—one hand on the exercise book, the other in the hair. Poor fathers—they are at home telling their neighbors, 'my daughter is in college' with a big mouth. They don't know that the poor girl is busy, not reading, but fighting a war with lice! But today we offer you a once-and-for-all remedy to these humiliating and unwanted guests.

"It comes as a cream. Yes, the cream stinks. But do lice not stink? Just massage this well-prepared cream into your scalp and wait for the result. Do you know the result?"

"No," the crowd chorused.

"We are listening," someone said.

"Then here it is. There will be a march past from your hair onto your neck, then shoulder, then your clothes. In the queue will be the grandmother of lice, the grandfather of lice, the mother—"

"Of lice," chorused the crowd.

"The father."

"Of lice."

"The daughter—"

"Of lice."

"The son—"

"Of lice."

"The grandchildren—"

"Of lice."

"The great grand children—"

"Of lice."

"The entire family of lice from generation to generation, will effect a march past from your head. You know why?"

"No," chorused the crowd, by now, in frenzy.

40

"Because this cream is no respecter of lice of any age or sex."
He paused to allow the crowd banter on the delivery so far.

"One warning, my people. After applying this wonder
cream, wash your hands. We don't want you to join in the march
past. Lest I forget, this cream fights lice. Yes. But it has other
uses. It can successfully eliminate bedbug from your house. The
powder form does that. The cream can cure eczema, ringworm,
insect bites, and even the one the white man calls skin cancer.
That one will be strange to you but to us, it is common and easy.
Cancer is a disease. It is not the same thing as Eka Nsa or Nsa's
mother.

"Finally, what can kill lice on the head can kill lice on the
pubic area too. Can you imagine that? Pubic lice! Only the very
dirty have that one. Don't invite me to apply the cream on you
if you have pubic lice, particularly if you are a married woman.
I don't want to die young. My children are still in school." There
was general laughter by the passengers.

"*The medicine is good*," they chorused.

"This preparation is local, but I had to undergo serious study
under experts in the *United Kingdom of America*. My pleading with
the white man yielded fruit. So the cream is quite cheap for two
shillings and six pence. You can get a jar that will set you free
from the tyranny of lice and other skin diseases. Only a lucky
few who are fast will get it." Again there was a rush by the same
men that rushed for the previous drug.

"No, not for men, unless you can prove that your wife or
girlfriend has lice or that you have inherited some. Girls first."
He looked at the girls around. They squirmed and giggled shyly.

"Where are those beautiful schoolgirls? You are shy now. But
remember to tell the world that '*the medicine is good*' was behind
your freedom." One girl dared to buy, and then there was a rush.
In another ten minutes, the sale was over.

"Thank you, women and men, girls and boys. I will see you
again if you can afford another five shillings for this trip. Some
people say that traveling in this ferry is cheap. It is only he who
has not tried to catch the *Odudu** bird that says it is a coward.

41

Five shillings is a lot of money. Ask me." He left as unobtrusively as he had appeared.

The laughter and small talk were yet to die down when a young, rather extravagantly handsome man sauntered to what can be described as the center stage with a not-too-handsome man by his side. The handsome young man had curly hair on his head, slight pencil line on each eyebrow, and a grayish rogue on his cheeks. Ekam was shocked to see a man with a "permed" hair and female makeup. But what astounded her most was the pair of earrings on his two ears. This was city indeed, even on water!

"Shiner, Shiner," the crowd chorused as the young man arrogantly dropped his plastic basket that contained assorted tins of shoe polish and brush of various colors and sizes. His "Abdul" pair of shoes shone like mirror in the sun. One could easily see one's face on it!

"People, I greet you," he said. There was applause. The shoeshine boy then adjusted his skintight jean trousers and body-hugging tergal shirt and did an "ajasco" dance that he stopped abruptly just when the crowd thought he would fall. There was wild applause as the crowd, irrespective of age, sex, and social status, cheered and hooted.

"Thank you, soul *broders* and *sistres*," the shoeshine boy said, speaking in an affected voice. "For those of you who are the Johnny Just Come alias JJC in this ferry, or those who just came from one village which is yet to see the white man's light—" The applause was simply deafening. Once again, Ekam felt a thousand eyes on her. She swore under her breath, cursing her fate for making her a product of a backward family. Her self-righteous anger was, however, drowned as Shiner continued.

"I don't have much to say today, lest I cut my tongue. After all, how much are you going to pay me for all the grammar and knowledge I went to the white man's land to learn? From London to Liverpool, from Washington to Toronto, from—" Again, the crowd was so ecstatic that a newcomer could not fail to show bewilderment.

"I am here with great news," Shiner said with one hand in the back pocket of his trousers. He pulled out the snow-white handkerchief that had one end hanging out of the right-hand pocket of his trousers, wiped his face, and smiled. "Don't be like me. That is the great news. I wear this pencil trouser and tell fine girls that I am a show boy. When I reach home at night what do you think will happen?"

"Tell us, tell us," the crowd chorused.

"I have to squeeze my face like a he-goat before I can remove the trouser, which my bro that lives in America calls cigarette pant." He paused for the audience to laugh to their fill.

"That is what happened to a young Lagos boy the other day. He wanted to attract fine, fine girls. So what did he do?"

"Tell us, tell us," the crowd chorused.

"He decided to wear *sorpedo.* Now, that is a costly shoe. Since he was an applicant, he went to the market to reap where he did not sow. When the police caught him, *hm,*" he paused, relishing the suspense as evidenced by the dead silence.

"They beat him till his mother could not recognize him again." The crowd laughed heartily.

"So, my friend, call him Boy O' Boy was requested to pay twenty pounds to the police. Twenty whole pounds!" The crowd whistled, some in derision, some in genuine pity.

"If he could not buy the shoes on his own, how could he pay the police?"

"Tell us, tell us."

"But pay he must, for police station is like a juju priest's shrine. Whether you are guilty or innocent, whether you get what you went for or you don't, whether you are the complainant or the accused, you must drop something. Only God will protect us from our protectors!" The crowd genuinely chorused, "Amen."

"Let me complete my story. So how did he pay for his freedom? He sold his father's land, his mother sold all her clothes, and yet the money was not enough. So he had to sell his own clothes." The crowd laughed and booed at the unseen fool.

"So my friend ate three pence worth of food, yet his 'shit*' was worth nine pence." After another pause for the laughter to die down, Shiner continued, "He is not alone. That is what I did when I tried to copy Bingo, my dog. As Bingo cracked hard bones, I swore I would do the same. 'Krack' went the bone. And what do you think I threw out of my mouth?"

"Tell us. Tell us."

"Pieces of my own teeth! As I don't want fine girls to run away from me because I am toothless like Nsọ, my grandfather, I have learnt to leave bones to Bingo.

"So, instead of stealing, or doing what you cannot, let Shiner polish your old shoe for you. You can deceive girls by telling them that you buy a new pair of shoes every week, even when your shoe is as old as Nigeria's independence. For only one shilling, Shiner will give you a brand-new secondhand pair of shoes. Get all those girls as soon as you land at Calabar wharf. I don't mind shining even the ones that smell because the owner forgets to wash his pair of socks after wading through water. Bring them. Yes?"

Two men rushed their pairs of shoes to him. In another fifteen minutes, Shiner was furiously polishing shoes just to keep up with the demand. As the small talk continued, he sweated away on rotten and not so rotten shoes.

Meanwhile, his mate, call him Eka-Inua, took over the talking. He had a small plastic bag with him.

"Ladies and gentlemen, papas and mamas, boys and girls, listen to me and listen carefully," he commenced. "Even if your shoes are with Shiner, what he does is not your business. I need your ears. The message I have is to save you embarrassment or something worse. If the inner part of your ear is dirty, get to the lower deck for I saw some baskets with fowls in them. What would our people not carry in a boat? Now manage to pluck one feather from one fowl and clean your ears.

"My bros here told you not to stretch to get what you want. Okay, but be careful before you find out what Mr. Frog found out. Do you want to hear?"

"Yes," the crowd chorused.

"Mr. Frog was used to jumping into any water where the water was standing at attention like the human beings made of stone you find at Ikot Obio Ofọng.* If the water was moving, it would still enter provided it was not running 440.* In fact, it prefers water that treks or is standing at attention. But one day, it jumped into hot water. That is when Mr. Frog concluded, 'So there are two kinds of water in the world!'" He waited for the laughter and small talk that came in the wake to subside and then continued.

"Now to the real story. My friend, call him Ikopo, an applicant with primary six wanted to attend a big men's party and eat such foods as jollof rice, chicken *pili pili*, fried lizard, and goat food, alias salad. He approached a wise elder for assistance on what he should do. The man told him to dress like the big men that were expected at the party. The wise elder however cautioned on something.

"'My son,' he said, 'when you go in there, watch what every person is doing and do the same thing. When they pick one piece of meat, pick one, not two, even if you are dying of hunger. When they pour a few drops of White Horse into their glasses, do not fill yours. After all, whisky is not *kai kai*.* When they smile and bow, do the same, even if you have a boil in your cheeks and severe pain in your neck. But watch, when they begin to speak, take excuse, tell the nearest person that you want to go and urinate.' Do you know why?"

"Tell us, tell us," the crowd chorused.

"Because they may request you to say something in English of course! And as sharp people who want to hide the shame of their ignorance would say, 'English is not our mother tongue.' So run like a dog, your tail tucked between your legs. If a friend asks you outside why you left in a hurry, tell him what the dog told its friend. Do you know what the dog said?"

"No, tell us," the crowd chorused excitedly.

"'My brother,' the dog said. 'When you go near human beings, watch out. As soon as they bend down, change your gear

45

and run hundred yards, for they are most likely going to pick a stone and throw at you.'" Again he allowed the discussions that followed to die down.

"Thank God Isopo obeyed the words of elders because they are what?" The crowd chorused, "Words of wisdom." "Forget that he looked like a he-goat wearing a coat. The oversized coat stood one mile away while his body stood another mile away. Also forget that he virtually slept in the toilet for the next two days because his stomach was not used to the kind of food he dumped into it.

"This evening, I came to show you another way of at least looking like a big man. You will not need to tie a rope around your neck like a Christmas goat and be dragged into a party hall. This thing the white man calls a tie can really tie you to death if you are not careful. We like to be free, that is why we use big loincloth and ordinary polo.

"You can look like a big man if you are fat and your cheeks are full of oil. Simply swallow this blood capsule twice a day, better still, once, except if you are as dry as stockfish. Within three months, your cheeks will be round and there will be oil all over it even in December. Be careful-o. It will make you eat like a pig that has delivered twelve children. If you are a laborer who is struggling to eat one plate of *garri* a day, I won't sell it to you—because you will steal! Now, this capsule is only two shillings and six pence a card. Those of you who like to wait for the seller to remove something from the price, you will be disappointed. We shall not, for as our elders say, you learn to die by sleeping. Learn how to be a big man by paying big for the future. Yes, let me see the hands of the future *mononias** of our country." Soon the man's bag was as empty as his face, which told the onlooker nothing about the authenticity or otherwise of his drug.

*   *   *

Ekam turned to look at the water after the humorous distraction. She could not discern much. Far off were tiny streaks of light.

When the boat was a little closer, she noticed that the lights came from a fishing camp. Thatched houses stood on stilts. Small canoes bobbed on the water close to the huts, doing upward-sideways dance to music they alone could hear. Wooden bridges crisscrossed the hamlet, woven the way women's hair is woven by a deft hairdresser. The bridges were in fact intracamp roads. The fishing village housed fishermen and their families, their main occupation being fishing and smoking of fish and crayfish. How people live there comfortably made her shrug in amazement.

Again, her reverie was interrupted. This time by a young man who was deformed in the feet.

"Women and men, boys and girls, my name is 007. I have a song to render to you. If my song moves you, dip your hands in your pockets and give a deprived man a means of livelihood. My song is titled *Look at the child's face, not the feet*." He proceeded to sing the song that implored listeners to look at his face rather than his feet, which were victims of a disease. This was a case of a one-man band. With two sticks as the only instruments, 007 used his mouth to sing as well as provide the guitar, drums, and other accompaniments. His performance drew applause, tears, and where possible, pennies from donors.

The song was apt. He might have been a victim of polio at childhood. He looked stunted. His legs twisted such that he galloped rather than walked. His face was rather deceptive. At a distance, one would pass him for a child. But a closer look kept one wondering where to place him—boy or man. All the same, 007, though also an itinerant money seeker, provided a relief, a refreshing difference in genuineness that the other performers obviously lacked and obviously did not need for success in their trade.

With the end of 007's performance, Ekam again looked outward. What she saw was simply ecstatic. Rows and rows of light shimmered like a million stars in the distance. She could not quite comprehend that. Houses were not evident, just rows and rows of twinkling stars!

Etefia, who always seemed to know exactly what the girl thought, quietly said, "That is Calabar." She was startled. She did not know when he stood by her, how long he had been there, and how he had read her mind. Nevertheless, she was grateful for the information and the relief that she felt, for at last, the two-and-a-half-hour journey from Oron to Calabar by ferry was coming to an end. She, however, told herself that if she is to survive in the city that was close by, she needed to be alert. She must not let herself go and be so absorbed by anything such that she became dead to her surroundings. Such apparent carelessness could prove fatal. And as for men, she decided to be extraordinarily alert for it appears they could creep and attack without being noticed—like a mosquito—till the pain of the bite shakes one up too late. She recalled that her uncle had once said that men are like and unlike lions. Men, like lions, can kill and eat; but unlike lions that roar before attacking, men can attack without making the faintest noise.

Whether the point made by her uncle could be applied to city men—expected to be gentlemen—would soon be seen as the lights she saw changed to buildings with men living in them.

BOOK II

Chapter 5

It was Ekam's belief that first impressions are not only important, they could actually be critical. It was convenient to hold such a view because the world and they that dwell therein are so difficult to read that it was good for one's sanity or at least one's blood pressure to believe in something. Deep down, the girl knew that first impressions were the most deceptive of things.

On the first day following her dramatic change of environment, Ekam woke up early in the morning to very strange sounds—car horns, admonitions from loud speakers attached to churches, frenzied activities of people, other sounds of day, and so on. To city dwellers, these were commonplace. As a matter of fact, the absence of such din would be viewed as very strange. To the girl that had just arrived from a village, it was a huge contrast as she was used to the eerie silence broken by early birds and insects and a few humans talking quietly on their way to the stream.

The mistress of the house, Mrs. Nduke, popularly called Mama Eno, had allowed the village girl to sleep far beyond acceptable time. Ekam in fact woke up by herself, just before the national news on the radio at seven o'clock in the morning. She felt guilty, but pleasantly surprised that her mistress had let her sleep that long. *She must be a kindhearted lady, a mother even to a househelp*, the girl thought. That appeared uncommon and gave her an initial, well, first impression of Mrs. Nduke.

Ekam was slightly taken aback, however, when she was told to take her bath before assisting in the chores in the kitchen. Although she was used to early baths in the village stream, she thought she would have been allowed to complete the smoky affair in the kitchen before bathing as she believed she was neither smelling nor too dirty to touch food items. She, however, shrugged off the uncomfortable thoughts, rationalizing her mistress's action with the thought that it might be one of the unwritten rules of the family. In any case, it amounted to the same thing that obtained in villages as children normally had their bath in the village stream before commencement of domestic chores that included cleaning of the premises and cooking. What she, however, did not like was the way it was said before male relations that lived in the house. That made her feel dirty in and out and very much uncomfortable.

Mama Enọ, a woman Ekam learnt quite early that she was in her midthirties, who however looked like someone in her late forties, was said to have been married to Mr. Nduke for about fifteen years. She was portly build, bronze in complexion with a round head that bore fairly bulgy eyes, a blunt nose, and two well-formed lips. A few "fittings" on the face as well as several strands of gray hair gave an impression of a woman on the wrong side of forty but were not strong enough to blur the youthfulness in her. The gap between two of her upper incisors and the dimples on her cheeks ensured that she caught the attention of people and gave her out as a pretty woman. Ekam was not sure even after watching her for nearly eighteen hours whether her character would be as pleasant as her looks.

Morning chores over, children off to school, and the man of the house off to work, Ekam was left alone with Mama Enọ. The lady was so lively and agile that Ekam felt quite dull and lazy. She, however, managed to rush through tons of sweeping, dusting, scrubbing, and washing in and around the apartment.

After a good breakfast of bread, tea, and fried eggs, Mama Enọ announced that Ekam would accompany her to the market—the Watt Market—among other places. The girl could hardly contain her excitement. Mama Enọ understood.

"My child, I hope you will not be disappointed by what you will see," the woman said casually. Ekam was surprised that her mistress could read her thoughts.

"Watt Market is one of those places or things that are greater in stories than in real life," the woman said and continued, "what you will see will not be different from what you have seen in your village, except that there may be more things—more sheds, more shades, more goods, more people, and of course more dirt, mud, and stench. As a matter of fact, the last three are the distinguishing factors for the average village market hardly has any dirt, mud, or stench."

The last bit was not enough to dampen the excitement of the girl. She hurriedly put on her "Sunday best," a fairly used pleated skirt given to her by her auntie who used to visit home from Lagos every three years. Mama Enọ gave her a pair of earrings and an old pair of shoes in place of the rubber slippers she arrived Calabar with, which she had intended to use. Of course, the use of a head tie was not acceptable to Mama Enọ.

"You are in a city, dear girl. Head tie is for church only," she instructed.

The girl's excitement was soon slightly dampened as they walked from the house on Dr. Dean Street toward Mbukpa Road to catch a bus to Watt Market. A "good" neighbor of theirs had accosted Mama Enọ and asked a few unpleasant questions.

"*Aha*, Mama Enọ, you did not tell me you went to the village?" The neighbor, whom Ekam later on learnt was called Madam Mbehe, asked.

"What makes you think I went to the village?" Mama Enọ retorted.

"This small sister of yours must have dropped from the sky then."

"Anything is possible these days, after all there is an aerodrome in Calabar."

"*Hahaha*. And there is one in your village."

"My friend, I am going to the market. I'll see you when I am back."

"Of course you are going. But first, tell me, is this your sister?"

"How is that your business, my sister?"

"It is my business-o, for when a neighbor is awake because of a problem, another neighbor cannot be asleep."

"And what will keep us awake? Anyway, this girl is my househelp."

"*Ehen*, I said it. If you picked your husband on the road or plucked him from a tree, it was fifteen years ago. These days, husbands, I mean real husbands, are not easy to come by. This girl is too beautiful to be a house girl. If you are unlucky, you could sooner than later be turned into a spectator of the house you have labored to build."

"Are you not wicked? How can you say such things of a tiny girl like this?"

"O yes, tiny. I never knew you could be so stupid. Are you living in this Calabar at all? Or have you blocked your ears to happenings around? Do you think your days of premarital innocence are still here? Are you not aware that there are more virgins in the cities than in the villages? Pump milk and eggs into this girl for another three months and see if that bare chest will not develop fat mounds overnight. Before you know what happens, Oga will be dreaming of straight breast that he can have right under his roof! You do not only have to have eyes behind your back, you need some on each side of your head. My conscience is clear because I have warned you. To be forewarned is to be forearmed, that is what my teacher taught me in Standard Two, twenty-five years ago. I find it handy."

Ekam had heard of busybodies, but she never knew they could be so brazen. Backbiting is an art among women anywhere, but the biting is behind, not frontal as had just happened. The young girl had come face-to-face with the realities of city life with that episode, less than twenty fours of her arrival.

From that moment onward, Ekam, a rather sensitive girl, noticed a change in Mama Eno's attitude. She had continued to chat up the little girl, but once in a while, her voice trailed off, indicating that her attention had wandered. Ekam decided to ignore this development if she was to enjoy her first trip into Calabar as a resident.

*　　*　　*

"Why do you wear such an expression on your face?" Mama Eno inquired from Ekam. The question arose from the surprise on the girl's face following a complaint by Mama Eno to the effect that was tired of walking. Tired of covering only about two hundred yards on foot! The two had trekked from the house along Dr. Dean Street to Mbukpa Road, the axis road that links a vast residential area, Mbukpa, to the business district on Calabar Road. To Ekam, that was like a toss for a start of a trip from her family house in the village to the village stream. An average village girl should regard a five-kilometer trip as a normal distance on foot for one day.

At the junction between Mbukpa, Imo Street, and Afokang Street, the pair joined other commuters bound for several destinations that terminate at the Watt Market. A rickety Volkswagen bus came along and screeched to a stop. The bus boy jumped deftly onto the ground, practically ordered the occupants out and proceeded to "load" the bus. Mama Eno and Ekam hopped in, sitting at the backseat, sandwiched between two rather uncomfortably fat women. A man sat by the side as one of the five passengers on the rear seat. The man shifted and shifted, squirmed, and hissed. The conductor shouted an instruction.

"One person move forward, one person move back. If you don't want to manage, drop, go, and buy a car. This is public transport."

"Sit there till those overfed women press the intestines out of your gut," one commuter, a man sitting on the next row, said.

"Your grandmother is overfed, you motherless son of Adam," one of the women blurted out.

"Do you mind these vagabonds?" the other said.

"Me vagabond?" the man retorted. "Take time, woman. My grandmother did not live as long as you and yet she never saw her second childhood." This invective did not go down well with the women who can tolerate a lot of things other than a suggestion that they are old. They almost tore the man up. The man jumped out of the bus. The driver, however, insisted that the man must board again otherwise he would not drive off.

"Go in my brother. This is neither their husbands' farm nor their kitchen," the driver said. The abuses that were heaped on the driver were enough to last a decent human being a lifetime. The driver drove off after the man was offered a seat at the driver's cabin as one of the three passengers. The stream of abuses, however, continued unabated throughout the duration of the trip, which due to regular stops and potholes, lasted for nearly forty-five minutes instead of fifteen minutes that a straight drive would have lasted.

The bus ride took the group through landmarks such as the Mbukpa Market; the headquarters of the Brotherhood of the Cross and Star, a spiritual organization; the Qua Iboe Church, all on Mbukpa Road; the Edgerly Memorial Girls School, a high school for girls; and the Apostolic Church grounds both on Edgerly Road. The bus turned right into Chamley Street where Mama Enọ pointed out to the right one of Calabar's premier hotels, the Manila Hotel. Thereafter, it turned left into White House Road. Then at the junction with Calabar Road, the driver made a sharp right run, which made the passengers to bump into each other. Abuses on the driver were many. Calabar Road is the longest axis road in Calabar that traverses the business district and links the highway out of Calabar to Ikom, Ogoja, and the northern part of Nigeria.

Within a few minutes of entering Calabar Road, the tempestuous bus ride terminated at the roundabout close to Watt Market. As each passenger disembarked, he or she hurled an invective at either the driver or the conductor. Ekam was too dazed to say anything. It had been a mixture of fun, fear, and fantasy.

"This is Watt Market," Mama Eno announced. She did not say this quietly. A number of those who heard turned and stared at her then at Ekam and nodded knowingly.

"To your right is Fosbery Road. Calabar Road continues after the market. To your left is Egerton Street. I hope you can find your way here by yourself tomorrow," she concluded. Ekam was surprised that her mistress could think of sending her out on her own after only one trip out of her residence.

*   *   *

The first place they visited that day was a bank, the Calabar branch of Standard Bank of Nigeria located on Calabar Road on the northern end of Watt Market. Ekam found herself inside a bank building for the first time in her life. Mama Eno was there to draw some money for her shopping.

Standard Bank was reputed to be a conservative bank. The building confirmed this. The staff with their austere clothes and severe mugs confirmed this. They smiled once in a while when a relation or friend or a big-time customer came in. Other customers appeared to be regarded as the figures and numbers the staff dealt with—impersonal, troublesome, but a necessary evil. The policemen outside, tired looking but alert, nervously fingered their rifles.

There was a large crowd inside, quite a number leaning on the wooden counter. The crowd was a noisy one. From a man who sat by Ekam, it became obvious that salaries had just been paid. Everyone wanted to withdraw money. Ekam wondered how the bank could have enough money to meet the demands of the noisy and jostling crowd.

The girl also noticed that the entire banking hall was filled with documents. Files, papers, cards, notebooks, more files. The staff moved about endlessly, writing, making entries, answering questions, listening, and once in a while, screaming. She felt sorry for them. A banking crowd can tax even the most staid of human beings. How these people worked without making mistakes, at least such as would have led to a collapse of the system, was to the girl a mystery. A few words entered her vocabulary that day: *passbook, check, bills, teller, withdrawal, deposit.* These were some she could recollect for they were used so often that she thought those were the only words used in the bank.

There were several distractions too.

"Mr. Clerk, return my check if you are not going to pay me? I have been here for the past three hours!" barked a man.

"I wonder-o. These people think we are jobless!" exclaimed a woman.

"Favoritism is killing this country. Nepotism, godfatherism, bribery, corruption and—"

"How do these come into a bank, Mr. Headmaster?" inquired someone.

"You don't know? My colleague came here only ten minutes ago. Now he is gone, just because his brother works here," the man responded.

"So that is the meaning of negoti—what did he call it?" inquired another client.

There was prolonged laughter.

"There is nothing you will not hear and see in a bank."

"Allow the man to display what he learnt at school *bo.*"

"If he is a teacher and he teaches our children 'ism, ism,' how safe are they?"

"Or we the parents?"

There was no end to the small talk. It was obvious that it took off the tedium and boredom of endless waiting.

Perhaps the most exciting aspect of Ekam's first encounter with banking was watching the paying cashier at work. He would shout a name, then on response by the person concerned, proceed to count fresh notes with such deftness and speed that made the girl feel dizzy. He would then make some entries on a piece of paper after asking the person, "How much is your check?" Ekam did not know why that question should be asked when the check was in front of the cashier. Nevertheless, the process continued, ending with the cash being handed over to the payee. The anticlimax would, however, come when the payee does the counting of the notes just received.

One after the other, Ekam noticed that each payee moved slightly away from the cage and proceeded to count the money received, often with someone to help in the exercise. The procedure was long and laborious, taking probably as much time as it took the cashier to pay twenty people. Take for instance payment in one pound notes. Five one-pound notes would be counted, twisted between two fingers to ensure that only one was counted each time. Then one of the notes would be folded into two while the other four are slotted inside. That made five pounds, which was then kept aside. This process would continue even if a thousand pounds would be counted. On completion of the exercise, the folded notes would be recounted and the arithmetic done. Spittle would be generously employed in the process. It was not uncommon for some people to approach the paying cashier to complain of shortage of some amount. The patient cashier, though with some irritation, would suspend further payments, recount the notes, and hand back the money with a baleful look accompanied by hissing from others waiting to be paid, who may later on be involved in the same mess of asking the cashier for a second count. How the cashiers paid without overpaying left Ekam in no small wonder.

After what must have been at least two hours, Mama Eno was ready to go. She complained bitterly about the time wasted. To Ekam, it was nothing more than three minutes. Time is measured scientifically in seconds, minutes, and hours. Mentally, it depends on who is going through time and the circumstances. One man's five hours could be another man's five minutes.

At the gate of the bank, Mama Eno met Madam Mbehe again. Ekam wondered silently why they had to meet the petulant woman at every turn.

"Are you just coming?" inquired Mama Eno.

"Yes," Mrs. Mbehe responded.

"I pity you. I guess you will get your money tomorrow."

"Me. Before you reach the market, I would have received my money."

"You did not tell me your sister is here."

"My dear, I have neither sister nor brother here."

"You grease their palms then."

"How much do I have? Don't you know me? By the time I shout and abuse two of them, the accountant will come in person and get me what I want."

"I trust you." There was a pause during which Madam Mbehe looked searchingly at Ekam. The girl squirmed in discomfort

"*Aha*, you this woman, you like trouble-o."

"How do you mean?"

"Are you sure this village girl hasn't got sticky fingers?"

"I don't think so."

"How do you know? She came only last night."

"I think she is good girl."

"Well, I hope so too. There is no need looking for trouble. You don't have to be like the frog which invites rain on itself."

"Until she disappoints me, I shall try and trust her. She is from a good family."

"Thank you very much. If she were from that good a family, why is she coming here as a housemaid?"

"The parents want her to learn one or two things about life outside the village. She will go to school next year."

"That is what they told you. That is what they tell everybody. What actually happens is different. I hope the one or two things she will learn will not come from your husband. Take my advice, watch this girl."

"Thank you. I'll see you later at home."

"Only God knows why this woman came my way," Ekam thought to herself. "Her househelps must be house slaves," she thought.

Mrs. Nduke and Ekam then walked out of the bank. Both walked briskly past the post office, another busy spot. Opposite the post office stood the African Club. Ekam later on learnt that it was a place for drinking, games, and parties but reserved for members only. The state library shared the same boundary with Watt Market on one side while the motor traffic division of the Nigeria police shared a boundary with same market on the other side. Ekam felt that the police station could be excused. But her idea of a library, elementary as it was, could not fit into the one located contiguous to the biggest market in the municipality.

*   *   *

Watt Market. Again, another landmark big in name and great in history, but small in size. But for the muddy footpaths and jostling crowd, one can walk the entire length of the market in ten quick minutes! Many markets where Ekam came from were twice the size of the Watt Market, but relatively less known or completely unheard of.

Watt Market was located at the city center. The market operated daily except Sundays. The myth behind it is that an oak tree stood where the market now stands. A water god inhabited the tree. When the people wanted to build a market, they decided to cut down the oak tree. The inhabitant of the tree wept and wept. The tree was cut down all the same. Still weeping, a pool of water that was by the base of the tree migrated to the Calabar River. As a result of the history behind the market, of which only the true indigenes can give more in-depth analysis and rationale, all attempts by the government to move it from its present site had failed. The people resisted such moves. A road had to be built round the market that took more time to move, from the post office on Calabar Road to join the other side of Calabar Road. A detour through Ededem Street and Bedwell Street to the other side of Calabar Road made the journey longer. Watt Market, apparently named after a white missionary, James Watt, stood right at the center of Calabar town.

Chapter 6

"Betrayal, wickedness, a demon!" Ekam screamed, looking for more derogatory words to adequately qualify her object of hate.

"Take it easy, Ekam. Look at that event as a lesson in your life," Ekam's friend Enọmma said soothingly.

Ekam was still fuming. She had cause to fume for she was trying to relive the experience of her seven-day stay in the house of Ekebo. Enọmma was Ekam's only friend in the city of Calabar, a city she now regarded with dread following the experiences she had had since her arrival. To her, the beauty and serenity of Calabar were no more than mere masks underneath, which lay corruption, dirt, and treachery. In her short stay in the city, she had gone through the wrong sides of a jealous and petulant housewife, busybody neighbors, lecherous men, and worst of all, a treacherous townsman whose residence she saw as any port in a storm rather than a true refuge.

"If one cannot trust his brother, who then can be trusted?" Ekam asked, spitting in the process as if the spittle contained the venom that was eating her.

"Maybe the end of time is here," Enọmma said gravely.

"When friends will become enemies, fathers will betray daughters . . ."

"And brothers will become rapists," Enọmma concluded.

*　　*　　*

Since Ekam moved her meager belongings to Enọmma's one room dwelling along Mbukpa Lane two days earlier, she had been crying or moping endlessly. Enọmma's was the only place she could go. She was aware that her father's stepbrother was in Calabar. In fact, she had visited the man on two occasions. But she could not go there, not because she could have been turned back, but because she felt she could no longer trust any man, particularly her kith and kin.

Enọmma was a childhood friend. She hailed from the neighboring village of Obo Atai. Her father was a schoolteacher at the primary school at Ekam's village in Oboyo. The two girls had met at school and had been in the same class from ABC, as it was then called, right through to elementary six. Their relationship had been very good despite the age difference, as Enọmma was about five years older than Ekam.

Enọmma had left for Calabar upon completion of her elementary education. She secured a job with an office furniture company called G. B. Olivant or simply GBO. GBO was of the UAC Group and was one of the blue chips in the country. Enọmma was one of the cashiers in the company. After working for three months, she rented a room that she called Enọmma's Little Room of No Regret. She picked that up from the Little House of No Regret on Aka Road, Uyo. The two met by accident one day in Watt Market. Since then, Ekam had been visiting Enọmma whenever she had a few minutes to spare.

Patience was one of Enọmma's greatest assets. She never seemed to be in a hurry to get anything through. To her, things that endure are those that were crafted over a long period of time. Take nature for instance, the timelessness of the hills; the order, timely, and perfect change of baton between night and day; the shell of an oyster; the streams and rivers; even the circles in the stem of a tree that one can see after it has been felled by man that does not know how those circles came about and how many years it took for an oak tree to become as tall and as large as it is. She had come to the conclusion that the principal reason man dies so quickly or why there is so much inconsistency in human beings is because God made man in just one day. The master craftsman certainly made just that one mistake. Probably God in his omniscience did not intend to have man as a perfect creation.

Watching Ekam as her emotions flowed and ebbed was both exciting and exacting. For two days, she had refused to talk, eat, and take a bath. Sleeping was in fits, punctuated by nightmares and screams. "Leave me, leave me you dirty old man," was what she kept saying with long beads of sweat covering her body, following what appeared to be a fierce struggle.

"You are supposed to protect me as a father. Why are you now killing me?" she oft repeated.

Enomma had finally succeeded on the third day to get Ekam to take a bath and to eat. She had seemed to be a little composed on that day. She had even smiled. Enomma now felt it was time to get her talking.

"I am happy that you are coming back to life, Ekam."

"Yes, and thanks to you for understanding me."

"I shall understand you better when you tell me your story. As I had said before, unloading your worries by talking could give a wonderful relief."

Taking a deep breath, Ekam sighed, adjusted her dress and her sitting position and allowed her mind and mouth to reminisce on the events of her seven-day sojourn in the house of Ekebo.

*   *   *

The journey to Ekebo's house was not voluntary. It was simply that it was no longer possible for Ekam to absorb any further insults and slaps from Mrs. Nduke. Apart from the physical danger Ekam faced, her pride was being seriously assailed. Things had deteriorated gradually, but the situation in the house was still bearable until Mrs. Nduke joined a group that comprised married women of her age group. It appeared she became more and more disagreeable each time she returned from a meeting.

Then one Saturday, which happened to be Ekam's second anniversary of domicile in Mr. Nduke's house, her mistress had woken up in the morning, looking rather bellicose. It was a day following one of those club meetings. From the first minute, Mrs. Nduke started raining abuses at Ekam. The first one was "daughter of a witch." Ekam, as usual, shrugged. Probably her mistress had gotten out of bed on the wrong side. The abuse continued unabated the whole morning. "Daughter of a viper," Mrs. Nduke had called her househelp.

The atmosphere in the house had become so tense that Ekam could not carry out her normal domestic chores. When she tried to bathe the children, Mrs. Nduke shouted, "You want to bewitch my children, leave them alone, after all how do you know you will have any?" Ekam tried cooking, but the woman shouted, "Heartless murderess, who will eat your food?" The girl wanted to do the laundry, "with your third eye you will see through those dresses," was Mrs. Nduke's reaction. Ekam attempted to pick the bucket to fetch water. Madam flew at her, almost scratching out her eyes, "You poisonous snake, who will drink your water?" With such consistency and tenacity, it was obvious that the woman was setting the stage for a showdown.

The drama continued till the man of the house intervened. Then all hell was let loose.

"Neighbors, where are you? Have I not been saying it? Do you need any further proof? Will you sit by while this village prostitute, this bastard, this homeless and shameless daughter of the devil snatches my husband? I have sweated in this man's house for seventeen years now. I have endured his abuses during his hours of frustration and helplessness. I have fed him, his children, his brothers, sisters, and uncountable cousins. I have been the source of his inspiration, growth, and success. See, now that he has become a man, what does he do? He kicks me out of the house with the left foot. In my place he brings in a good-for-nothing semiliterate village girl. See my seventeen years of suffering going down the drain, see . . ."

66

A few slaps administered by the normally staid Mr. Nduke worsened an already very bad situation. Mrs. Nduke let go of her loincloth, tore her blouse, scattered her hair, and proceeded to tear Ekam's clothes to bits, all the while screaming at the top of her voice. It took two male neighbors some energy to release Ekam from the vicelike grip of her mistress. The girl was by now bleeding from her face and chest. Ekam took a beeline immediately she was free, leaving behind a screaming Mrs. Nduke. She was thankful that she had hanged out a few clothes to dry outside. She snapped a blouse and a skirt off the clothesline, hurriedly dressed and escaped.

"It is not that I could not have given that woman a good beating," she had told Ekebo, her 'savior,' the night after the incident. "It is that I was brought up to look at all women as mothers, and all men as fathers. I was taught to respect my elders. How would I face my parents and my Sunday schoolteacher if I had as much as given that woman just one slap, which she actually needed—and deserved?" she concluded.

"You did a good thing by turning the other check," Ekebo had responded gravely in a tone that was a mix of anger and admiration. He had cut a figure of concern at the plight of an innocent girl who been unjustly assailed by an irate housewife.

"My sadness is that because of me, a perfect gentleman lost his temper and beat up his wife." She paused, sighed, and continued, "A man must never slap his wife. My father has never done it. And my uncle told me that if a man beats up his wife in the presence of his sons, the sons will also beat up their wives. Unfortunately my master's sons were there when my master beat up his wife, I suspect, for the first time."

"He probably could not hold himself much longer. A bad woman is a bad woman," Ekebo said. Ekam had sighed again and again.

"What was the reason behind her action?" Ekebo asked.

"She accused me of tempting her husband. She said I was trying to take her husband from her and that the man was no longer interested in her."

"How can a little girl like you tempt an old man like that?"

"I wonder."

"Probably it was the other way round."

"The man never showed any interest in me. He is a respectable man."

"I would be surprised, my dear girl. Respectability is not one of the words common in this man-woman business."

"That may be so. But this particular man is kind and he is like my father. He would not try something stupid."

"Stupid? I don't know about it being stupid. Probably the wife was trying to stop the man from making any move. He would have tried to 'approach' you a little while later."

"You talk as if it is something that must be done. Some men still respect themselves."

"I suppose so."

Ekam was too occupied with her raw experience early on to have noted the veiled threat in Ekebo's submissions. She felt quite at home in Ekebo's two-room apartment. This was home.

Ekebo hailed from a neighboring village but was said to have some distant blood relationship with Ekam's mother. Ekam regarded him as an uncle and father particularly after her raw experience at Mr. Nduke's house. She had met him a number of times while she lived at the Ndukes.

Ekebo lived in one of those nondescript bungalows that lined the streets of Calabar. It was one of those houses built to accommodate tenants. The external walls were painted white with a blue paint lined at the base. The fascia board of the roof was also painted blue. The house had twenty rooms in all, with the main building having twelve rooms while the two extensions behind bore four rooms each. The conveniences and cooking area formed a block at the back, leaving a space in between as washing bay and for relaxation.

Ekam had noticed on entering the house that the walls were very dirty. Years of scribbling with dirt, chalk, and oil left the walls in multihues with brown dominating. The backyard, as it was popularly called, was shiny green, filled with leftovers of food and human waste deposited by the numerous children in the compound. The bathroom defied description. The toilets, two in number, one for each half of the building that implied occupants of ten rooms, were of the pail system. Clearing one's bowel was always an ordeal, except after the washing of the toilet, which was carried out once a week by one of the occupants on a rotational basis.

To Ekam, these objectionable aspects could be borne. Mr. Nduke lived in a three-bedroom flat with modern conveniences of which she had ensured strict cleanliness. But it was not a home to her. Home is where one's mind is at rest. Home is where one feels wanted, where one is not an alien, where as one man put it, "you can ease yourself just about anywhere and no one says, 'we don't do such things here.'"

Ekam's first night at Ekebo's was uneventful. She had eaten a good meal of rice and red sauce with four solid pieces of meat. That type of meal was common only on Christmas day. The meal was prepared by Ekebo, who had earlier treated her wounds by bathing and cleaning them with warm water that had some drops of Dettol antiseptic solution introduced. Ekam had felt very comfortable following the first aid. She then relished the food presented before her. The food tasted too good to be the handwork of a man. Had she not seen Ekebo cook the food just outside the door of the sitting room, she would have thought a woman had prepared it.

Ekebo lived in two rooms, one serving as a sitting room, the other as a bedroom. The sitting room was well furnished. There were easy chairs—one two-seater and three singles—and a table with drawers on top of which were some books and a reading lamp. At a corner stood a "radiogram," a hi-fi boxlike radio cum gramophone machine made by Grundig. Few men could boast of such instruments at that time. Ekebo sure had taste.

A refrigerator stood close to the door that opened into the bedroom. Ekam could not quite make up her mind whether this gadget, an Electrolux product, should have been better placed in the bedroom or in the sitting room. Ekebo preferred it in the sitting room, more as an item of furniture to boost his ego than as an instrument that provides convenience. The sitting room was carpeted with linoleum covering, wall to wall. Ekebo's idea of living marked him out as one with high taste. Why he did not have any woman living with him baffled Ekam, for men with much less household furniture and equipment that epitomized comfort attracted as many women as they wanted. The only uncomfortable aspect was the red bulb in the bedroom. Bachelors were in love with bulbs of different colors in their apartments. Ekam's favorite color was not red, and for it to adorn the bedroom and function in the night when someone's eyes cannot be seen made her squirm.

The second day of her sojourn was equally uneventful. She had gone to the market with a good one-pound note in her purse. One pound! She had bought and bought a whole lot of things, including a handkerchief, panties, a pair of earrings, and a scarf, aside from the food items that she carried home in two big bags. She had wondered why a man could part with so much money for one shopping trip. It was in fact the largest amount of money she had ever handled for expenses in her life. Probably Ekebo was trying to impress her? *Probably.* She could not fathom the reason. It also could have been because he likes living well. He liked living for today for tomorrow is unknown, which is probably why he had the nickname *man-die-go.*

* * *

The compliments lavished on Ekam by Ekebo following her preparation of food left a very pleasant feeling in her far into the third day of her stay at her new residence. The day ended well when Ekebo took her to watch a popular movie at Patsol Cinema along Bedwell Street. Ekam had never had the opportunity to participate in the nightlife of the city. What she had dreamt of seemed to come alive as from that night.

Outside Patsol Cinema, a movie house owned by a Mr. Patrick Solomon, a naturalized Nigerian of Lebanese origin, Ekam saw a motley crowd of mostly young people. They appeared in various colors of apparels, makeups, and hairstyles. Both men and women smoked cigarettes, the latter to Ekam's utter consternation. As it happened on the ferry trip from Oron to Calabar when Etefia was by her, Ekebo watched Ekam's reactions with amusement but in silence, once in a while throwing light here and there on certain behavioral aspects of the crowd.

At the gate, Ekebo paid a total of four shillings, two shillings for each of them. The man at the box office tore two tickets and handed them to Ekebo with a wink and a knowing smile.

"How now?" Ekebo asked.

"Life is hard, my brother," the ticket man answered

"Man must live."

"Or man-die-go."

"This is your new catch?"

"Well, she is my sister."

"I hope not Owerri sister-o?"

"No."

The conversation was stopped by shouts from the impatient crowd behind.

"*Oga* move now; time is going."

Ekam and Ekebo were virtually shoved into the hall. On entering, the girl stopped and looked around, her mouth wide open. To her, this was quite a hall. Apart from the assembly hall of the village primary school and probably the church hall, she had never seen so much space within four walls. She stood still until Ekebo gently propelled her forward. She sat down on one of the seats arranged in rows. With the bright lights still on, she took a good look at the hall.

Directly in front was a wall painted black. This, Ekebo explained, was the screen. Rows and rows of metal chairs were evident, arranged at different levels of elevation such that everybody could see the screen clearly irrespective of where one sat. On looking back, Ekam saw two openings with what Ekebo called projectors pointing outward. She could also see various doors marked "Exit" at various points. At the left, close to the

71

screen, she noticed two other doors with the inscription, "Female Toilet" and "Male Toilet."

It did not take another fifteen minutes before the entire hall was filled to capacity. The conversation was by now deafening. Some people sitting close by were competing with each other, trying to give a full run down on the film that was about to be screened, which had John Wayne as the central figure or "actor." As time wore on, there were mass catcalls. As the whistling rose to a crescendo, the lights went out, making Ekam to grab Ekebo's hand. Ekebo told her that the lights out signaled the commencement of the film.

The girl could not say at the end of the film whether she enjoyed what she saw or not, for there was so much noise, so much smoke from numerous cigarettes, heavy fumes of alcohol, and even at a time, a mild stampede following a fisticuff when two watchers could not agree on who was a better fighter on the screen. The men were so crude. They spoke at the top of their voices, abused each other, punched people once in a while, and were exceptionally rude to girls. She felt that the tension and fear were not adequately compensated for by the thrills of the film. She told Ekebo emphatically that she would not visit the cinema hall again, unless there was a place the crowd could be more civil.

*   *   *

Her misgivings about the rawness of men following the outing of the previous night could have quickly evaporated had Ekebo not sprung a surprise the night of the fourth day. Things had gone on smoothly till it was bedtime. Ekebo had come into the bedroom, gently shook Ekam, and requested to be allowed to sleep on the bed. Hitherto, he had slept on the couch in the sitting room. His gentlemanly approach made her feel guilty. Can you imagine the owner of a thing humbly requesting to be allowed to make use of what is rightly his? Ekam had rather suggested that she should go to the sitting room. Ekebo had flatly refused. It would be unbecoming of him as a host to allow his guest to sleep on the narrow couch while he slept on the bed. Though she felt uncomfortable, she had acquiesced. Sleep did not come early as this was the first time she was spending a night on the same bed with a fully grown man. As Ekebo did not disturb her except for occasional touch by a stray leg or stray hand, she slept off.

It was when she woke up with a start in the wee hours of the morning to find herself in Ekebo's arms with the man breathing hard on her that she recoiled and felt that men just could not be trusted. All he could say was that he had lost self-control for Ekam was so beautiful and desirable that it would take more than a man to resist her charms.

All morning, Ekam could not hide her discomfort and resentment. Ekebo was not just a fellow townsman, her kith and kin, but had some blood relationship with her. A lot can be tolerated in her village. Incest was absolutely an unacceptable behavior in the community. Unfortunately, the limit of blood relationship appeared to be extremely elastic, forcing people to seek spouses outside their villages so as to play safe. The uncomfortable aspect was, however, that Ekebo could marry Ekam as the blood relationship was a little distant. Despite this, she felt any intimacy with Ekebo was revolting and unacceptable.

As if to make up for his misdemeanor, Ekebo took Ekam to a spiritual revival service on the fifth day. The service started just after dusk and lasted till almost midnight. Ekam lost touch with events as the preacher started preaching. The man had dwelt on two items—the ungodliness of all other churches except his own and generous donations. Ekam believed in the Biblical injunction that men should not judge each other. The overemphasis on generous donation also turned her off. By the time she went home, she was as unhappy as she was before she went there. The purport of Ekebo's decision to attend the service was also not clear to her.

*   *   *

"Don't you city people ever stay indoors for one night?" Ekam asked Ekebo when he said he had something lined up for her sixth night at his end.

"In the city, there is neither day nor night," Ekebo had responded, throwing his arms wide and allowing them fall by his sides making a clapping sound.

"In the city, you work throughout the day. For you to live long, you must enjoy the benefits of your efforts and it is only in the night that somebody can enjoy. So you work hard and enjoy hard. And you must know one important thing, the money made in Calabar must be spent in full in Calabar."

"That is why you people forget home people."

"And when we finally leave at old age, we put our belongings in a pillow case like the infamous Efik Udo Ibanga."

"You put it so casually as if it is a good thing."

"I say it so casually because it is accepted as normal."

"Normal?"

"Yes, normal. When something—even the bad—is accepted by a majority, it becomes at least normal, if not good."

"What about sleep?" Ekam asked.

"Sleep? Well, that can take place anywhere. In the office, at the shop, in the church, even on the steering."

"No wonder we have many accidents on our roads."

"Witches and wizards cause accidents."

"You wouldn't blame witches when the drivers themselves cause the accidents."

"My dear girl, our society is one which seeks scapegoats for everything. You know the brakes of your car are faulty. You jump into the car and drive off. You run into another car. What do you say? Some witches are hungry for blood."

"If you know that much, why don't you spare some nights for sleep?"

"I don't own a car, my dear. If I sleep, I do so in the office."

"The work suffers, isn't it? Yet you are paid from my father's tax money."

"Like the pig said to the piglet, when you grow up, you will know why I am always plowing the soil with my snout."

"Is there no way the city dwellers can be made to change their love for nightlife?"

"No matter how much rain falls on the *editan** leaf, its bitterness will remain. Let us not talk of changing people. Let us talk of changing our circumstances. If I were rich, I would own a television set. There would be no need for me to take you to a rowdy cinema hall."

"Would being rich stop you from going to bars?"

"Not likely, I must confess. Yes, I can buy beer at home if I am rich. You can cook the most delicious pepper soup for me, but money can never pay for the company of friends, their conversation about girls, their sexy demonstrations, political discussions, and others which you get only when you spend some time in a hotel." He paused to let that bit be assimilated.

"Talking about hotels, I am planning to take you to the city's number one nightclub—Luna Nite Club on Fosbery Road. That will be on Saturday, and although you are so young, I expect you know what Saturday night means in a city." Despite her revulsion at unending night activities, Ekam smiled at the idea of a night at Luna Nite Club.

While she excitedly looked forward to a great time at the club she had heard so much about, she had to manage through the Friday night event. It was a wake keeping. One of Ekebo's colleagues had lost his mother. Ekebo had to attend the all-night ceremony of preparing the dead for the trip to the world beyond. Or better still, a night for the living to revel, eat free food, and drink free drinks, leaving the family to pay the debt for many years after the burial. Very importantly, vigil night afforded opportunity for lads and lasses to strike dates or consummate relationships that could leave one of the parties heavy for nine months after.

Wake keeping is one of the ceremonies that make up city life. Such ceremonies, of course, obtain in the villages. In the city, there is a touch of class, with the eatables, drinkables, and decorations reflecting the financial means of the family of the deceased. It is one of the occasions during which people display their wealth purely for public relations purposes or as an ego trip. In some cases, the deceased are known to have died of malnutrition or neglect.

The goings-on at the wake keeping did not make much impression on Ekam. The usual things happened, the gossips; the lewd or hateful glances; the drunken brawls; the quarrels among family members and rivals; the fight over food and drinks; the protests by those who felt cheated by stewards; the sometimes irritating activities of praise singers; the professional criers who turn weeping for the dead into an art; the music and the dance; the endless meetings, whispers and consultations; the rowdiness; and all those odd activities that make up a wake keeping event. One outstanding thing about wake keeping ceremonies, Ekam recalled, was that men and women have been known to lose their spouses to other men and women while parents could go home without their daughters.

As was usual, those who attend the all-night vigil wake up rather late. Ekebo woke up late. So did Ekam. As the events of the previous night were not worth remembering, she decided to focus her imagination on what lay in front, for as elders would say, what lies in front is greater than what is behind. Ekebo, however, rushed off to work, putting in the half day to midday before returning home to prepare for the night's activities.

*   *   *

At about seven o'clock, Ekebo, in the company of Ekam, arrived at Fosbery Road from the Watt Market end. Although the Atomic 8 dance band was reigning at Olympic Hotel close to the Fosbery Road by Bedwell Street junction, the pull of Luna Nite Club was much stronger. The pair strolled casually toward the club, hand in hand. To Ekebo, there was more to holding of hands. There was pride on his face as he sucked in the jealous glances of amorous sons of Adam. To Ekam, now a full sixteen-year-old, fair in complexion with a devastating figure barely covered by the 'tight knee' dress that appeared to have been made by the gods just for her, holding hands with Ekebo was more of that of a girl who needed protection by her uncle from the claws of the lions that lined up the streets ready to pounce and devour her.

All along the route to Luna Nite Club, young men and women stood by the sides. As men are wont to hang around such places, she was not bothered. What surprised her was the number of women moving aimlessly up and down the street.

"Who are these women?" she had asked innocently.

"Free women," Ekebo replied

"You mean they came here unaccompanied?"

"Yes."

"What for?"

"To look for men."

"I thought men look for women."

"The reverse can also hold."

"What happens when they get the men they want?"

"What normally happens when women get the men they want. Only in this case, there will be a price tag."

"Who pays?"

"The men of course."

"You mean any stranger can just come and pay for a woman here and take her away?"

"Just for the night. Just for the night."

"Suppose the stranger is a ghost?"

"This is a city. We don't talk of ghosts in the city."

"Suppose the stranger is a bad man? Suppose he is a highway robber?"

"That is one of the risks of the trade. To make money you have to take risks."

"Must a woman risk her life just to make money?"

"If need be."

"Bro, why do these women do such things?"

"Because they have to survive. They have to pay rent to the landlords. They have to buy dresses and cosmetics. Above all, they have to eat."

"What a way to get money! Why can't they do some other thing?"

"They may have had no alternative. Some of them are illiterate. Some are semiliterate. Most have no respectable jobs. Some have jobs but their salaries are so small that they cannot meet most of the important things they need. So they look for other sources of income by night to add to what they make by day."

"But these things do not happen in the villages."

"Because in the village peoples' wants are few and simple. The money they make can meet what they need as well as what they want. What they cannot meet, family members, friends, clubs, neighbors, and even the church can help out. In the city, the demands of everyday life are so many. Yet the means to meet them are piteously limited. To cap it all, it is every man unto himself and God for us all."

"Why can't people go back to the village instead of doing things that are wrong just to remain in the city?"

"The pull of city is too strong, my girl. Everybody feels it, including your humble self. The village is denied so many basic things—electricity, tap water, hospitals, good schools, good roads, buses, and taxis. The absence of these things makes life very uninteresting. You cannot live again in a village if you've lived long in the city. The best thing is not to come at all. The city beckons, draws, and traps those that are not careful. I am sure you would not think of going back to the village now."

Ekam could not give an answer to that. She had just started having the taste of city life. It would be difficult to give up all the comfort and all the easy living she had become accustomed to within such a short period of time. The idea of seeing one's way around with light from dried palm fronds was not too enticing. One only needs to flick a button on the wall to have light that shone on and on. Now she could have as much water as she wanted by simply turning a tap. She did not need to make a one-hour trip to a stream for just one pot of water. Nor did she need any more to go through the art of lifting pots at the stream. Or even of putting them down at home. The list was endless. But most importantly, nightlife, which she had heard so much about and to which she was now being introduced, was one thing she could not afford to let go.

*   *   *

The pair had by now reached the nightclub proper. With neon lights, Luna Nite Club stood out along the street. The clubhouse was in fact a bungalow that once had tenants. With generous painting, lights, and posters, the place now stood out as an abode of enjoyment.

With ten shillings, Ekebo and Ekam gained entry into the club. The hall was not big compared with Patsol Cinema. It was of an L-shape covered with colorful canopies. At the middle was the bandstand. A signboard announced that on the stand was the Luna All Stars led by Bustic Kingsley Bassey, a musician of no mean repute.

As the hall slowly filled out with revelers who sat on the metal chairs that surrounded round wooden tables, the band started warming up for the night's activities. While the drummer tested the drums and cymbals, the guitarists strummed away, giving out various notes, bending forward and backward to adjust the strings once in a while. The men on the horns blew away carelessly, giving out discordant notes. They routinely wiped their lips with their palms while their equipment that had knobs all over were wiped with pieces of cloth.

One of the men ran all over the stage, touching one thing or the other, connecting and disconnecting wires and connecting them again. Finally, a young man in a rather weird attire took the microphone, blew air into it, used the four fingers of his right hand to hit the instrument several times, and then said, "Hello, hello, testing the microphone one, two, three." He repeated this so many times that Ekam felt like going to snatch the poor suffering instrument from the man. This activity she had seen several times at local dances. Vocalists were so fond of toying with the microphone, always shouting "testing, testing the microphone, one, two, three." Probably this made the instrument to work better?

As the band played the first tune, the inflow of people into the hall increased rapidly. Ekam could see some white men moving around, inspecting the band, the bar, the lighting, and chatting with some regulars. Apparently, these were the owners. She had heard about this particular group—the Lebanese—who seemed to be everywhere, especially in entertainment and trading. Ekam had also met them along the Marina, where they owned a number of grocery stores and garment sales outlets.

By now, a few people had gone to the floor to dance to the good old highlife music played by the band. Ekam could pick out tunes by Joe Mensah of Ghana, Cardinal Rex Jim Lawson, Celestine Ukwu, and Etubom Rex Williams, all Nigerians; and some from Bustic himself. Once in a while, some rock music popularly called "soul" came on. So did reggae. At that time, James Brown and Jimmy Cliff represented the epitome of soul and reggae, respectively.

Ekam was so carried away by the goings-on that she did not notice that she had finished one bottle of Star beer and was onto a bottle of Guinness stout. Ekebo urged her to take some more.

"If you want to dance freely without feeling shy, you must make yourself *high*. To be high, you need more alcohol in your system."

It was not that she had never taken a beer in her life. No village lass would say that truthfully. It was that she had never finished a bottle before. Now she was even mixing the varieties. She began to feel light-headed and actually felt like dancing. And she danced. It was true then that alcohol could make one dance without feeling shy.

The effect of alcohol did not, however, make her miss the face and feet of the young man that was billed as Saturday night special. She remembered him clearly. It was the same 007 that she had seen over two years earlier on her way to Calabar from Oron. 007 performed as usual, drawing applause, sympathy as well as shillings and pence from the crowd. He certainly smiled home at the end of his performance.

Another side attraction was a young man who danced *ajasco* with a special music. He performed so deftly with his feet that the movements at a point made onlookers feel dizzy. His choreography drew applause from the crowd. A few coins and notes also changed pockets. Of note during this performance was a girl who went to the young man, danced with him at a rather close range, and then pushed a five-shilling note right into his panties. This drew applause from the revelers.

The variety also included a dance drama, fire eating, a show of strength by a "superman" among others. A lady vocalist who did a belly dance drew applause despite the poverty of her voice. Everything, good or bad, weird or normal, added color to the Saturday night at Luna.

By the time the revelers left for home at about three o'clock in the morning, they were tired, but happy. Ekam virtually walked on air all the way home. The cool early-morning breeze cleared a bit of the fogginess in her brain and eyes before she reached the house. However, she looked forward to immediate sleep on reaching home.

This was not to be. On reaching home, Ekebo locked the door, undressed fully, revealing his manhood to the consternation of the girl. She turned her face away. He only laughed, a boisterous, bawdy, and mocking laughter. Gently dragging into the bedroom, the little girl who was by now very frightened, he proceeded to undress her. The girl's resistance, pleadings, and threats of a scream made no difference. A few minutes later, Ekam had lost everything—her dress, her trust in men, an abode, her pride, her innocence, and her virginity.

Chapter 7

"What did the fool say in the morning?" Enǫmma asked Ekam after she had told her story.

"He looked very sad. He looked guilty. He apologized, blaming the devil for forcing him into a wicked act," she replied.

"Poor devil. He gets blamed for all the bad things men do."

"Enǫmma, why do men do such things? Must they force their way through?"

"They can give a dozen reasons for their actions. Don't forget women too sometimes force men into the act."

"Impossible."

"So you think. Rape takes place when one person is forced into a sexual activity. The force can come in many ways."

"This kind of thing does not happen in the village."

"It does, but it is very rare. The demands of city life force men into things they would not normally do. Meanwhile the women in the city expose themselves to rape by the way they dress, the way the walk, the places they visit."

"How did I expose myself?"

"You walked on your two feet into the lion's den."

"Why must the women always bear the blame? I trusted somebody."

"In the city, you need not trust anybody. Not even your father, for he can sell you to the next buyer, just to raise a few pounds for some bottles of beer."

"Who would have thought that the quiet and innocent-looking Ekebo could do a thing like that?"

"The calm and innocent-looking men do the worst things. Like the sea, they are calm on the surface while underneath, monsters dwell in thousands. Remember that his name is Ekebo."

"Who would have said? Who would have thought? He bears just the right name. But Enomma, you have not told me why men commit rape and how the victims can come out of the bad experience."

"There are theories and there are theories. I think that these men are trying to take out their frustrations on others."

"Why in the cities?"

"Life in the village is very simple. Expectations are few and simple. A man who needs sex either gets married, and cheaply too, or he talks to a woman that is of interest to him. What he needs most is his readiness to shake off shyness and the dread of failure and put his case forward. His power of persuasion is important.

"In the city it is different. You need to have more than a good command of the English language or whichever language the woman understands. A man needs not just good English but also pounds and shillings, for grammar does not put food on the table. The lady needs certain things to make her presentable and to meet city standards. Whoever wants to have her should be prepared to part with a few coins. That does not make all women prostitutes. It is just that a woman has to be taken care of by men. That is what the society accepts. For the man who is unable to pay for what a woman can offer, rape could come into his mind if he is unable to bear the pressure that nature has put on him."

"Sad, isn't it?"

"Yes, it is. We don't have to blame all cases of rape on lack of money though. One other reason is that it could be a way of showing that a man is more powerful than somebody else. Look at it this way—in the city, there are several levels of power. A messenger in the government ministry is oppressed by many people, from the governor to the clerk in the office. On the road and beyond, the police harass him. He is disturbed at home by his landlord, treated badly his wife and his children if he has them. There could be a strong desire in him to subdue someone so as to prove that he is a man. He attacks a helpless female.

"This does not happen in the village. The system in the village is very simple and straightforward. There is the village head, the village council, the ward heads, the family heads, and the heads of different societies. There, age is the most important thing. A young man first needs to behave well, contribute to the activities in the village and wait. As the elders die, young ones move into the vacant positions. These days, one can become a village head by working hard to make himself somebody even when that person is not from a royal family.

"In the city, an office messenger must forget about being a permanent secretary in his lifetime. For not only will it take him years of education to be prepared for the job, he will need more than hard work to become a permanent secretary, such as 'man know man.' The city breeds frustration and it encourages crime."

"Are you trying to say that Ekebo was right?"

"Not so. I am only trying to tell you that there is no point in living in the past. The milk is spilt. It can never be recovered. You can be a virgin only once. You have to wake up and live. If city people were to worry about past things, they would not live to be forty years old. As long as you survive any misfortune with your life, health and freedom, you push such behind you and get on with the business of living. What is in front is greater than what is behind."

Ekam sat quietly for some time, thinking about Enomma's words. She recalled her dream of the city as a place where life held the best for the residents. What she was now being exposed to were great contrasts that she realized were the realities. It was time for her to wake up from her world of ideals.

*   *   *

After Ekam had poured out her heart to her friend, she slept like a baby throughout the night. It was one of those nights one is said to have a dreamless sleep. In the morning, she woke up feeling refreshed and revitalized, apparently ready to face the world again.

"I told you, didn't I?" Enomma enthused.

"What didn't you tell me?" Ekam asked in the way their peer group members would ask.

"That you will feel a load lifted off your shoulders as soon as you tell your story," Enomma said.

"You were right."

Throughout that day, which happened to have been a public holiday, the two young women chatted away. It was as if nothing had happened that nearly ruined the happiness of one of them on a permanent basis. Their conversation ranged from childhood fantasies and realities to adulthood realities, hopes, fears, and expectations.

More current issues were also discussed, prime among which was Ekam's future. Although it had crossed the minds of the two girls, none of them dared to moot the idea of Ekam going back to the village. That would be unthinkable, impracticable, and in fact, unrealistic. This was because neither of the girls believed that the village was a good alternative to the difficulties of city life. And in any case, Enomma's belief and Ekam's acceptance of the fact that what lies in front is greater than what is behind made them regard a return to the village an unrealistic option at that point in time.

Since going back to the village was out of the question, staying in the city was the only option. However, the girls knew that even with the economy being at high noon as a result of the oil boom, a sensible person could not stay at home all day doing nothing productive. The pace of economic and social development in Nigeria had left a dent even on the concept of "full-time housewife." Women craved for and where they got it relished their financial independence made possible by paid employment.

A number of options were discussed and discarded. Ekam rejected several suggestions. For instance, Enomma suggested that she could serve as a steward in one of the hotels or numerous eating houses in town.

"God forbid!" she had exclaimed.

"Why?" Enomma had asked.

"Those places! *Hm.* I used to help a neighbor once in a while when I was living with Mr. Nduke. So many men used to eat there. *Hm,* stewards. Imagine dirty old men with their palms that are as rough as the bark of a tree, that have old fingers that end in dirty fingernails—"

"*Ah ah!* What bad-mouth, Ekam."

"It's true. Those old men can hardly keep their hands off people's children."

"You can gently tell them off."

"Wrong! They would think it is the normal way girls behave. They simply go on, touching far beyond the hand and shoulder and upper back. I hate them. Do you know that a lot of men who go to eating places and drinking parlors do so not because they want to eat or drink?"

"Which is why operators of those places prefer to hire attractive young girls." Enomma agreed. There was brief silence as the two were lost in thought.

"Will you then serve as a shop hand?" Enomma asked.

"Not me. When the owner cannot manage his business, he turns around to blame an innocent attendant, accusing him or her of stealing. Call me what you like. Accuse me of everything else, even murder—"

"Even murder?"

"Yes, even murder. Our society hates people that kill, but is ready forgive them. Stealing? No way. So don't accuse me of stealing."

"You can be an attendant in a pool company," Enomma suggested.

"Heaven help me!" Ekam exclaimed, throwing her hands over her head in exasperation.

"What is wrong with that one?" Enomma asked.

"Those illiterate stakers! Those irresponsible gamblers!"

"Stop it. There are a lot of respectable people in the business."

"Don't tell me that. Whoever goes to put his money in a game that is to be decided in the future and in a location thousands of miles away! Liverpool is playing Everton, Manchester City versus West Ham." Then feigning seriousness she said in exasperation, "Oh, only one is cut." The two girls burst out laughing.

"Perm two from three equal six lines," Ekam continued.

"You got it wrong," Enomma said laughing.

"I hope you don't involve yourself in that hopeless business."

"Call it what you may. What I know is that a lot of people have made their money as agents or forecasters or bookmakers."

"From hopeless stakers, isn't it? Banker draw." They laughed again.

"It is not your business what goes on there. Mr. Good is not another name for the game. What you go there for is your monthly salary plus bonus every Friday or Saturday depending on the season," Enomma explained.

"Which one is season?" Ekam asked.

"Australian or English," Enomma replied

"This one that you know so much about the business, I hope you are not a victim."

"Not directly. My friend Edet is an agent."

"No wonder. A person praises what is hers."

"All I am saying is that you should get a job in one of the pool houses."

"I won't. Do you also know that the owners of the pool houses demand sex from the girls that work for them? If you allow them, they dump you when they are tired and want a new girl. If you reject them they regard it as stubbornness and sack you, as if sex is part of the agreement."

"Some believe it is their right."

"That's just it. So count me out of the family of the suffering pool workers—poor pay, too much work, abused by stakers, laughed at by friends who have better jobs, and disturbed by their masters for sex. That is one job Ekam will never be involved in."

"So what else can you do with your qualification and experience?"

"You suggest. You have been here longer than I."

"What of learning a trade?"

"Such as?"

"Dressmaking."

"A seamstress? I hate that group too. My reason? They are lazy. As you get close to their shop that is always located such that they can see visitors, they rush and put your cloth on their machine. When you arrive they dance around you." She tilted her head to one side and said, "'Oh, I am almost through. *Em,* I have been too busy-o. Please come in a week's time.' Meanwhile, as soon as you leave, the person removes the cloth from the sewing pin and hangs it till the following week. Yet they are poor." The girls laughed.

"Besides, who told you I can be an apprentice for three years! Three good years of standing around watching madam cut pieces of paper, asking you to stitch, sending you to shop for her, cook for her, wash for her, do all the duties of a housewife except spending a night with her husband—"

"Ekam. You are bad-o."

"It's true, isn't it? Apprentices are househelps. They spend not less than two of the three years of training working in madam's house."

"When you are free and on your own, you will do the same thing to your apprentices."

"I have a conscience."

"This is serious. You can't work in a pool house. You can't stand restaurants and bars. You can't be a househelp again. You find apprenticeship boring and unattractive. So what are you going to do?" Enomma said in exasperation.

"Sorry that I am a burden to you."

"For God's sake. That you are staying with me is not the reason for my wish that you should get yourself something to do. You must get a job, for the devil—"

"Finds work for the idle," Ekam concluded.

"I hope not you. Meanwhile what is you plan?"

"I would like to work in an office," she said with pride.

Enomma looked at her innocent idiocy with pity rather than with disdain.

"An office is where you put in a hard day's work to earn a living," Enomma said.

"I mean a ministry."

"I see. That confirms that you are a lazy person."

"It does not follow."

"You are right, and you are wrong. Nine out of ten workers in the ministry just go the office to avoid query. They spend the day gossiping, moving dirty and torn files, sleep, then wonder when salary will come."

"It is not as bad as that."

"Because you like it. I am speaking from experience. Meanwhile, with your qualification, a job in the ministry will at best hurt your pride. You can only be a cleaner, tea girl, or messenger."

"I will manage."

"And become a manager. Anyway, suit yourself," Enomma concluded and shrugged. "Come-o, why is it that everybody wants to work in a government office? How will our private sector develop?"

"Well, I am not going to set the foundation stone for it. I can only assist when I grow up."

"Well done. Meanwhile, what else can you do?"

"I can work in a private clinic as an attendant."

"Why do you like that one?"

"I will have an opportunity of learning a little medicine."

"What kind of medicine?"

"Many. Analgesics, sedatives, purgatives, and the pill."

"Which one is the pill?"

"Birth control pills."

"You must know that one! Come to think of it, where did you learn those things?

"There is a chemist next to the house Mr. Nduke lives. I used to spend some free time there apart from the restaurant I mentioned earlier. I was very much interested in pills."

"Why?"

"Because it is important for a girl. You should know that."

Enomma paused for reflection. She wondered at the great contrasts in the girl before her—at one point naïve, at another wiser than her age.

"Since private clinics are few, what else would you want to do?"

"Business."

"Which is to say?"

"Trading or contracts."

Where will you get the money to start off?"

"Here and there. When it is time for that, something will happen."

"I see. And what will you trade on?"

"*Ah*. There are so many things."

"Once it is not flesh trade."

"You shouldn't have said that, Enomma. That is very unkind. I may be poor, now. I may be homeless. But I am still from a good home."

"I didn't mean to hurt you. I just want to make sure you are aware of all the options and that you know the way our people think. Whatever you decide on, it should be good, acceptable to the society, and it should be the type you can carry out without too much stress. Your friend here will stand by you."

"Thank you," Ekam said.

*   *   *

Two years after Ekam moved to Enomma's house from Ekebo's, she had changed jobs four times, an average of two jobs per year. Jobs at low levels were easy to come by despite the movements of employable youths from the rural areas that were gathering momentum though at a slow pace. This was because of the booming economy that witnessed a lot of private sector investments and the desire of the governments at the various levels to touch the lives of citizens, particularly as the governments also had a lot of money to spend.

The girl's first employment was as a factory hand in a cottage industry. The Uwa's Clothing Industry produced ready-made dresses. The factory was a long hall, which had little or no vent for air movement. Light was provided through transparent roofing sheets strategically positioned on the roof. The factory was hot all day, reaching a peak from midday to about three o'clock in the afternoon. With bundles of cloth of various odors, sweat from several bodies of workers numbering about twenty, and the stench from a nearby drainage, the unhealthy mix of odors combined to make the working environment almost unbearable. Yet the laborers toiled on.

Enomma had introduced Ekam to the production supervisor who happened to be an acquaintance. She had seen an advertisement on a piece of chalkboard placed in front of the factory that read: *Production Assistants Wanted Urgently. Apply in Person Within.* What had attracted Ekam was in fact the big name "production assistant." Though she could not quite understand the meaning, she had believed that the longer, more complicated, and heavier the title, the more important would be the job, and by extension, the pay packet. She got the job but was surprised to find herself as one of the many that handled sundry duties on the factory floor where trained tailors were the kings. The daily routine of packing dresses ready for the market, and worse still, buying food for the tailors almost drove Ekam beyond the brink. Thus, after just two months, the girl called it quits and continued her search for a better job.

After leaving the cloth factory, Ekam sat at home for another two months.

"You must be bored my sister." Enọmma had sympathized.

"You can imagine me staying indoors all day," Ekam said heavily, spitting as if to throw away the venomous feeling inside her.

"But why did you leave that job? I keep asking you that question?"

"And I keep dodging," Ekam answered.

"Well?"

"I hated the job. The factory was too hot."

"But it was a job all the same. As our elders say, welcome back is better than how is home?"

"Or half a loaf of bread is better than none."

"You said it."

"Enọmma, staying at home is very difficult for me. But I would rather just leave home every morning and walk the length and breadth of this town doing nothing, than continue at that factory. I felt like a slave with the big name of production assistant."

"So what are you going to do?" Enọmma asked. Ekam paused and thought for a while.

"I honestly don't know," she replied with a shrug.

"How about working in a hospital?"

"Tell me more about it."

"Well. You'll be expected to keep the place tidy generally."

"By that you mean I'll be a cleaner."

"I did not say that."

"Call a spade, a spade. Probably you'll give cleaning some big title such as 'hospital assistant' or 'hygiene assistant.'"

"Don't be ridiculous. It is a job after all."

"Yes. A job where there is no respect for the worker."

"Are you going to eat respect?"

"We need it. Remember I am from a proud family—poor but proud."

"Think of other benefits of working in a hospital and you may change your mind. Recall that you once said you would prefer to work in clinic."

"What are the benefits?"

"Several. You will know more about medicines and how to use them. You can even learn how to administer injections."

"I have not been trained for that kind of thing. I don't want to do what is wrong. I hear some attendants even try to operate on people."

"That is not what you will be going for. You are from a good home. Your father cannot tell people what he is not. You cannot do something different."

"Don't bet on it. Oboyo and Calabar are not the same."

"There is still some morality in the city. While you can bend a few rules of decency to enable you survive the needs of the city, you can still maintain your self-respect by being your father's daughter. Call it principles."

"I don't know what principles mean. But I heard someone shout the other day, 'Principles you say! Principles. That word has no place in the city dictionary except for pupils in primary schools.'"

"I keep wondering what you will turn out to be."

"Don't worry, I'll be fine."

"Meanwhile, will you take up the job?"

"I'll think about it."

"The sooner, the better. Jobs in the city are not like marriage proposals. They do not wait for people to make up their minds when they feel like."

*   *   *

Ekam lasted just three months as a staff of Getwell Clinic and Maternity Home. It was a hectic three months. Most of the night, she would come home and find it difficult to eat.

"What happened?" Enomma asked the first day she went about with a face that portrayed revolting feelings.

"Blood. My God! I have never seen so much blood in my life."

"I thought you were strong."

"What has strength to do with it?"

"Inner strength, I mean."

"Not with blood. And I had to clean it all! Oh god, the smell. Enomma, I appreciate your concern for me, but I don't think I can manage that place. You know that cleanliness is a way of life in the village. We hate odors. That clinic smells so much. There is no way I can ever eat when I am through with a day's work."

"You will get used to it."

"I don't think so."

One day, Ekam went back home and collapsed. It had been a full day for her. An accident case had been brought to the clinic. The victim's intestines were sprawling all over. Part of his head was badly smashed such that white tissues, which Ekam later learnt were brain cells, were visible. The man's left arm and leg were crushed such that pieces of bones and flesh mixed together. Everybody could feel the agony. Even the doctor appeared to be crying. Probably he had not seen a case like that before.

Conveying the man from the car that brought him onto a stretcher was a burden. He screamed and wailed. There was general pandemonium in the hospital. Nurses rushed around with bags of infusions. The theater staff rushed to put on their clothing. Everybody was in a hurry. Yet after one hour, they came out looking sullen. The man had died. Ekam heard someone make a comment.

"Sometimes I don't know why these people bother about some cases. A layman should have known that the man would not survive."

"Medical people never write off a case until the patient breathes his or her last," another had said.

"Such agony. Such pain. Probably he is paying for his sin here on earth," yet another said.

"I wonder how you knew that," another interjected.

To Ekam, the task could have been less onerous and objectionable had it ended with cleaning up the mess. But she was instructed to accompany the corpse to the mortuary at the general hospital close to the wharf.

"That will be it!" she had exclaimed.

She could not, however, refuse. Though she felt extremely frightened, she nevertheless felt like seeing what was behind the perpetually shut doors of the mortuary. She sat with the driver of the ambulance and another staff of the clinic while the corpse was behind.

At the hospital, they met a mortuary attendant who took them to the mortuary. The attendant knocked on the door before opening. She wondered whether there was anybody alive inside. He then entered the room. Ekam vacillated when requested to follow.

"Come in, young girl. You are safe." She entered gingerly. Her eyes met one large white cabinet with partitions. The room was warm and surprisingly clean and odor free. Her confidence started coming on after about five minutes of survival in the room.

After a few activities that the girl could not understand, the attendant drew out one cabinet. Out came a still body that had a most ghastly face. The eyes bulged out, the mouth was agape with large teeth while the skin was soft and white. Ekam screamed and made for the door. She bolted out of the room and headed straight home, leaving behind her handbag, shoes, and an unclaimed salary at the clinic. She never went back.

*   *   *

A week after the encounter with what she decided to call a vampire after a horror film she had watched some months earlier, she recovered and was ready for another job. The nightmares were gone. The nausea had disappeared. She regained normalcy.

What she regarded as a lucky break came sooner than expected and from a most unexpected source. One night, Ekebo walked into the room occupied by the two girls. He looked penitent enough to be allowed to sit on the stool, which was the only seat available that visitors could use. Ekam had bought it because she felt that if a seat other than the bed was not available for male visitors to sit on, one was literally inviting the visitor to the bed, and by extension, an attempt that could be unwelcome.

"I hope you have forgiven me by now," Ekebo said, without even a greeting. Ekam did not respond.

"You have to appreciate the city, my sister," he went further.

"Who is your sister?" Ekam retorted.

"You are. That a wife has died does not mean that the two families are no longer in-laws. We are still from the same village. If I see your body by the wayside, I won't walk by, the way others might."

"It is your body that you will see, not mine," Ekam reacted in a tone loaded with venom.

"Of course if it is my body, you will not walk by."

"I will."

"Blood is thicker than water. And what is more, a case involving kith and kin is like the blood in your mouth—you find it difficult to swallow and at the same time, difficult to spit out."

"If you are the blood in my mouth, I would spit you out ten times before the snap of a finger," Ekam responded.

"That is what you think. What do you do with a millipede that is crawling on your stomach? Do you remove it with a knife? No. You use your hand to remove it because it is your body. It is revolting business but that is how it is done. And since there is no forest where bad and wayward people are thrown, you have to manage your bad brethren," Ekebo concluded, looking satisfied with his wisecracks.

"If you have nothing to say, and I believe you have none, I think this room will be more blessed without you." To emphasize her point, Ekam picked a broom and stood by the door.

"You want to sweep out my footsteps. Hear me out yet," Ekebo implored.

"Get out," she ordered.

"Take it easy, Ekam," Ekebo pleaded.

"You could be sweeping away good luck," Enọmma said.

"This man's first name should in fact be bad luck."

"Call me whatever you fancy but remember that one should not sweep in the night. You will be sweeping away your good luck," Ekebo added.

"Village talk," Ekam retorted. She moved the broom from one hand to the other.

"All of us in the city came from villages. We may behave like the white man, empty our bowels inside the house, eat fancy foods, speak through our noses, and walk like cats. It does not change the fact that we came from villages where we used pit latrines located far away from the house. At the latrine we empty our bowels of remnants of cassava *fofo** and assorted vegetables."

"Get out," she said, standing astride, her left hand on her waist, her right hand clutching the broom, and her head cocked to one side.

"See, whatever you feel cannot change the fact that we have something everlasting between us. The most expensive soaps in the world cannot wash away that fact."

"See the way you say it as if it's a great achievement. You are proud of the way that something was shared, shameless son of Adam." Ekam was becoming impatient as her anger climbed toward boiling point. She started to fret. Ekebo guessed that if he waited much longer, the young lady might act the way newsmen in the yellow press might be delighted in.

"Okay, I'll tell you why I came. If you don't like it, leave it. I would have played my part as a brother. Tomorrow, go to the Ministry of Works, Housing, and Transport. Since you walk about this town from dawn to dusk, I guess you know where it is." Ekebo paused to let the sarcastic bit sink in. Ekam only looked at him balefully.

"When you enter the office, ask the receptionist, that is, the girl sitting at the main entrance, after one Mr. Robert. He is the senior executive officer in charge of recruitment. He is a very good friend of mine. I have talked to him about you. He will assist you to secure a job in the ministry. Since you don't have a good qualification, you will not have to go through an interview at the Civil Service Commission, which you would fail anyway, for I guess what is in your skull is coconut milk rather than brain. Just go there. And behave yourself for the sake of my good name." Ekebo left the room without exchange of greetings. After he was gone, Ekam stood there for some time, undecided as to her next line of action. Enomma coughed.

"You have not started sweeping," Enomma said.

"I thought you were a friend," Ekam responded.

"I am. You see, like the raven said, on the day you are to pick a lucky thing, your eyes may not be looking at the ground."

"Can you imagine him saying that I should behave well for the sake of his good name? Good name indeed!"

"He didn't do what no other man has never done, my sister. Even now, he has insulted you and me badly. But all these good and respectable human beings you see are good and respectable in the daytime. At night or behind closed doors, they are a little higher than animals in the forest. He who is caught is a devil. He who is not caught continues to be a saint until he is caught."

"Ekebo is a devil any day."

"So you will not meet this Mr. Robert?"

"I-will-not."

"Come on, dear girl. Look at it this way, a man that owed you has come to pay back his debt. Why would you reject the repayment?"

"That is, you support him? I have no self-respect, Enomma? How can a man rape you, come for the first time nearly two years after, offer no apology but rather rubs salt and pepper on the wound and then turn around to offer you ice cream? Would you take it?"

"We are in a city. Here, dogs have wiped the faces of everybody with their tongues. We have no emotion, no pride. What we want is to survive even if the source of survival is from the person that killed your loving grandmother and later your mother and father. Ekam, whether you accept this offer or not makes no difference to him. He has been able to ease his conscience by going out of his way to search for a job for you. Meanwhile, don't forget some of the things he said show that he has been monitoring your movements. Ninety percent of the men in this town would behave as if they never knew you as soon as they have had their fill of you. He is a sinner, but with some residual conscience."

After three days of pleading, argument, and even a threat of ejection by Enomma, Ekam finally decided to give the idea a try.

"Is it not what you have always wanted?" Enomma had entreated. "A respectable job on a salary scale. You can now tell people, 'I work in the ministry.' And for that matter, the Ministry of Works. People will now look at you differently. It does not matter if you earn half of what you were earning at the clinic."

*   *   *

That Ekam lasted six months at the ministry was because of the respectability attached to the job and more because she feared that Enomma would throw her out of the bed-sitter they shared. Enomma had been showing signs of being fed up with her friend's inconsistency.

*   *   *

The ministry was one long bore. A few workers appeared to carry the whole burden of keeping the place afloat. Of course, they were branded "eye servants." It was common to hear some people tell such hardworking civil servants, "You think that this is your father's job or your father's estate. Relax man, ministry work never finishes. If you collapse today and die, another person will take up your position without any loss of continuity. And the ministry would not even buy a quarter of a page in the *Chronicle* newspaper to sing your praise."

Ekam found it difficult to adjust to the routine of arriving at the office on or before 7:30 a.m., signing the time book, searching for files in dust-laden piles in cabinets, sleeping three quarters of the workday, watching the clock for closing time, rushing to sign the time book at the close of business, and rushing home thereafter. The routine was too much for her. Despite her inconsistency, laziness was not one of her weaknesses.

The girl had been appointed an office attendant. She was actually meant to be one of the cleaners and to serve tea. But because she knew the senior executive officer, she was made to sort out files and mails, a job that was for clerical assistants with the West African school certificate (attempted) qualification. Favoritism was part of the civil service structure, so coworkers merely gossiped about Ekam's disposition. They could do nothing about it.

*   *   *

Ekam's woes as a staff of the ministry started when a new permanent secretary was assigned to the ministry. That was one man that had no scruples whatsoever. Apart from open embezzlement of public funds, he was notorious for running after girls in his ministry, even making love to them in his office. His appetite made no room for status of his target—single, married, widowed, divorced, graduate, semiliterate, name it. Girls were known to run away when he appeared, for he would fondle them at any place. The man could not be disciplined because he was said to be close to the high and mighty at state and federal levels.

Permanent secretary's first move on arrival at his new office was Ekam. She was instantly transferred to the permanent secretary's office. It was nobody's surprise as the girl was a beauty in her own right. One month into the posting, Ekam had slapped the man several times, and at one point, nearly bitten off his lips. During one particularly serious brawl, she received severe beating from the permanent secretary, who though short and stout, packed a good punch. After the fracas, the scandal was the talk of the town for almost one month. While Ekam spent two weeks in the general hospital for treatment and received unwelcome visitors, including members of the yellow press who eulogized her bravery and high morality, the permanent secretary spent nearly two months abroad on government sponsored "full medical treatment," including some time to enable him to recover from the "attack" by a junior staff. On his return, he was given an additional responsibility as chairman of the task force on Reformation of the Civil Service.

"This world is full of injustice." Ekam had observed.

"That is one lesson for you," Enomma replied. "Imagine a situation in which a dirty old man in a high office disturbs a young girl and all he gets is promotion."

"And I, an honest worker, only received a letter of dismissal. What a world!" Ekam lamented.

Sooner than later, the scandal had faded into the foggy memories of the people. Another event had taken over to give cause for new gossip. Life in the ministry continued "normally." The daily happenings were like ripples in a sea that may widen and widen and yet, like other ripples, end while the tide flows on without change in course. It needs more than a scandal to change the civil service. It needs something like a rechanneling or dam to affect the flow of the staid stream that is the civil service.

*　　*　　*

While the world moved on unperturbed, Ekam again found herself at home jobless and frustrated. Her celebrity status gradually waned. She had at first been ashamed and shy when people pointed at her as she passed by. It had made her stay indoors for some days. Then she started relishing the attention, particularly as the comments on her were positive—a well brought up, daring, and brave girl who could stand up against the high and mighty in the face of all odds.

As people stopped pointing and giving her the thumbs up, she gradually withdrew to herself and digested her loneliness. It was the way a bereaved family feels after a burial ceremony—when the crowd of mourners and revelers disappear, the quiet could be oppressive and distressing. One at best had to accept the desertion as a fact of life, knowing that the person in the grave was at a worse position—no neighbors, no friends, and permanent loneliness.

Again, Enomma was at the receiving end of Ekam's frustration. She continued to bear the financial burden of providing food, cosmetics, medical care, and rent. Ekam had always helped when she was working, usually handing over her entire pay packet to Enomma who would decide how much Ekam should keep as her pocket money, how much she should use for clothes and cosmetics, and how much she should put away as reserve for the proverbial rainy day. The rest would go to supplement their home expenses.

"Enomma, you are more than a friend to me. You are more than a sister. You are in fact a mother," Ekam said tearfully when Enomma brought up the idea of scouting for another job.

"Well," was Enomma's shy response.

"It is said that one's brother is out there on the highway. No blood relation of mine could have taken care of me or could have tolerated me the way you have. I have been a big burden to you."

"Don't say those things. In our culture, we are all our brother's keepers. And who knows tomorrow? You could be my savior."

"That would be the day," Ekam said hopefully.

During the night, Enomma woke her friend for a discussion. Ekam felt a twitch of fear tear through her stomach. The fear was also written on her face. Enomma gave her a reassuring smile.

"It is strange I know, to wake you up in the early hours for a discussion. But I tell you, a number of the great men in our society take their most daring steps from the decisions they reached in the discussion between them and their God after midnight."

"Well," Ekam said.

"I have given your situation a lot of thought," Enomma said and paused. Ekam could not help shifting several times, crossing and uncrossing her legs again and again.

"It appears your god does not favor employment."

"Well?"

"Probably you would be good in business."

"Business?"

"Yes, business."

"What kind?"

"I know what you mean. These days armed robbery, prostitution, and stealing by tricks are called businesses. I read in a foreign magazine the other day that selling marijuana is a multimillion-pound business. What would people not do to make money, even at the expense of lives, limbs, and people's sanity?"

"So what business do you want me to go into?"

"What you can manage. I suggest trading."

"How do I start? I have no money."

"That is what has been giving me sleepless nights. The problem is not really how to get it but whether I will lose what I can arrange for you."

"Oh, Enomma," Ekam said and embraced her friend. She wept on Enomma's breast while her head was caressed soothingly. She then raised her tearful face.

"Only God will reward you."

"Yes, but you have to assist God for as we were taught at school, heaven helps those who help themselves. You must also work hard, be careful, and be honest for honesty is the best policy, again, as our civics teacher taught us."

Ekam had heard all those idioms several times. She understood them but felt it was begging the question. Human beings from good homes should be honest. They must be hardworking and prudent.

"Enọmma, you know me well enough by now. I won't let you down."

"I want to believe you," she said and paused. "I have no alterative anyway."

"But where will the money come from?"

"You should first of all ask what you would sell."

"Whichever line you want me to go into."

"Okay, but what would you prefer?"

"Fancy goods. Fancy clothes. Fancy shoes. Jewelry."

"This girl, you are simply impossible. Funny enough, I thought along the same line."

"Oh, Enọmma," Ekam embraced her friend ecstatically, "the next question is, where?"

"Watt Market of course."

"I can get a shop in Watt Market?"

"Sounds impossible. My sister, in our country, everything can be arranged."

"This is more like a dream."

"Yes, but listen." Enọmma became severe. "You will have a shop in the market on a line dominated by men. You know that men are used to women selling food items, not ready-made goods."

"I like the challenge."

"It will indeed be a challenge."

"But from where will I buy my stock?"

"Good question. Hey, you are already a businesswoman. I knew I was right."

"Thank you."

"You will have to travel to Aba and even Onitsha to buy what you want at cheaper rates. This will give you bigger profit. If you buy from local wholesalers, your profit will be smaller."

"That will not be easy. I'll have to travel in lorries for days and nights, mostly nights. And in this country when the war has just ended, girls are not safe on the road."

"That is why I told you it is a man's world which you have to enter."

"I'll try. I promise you I'll try."

"Good. Let me tell you how we will get the money," Enọmma paused. Ekam's heart raced a little.

"I have been involved in an *osusu** for the past nine months. My turn comes up next week. I'll pick up twenty pounds." Ekam was astounded.

"Yes, twenty pounds. I also plan to get a loan from my office. Then I'll borrow money from my mother as well as from my boyfriend. I hope to raise one hundred pounds in total."

"I can't believe that!"

"You better do."

After further planning on the modalities for the business, both girls slept off in each other's arms. They woke up feeling a high sense of elation and satisfaction from the great expectations of the future. Enọmma successfully silenced the still small voice that nagged her, warning her against what was evidently a gamble.

*　　*　　*

The following two weeks were busy ones for Ekam. She visited the stall hired for her in the Watt Market and immediately got herself acquainted with the neighbors and others in the same line of business. This included a woman who gave Ekam the feeling that the trade was not reserved for men only. The woman also appeared to be motherly and supportive. While waiting for Enọmma to organize the funds, Ekam attached herself, albeit forcefully, to one man who showed her some tricks of the trade.

Two weeks after her discussion with Enọmma, Ekam in company of Enọmma's boyfriend, Edet, joined a team of traders for a trip to Onitsha. It was her first trip outside her native southeastern state. Since she was in the belly of the lorry, she could not say much about the route. She could not say much about Onitsha either, as she visited only the market and thereafter returned to the garage.

The most revolting aspect of her journey, however, was the unending stops at checkpoints. There were checkpoints mounted by policemen, soldiers, customs men, Board of Internal Revenue personnel, vehicle inspection officers, and others that she did not know. These lengthened the journey by more than four hours. It was a distressing experience.

She, however, forgot about the hassles as soon as she finished displaying the wares in her shop, assisted by Enomma and her boyfriend. She was ecstatic. Her elation was such that she let out a howl of delight. She was surprised that her neighbors did not get angry. Rather, they hailed her and asked her to "wash" her shop.

Edet's involvement in the commencement proceedings was strategic. Aside from the fact that he had lent Enomma some money (he rejected the idea of being a shareholder because he could not trust a green horn of which Ekam was), his presence made it look as if he owned the shop. The impression given was that Ekam was just a salesgirl. That did help as troublesome competitors were intimidated by the bulk of which Edet was. A six-footer in a place where the average height was five feet, four inches, Edet was regarded with awe. Coupled with his wide girth, stentorian voice, and extra large hands, the prudent line was for competitors to let him pass when he approached. All they however wondered was how Enomma, slight of build, was able to "carry" such a weight when "eyes are four."

Within two weeks of commencement of trading, Ekam had almost exhausted the stock in her shop. Men flocked there to buy but more to have a chat with her. She employed all her feminine charms to pull customers to her shop. When Edet took stock after two weeks, a tidy profit of about twenty pounds had been recorded.

"I told you," Enomma enthused to Edet.

"It could be a flash in the pan."

"It isn't. The girl is naturally gifted."

"Time will tell."

Enomma did not like that. Jimmy Cliff's music of that title came to her mind. "Time will tell," she repeated to herself. "But I hope on the brighter side."

Ekam generally did well given her lack of experience. She was, however, far from knowing most of the intrigues of trading. Each new day revealed one intrigue or the other by her competitors. One of the intrigues, as she later found out to her chagrin, was that they encouraged her to sell on credit.

"*Ah*, whoever succeeds without giving credit?" one of them had said.

"But what of that photo in your office which shows a fat man saying 'I sold in cash' laughing at a lean man who is tearing his hair and saying 'I sold on credit'?"

"That is not important. We just keep it there. You will drive away potential customers if you don't give credit. Credit means trust," another competitor had said.

Yet another, the woman she had met when she first came to the market, had said to her, "Didn't you see me sell to one woman on credit yesterday?" Ekam had agreed, believing that a woman would not trick a fellow woman. It was not until Ekam's shop was almost empty and up to half of her capital was stuck with debtors that she knew it was all planned. Business of the strain she was involved in was not for those who talk straight, think honest, and deal clean.

Six months into the business, Ekam was going to the market to spend the whole day with customers willing to buy, but no goods to sell to them. She spent a lot of time in ministries, trying to pry money out of her debtors. She fought physically on a number of occasions, one of which landed her in a police cell. It appeared there was collective shamelessness in government departments toward debt. It was as if it was part of the system to buy on credit—from food to clothing, rent to school fees. Brawls were so commonplace between debtor civil servants and traders that people hardly spent time to engage in gossip over such episodes.

*　　*　　*

As the fortunes of the shop dwindled, Enọmma became less and less friendly. She would scream at Ekam at the slightest provocation. Ekam, who still had high hopes, could not understand Enọmma's anger and persecution. One day, they had a blowout, which proved decisive to their relationship, nay, Ekam's future.

"Enọmma. Things will be all right."

"How? When?"

"Soon, soon I hope."

"They better be."

"But you know I did not misuse your money. It is business!"

"Business my foot."

"I can't understand your bitterness," Ekam blurted out in frustration and exasperation. It was obvious that she had made a fatal mistake. Enọmma had become uncontrollable. She called Ekam a lot of unprintable names.

"How would you understand? Was it your money? Did you suffer for it, you godforsaken daughter of damnation? I curse the day or whatever it was that brought you into my humble home. You have no conscience. One hundred pounds gone down the drain, and you show no regrets. And you continue to receive shelter and food from me. Have you no shame on your face?"

It was too much for Ekam to stand. She walked out of Enọmma's room, never to return. Later that day, she went to Edet, knelt before him, wept, and begged him to plead with Enọmma to forgive her and to give him time to pay the debt.

"I am on my knees, Edet. This is one thing I have done only to my father. Please talk to Enọmma. I did not steal her money. In six months I have not bought a new dress. Not even a handkerchief! I bought no earrings, no necklace. I loved those articles I sold but I never made use of any of them. My problem was lack of experience. I did not know that one had to go to school to sell successfully. I now see why Ibo youths remain as apprentice traders for years. If I have another opportunity I will do better. I am sad, but wiser."

Edet, despite his dislike of the girl, felt a twitch of emotion. There was no doubt that she was honest. She worked hard. She ate the lowest quality food during the day while she was selling. She had the pull and the will. Yet she was ill equipped for the rarefied world of business. He had nodded gravely and promised to talk to his girlfriend.

*   *   *

Ekam decided that given her experience, business is for those that have no conscience, those who would easily sell their grandmothers without batting an eyelid, those that are ready and willing to be mean. Business is for the hard-hearted. Ekam was too soft for the rough and tumble of that world. And so she crashed out, not because she was not in it with her heart, but because she could not manage the seamy sides of business. Edet went to Enomma to plead on Ekam's behalf. It was then that the harried girl was allowed to pack her clothes and go out to face a faceless world.

*   *   *

Ekam was determined to pay off Enomma. She was now initiated into the world of business where only the strong survive and "the end justifies the means" as what a new friend, Utitofon, more educated and more experienced, told her whenever she tried to show restraint in an activity. Utitofon had gone through "fire and brimstone" in her life and had been so traumatized by boyfriends and girlfriends that she decided not to have any friend but rather "close acquaintances," and for men in particular, "social brothers" even if intimacy was involved.

Ekam started off by joining a mobile band group tagged "Sound on Wheels," singing and dancing on stage. The late nights bothered her and so was the revolting feeling that people looked at her as depraved, for all band hands were regarded as dropouts, ill-bred, and ones without a future. As the days went by, she adjusted to all revolting situations and became part of the scene, starting off by being "stoned" with a solid bottle of big stout each time she was to mount the stage and later on with "igbo" or marijuana, which surprisingly and mercifully did not make her mad the way she had seen a number of youths that had been involved with that notorious "weed."

Along the line, she solicited men. It was terrible at first, but she warmed up to it as she remained under the cover of heavy makeup and headgear and also justified her acts by the big money that came in with so little physical and mental exertion. She gradually graduated into "refined" crime, particularly deceiving people in what the police described as "stealing by tricks." To keep her out of police cell, she retained any incumbent of the office of divisional crime officer as "friend" with generous gifts in cash and in kind.

Genius is genius and can be applied positively or negatively. Ekam was a very bright pupil in the primary school and always found her name, with little effort, among the first three as the headmaster read out the result at the end of every school term. Among her peers, she was the first to memorize the "times table" from one times one to twelve times twelve, and she could mold almost anything with mud. In sports, she was a star in the hundred-yard race and was always the anchor person for the relay race. Unfortunately, such brilliance was not tapped because of her background and location. It was because of her ability to do everything virtually well and out of proportion, including use of proverbs that her uncle Nte regarded her as his favorite child in the extended family. And her master, Mr. Ndukwe, recognized her brightness and said that much when he went to negotiate with her parents for her stay in his house. Many are the geniuses that are lost to the world as a result of lowly background that cannot finance the development of talent. Sometimes, such persons engage their abilities in negative engagements because such often come much easier and cheaper than the positive ones.

Within one year, Ekam had made enough money to pay up her whole debt to Enọmma. On the day she handed over the last five pounds, Enọmma wept. She apologized for putting her friend through all the mess for she was well aware of the way she was making money. She even invited Ekam to pack back to her apartment. Ekam was appreciative, but politely declined.

"I am too far gone, my sister. I cannot live your kind of life again."

"You can start all over again, Ekam. You can go to school in the evening."

"Who will pay the fees?"

"Well, you are making money."

"I should use money I make from men to pay school fees? No. Money I cannot use as offering in church, I cannot use to build my future. The money I make now is just for today."

"All the same, thank God you did not use that word."

"Prostitute, *eh*? I have avoided it by telling myself, not the world, that I don't have a room in a hotel." She shook her head sadly and suppressed tears. "I wish I were correct."

"I shall get you another job," Enọmma offered.

"I can never fit into a regular employment again. I actually came to the city because of the pull of the bright lights. It appears I have at last arrived where I belong."

"But your family, Ekam?"

"You did not think about that when you kept quiet as I moved from one bad place to the next, did you?"

Enọmma was stung. She could not reply. Rather, large balls of tears rolled down her chubby cheeks.

"I am sorry," Ekam soothed.

"You should not have been so unkind. You know it was the debt I owed that forced me to talk to you the way I did. Please forgive me."

"I understand."

"All the same, remember that when everything and everybody abandon you, you have one shoulder to cry on."

"I know, and I am grateful."

After further tears and assurances, Ekam left Enọmma with a mixed feeling. She felt elated that all she owed had been repaid, yet she felt she had lost a friend. Though she knew she could always go back to Enọmma and be welcomed, she also knew she could no longer trust her. It was terrible that she could no longer trust her kind, having also lost confidence in men.

Her family? That appeared to belong to another world. Although she was sure she would be welcomed if she went back to Oboyo, she knew she could not go—at least—not immediately. She had nothing to show for her sojourn at Calabar and did not want to be regarded as one of those vagabonds or victims of the saying that "money made at Calabar finishes in Calabar." Since she left home, she had made just one trip home—for Christmas. She was well received, but she felt empty as she had nothing to offer, even for her elder sister who had predicted that she would forget her mother.

The implication of her analysis was that she had no ground, what she felt was sympathetic, and solid enough to accept her weight without complaining. Her hitherto best friend was now a stranger, her family seemed so far away, and the intensity of reception was doubtful. She shuddered at the thought.

*   *   *

The next few months rolled by at such a dizzying pace that Ekam could not keep up with events. She hopped from one hotel to the next as a member of another group, the *All Starts Orchestra*. When the band was not hired, she went soliciting men. All she could do to hide her shame was to rationalize by telling herself that she did not take up a room in a hotel as prostitutes would.

Through such indiscriminate union with men, she missed her monthly visitor. The realization came after three months. Not only did she feel less agile, more tired, and often nauseated, "concerned" women started asking some uncomfortable questions.

"*Ah*, are you sure you don't have more than food in this stomach?" "Don't you think you require bigger clothes?" "*Hm*, this one that you spit all the time, are you sure you do not have worms in your stomach?" Snide comments and questions were endless, disturbing, and confusing.

As the days went by and Ekam found it more and more difficult to cope with the demands of the band as well as attendance at an evening school that she had finally decided to join to improve her level of education, she felt it was time to do something. She thought of going to Enomma but decided against it. That bond of absolute trust had been broken—forever! On advice of one of her former coworkers at the Getwell Clinic and Maternity Home, she went for a pregnancy test. She was confirmed to be four months pregnant. Four whole months! And she did not know. She realized that waywardness was not equivalent to being streetwise and that a girl needs more than formal education for survival.

Her next thought was abortion. The doctor at Getwell Clinic, a man she worked with during her brief stint at the clinic, read her mind and strongly advised against it.

"Medical science accepts eight weeks of pregnancy for safe termination. You are sixteen weeks gone. You could die if you try."

Ekam could not contemplate death yet. "How many Christmases have I seen? What have I enjoyed yet?" she asked herself.

Despite her revulsion at early childbearing and her sadness that she was not street-smart to have prevented the pregnancy (more so, as she did not in any way know who the father of the unfortunate child is), she decided against the risk of abortion. She, as usual, rationalized her decision by telling herself that she could not afford a safe abortion. And a quack? "God forbid! Not after the horrors I saw at the Getwell Clinic when victims of quack doctors were brought in."

As she could not go back to her village, had nobody to stay with at Calabar, and in any case could not stand the shame of meeting her friends and colleagues daily while carrying an unwanted pregnancy, she decided to go to a village at the suburbs of Calabar for the remaining term of the pregnancy. That was how she found herself at Akpabuyo, a sprawling farming community on the outskirts of Calabar.

She had decided to go to Akpabuyo for two reasons. Firstly, a friend of hers, Atim, had introduced Ekam to her elder sister who was living there with her husband. They had agreed to accommodate her as a farmhand. Secondly, while Akpabuyo provided a shelter away from her friends' attention, the name gave her the feeling that she was home. Some people described the place as the "sea" of Oboyo or the "first" Oboyo depending on the inflexion on the word "Akpa." Ekam, therefore, decided to go "home" and sort herself out.

*   *   *

After a five-month sojourn at Akpabuyo, Ekam suddenly reappeared in Calabar. The first person she met on arrival was her friend Atim, whose relations had quartered her during her stay at Akpabuyo.

"There you are, Ekam. You are back," Atim had enthused. "And you look so fresh, so healthy."

"Oh, thank you. The credit goes to you."

"And what about them?"

"Atim you are bad-o! Imagine that you have not seen your sister for so long."

"What about you? Does this town let people think about their people in the village? City dwellers only see their families during Christmas and probably Easter."

"Or when a family member dies."

"When they will go and spend money which they would not spend on the person while he or she was alive."

"*Hm.*"

"What about—?"

"Don't ask questions unless someone volunteers information," was Ekam's crisp retort. Atim had shrugged and kept quiet.

*　　*　　*

Not too many people were bothered about Ekam's sudden disappearance—and for that matter—reappearance. These were common happenings. Men could change location in search of better paid employment or even to escape from punishment following a crime they had committed. Girls could do the same, or like Ekam, go back to the village to off-load an unwanted burden only to reappear and start again where they had left off. Ekam was in the second category, returning from an unknown destination where she had gone for an undisclosed engagement, only to emerge and merge again into the city with such force it was as if it held eternal life and as if nothing of note had earlier happened. The one "good" thing she, however, did on her return was to register again with the Future Scope Evening School on Ededem Street.

What would a young girl full of life and indeed now more streetwise do indoors all day? No one would have expected Ekam to stay at home, wherever that was. She, as a matter of fact, had "no fixed" address since she returned from Akpabuyo. She, thus, hopped from one residence to the next, usually with men who were ready to accommodate her for as long their excitement about her remained. One thing she, however, swore not to do was to take up full-time residence in a hotel. "That would be when I would now call myself a prostitute," she had told Atim, when the latter had gingerly observed that she was going out with "too many men." The understanding that she was not a "professional" and was not "admitting" all comers did some good to whatever was left of her conscience.

Despite the fact that Ekam hardly had a man that she could be identified with and who would thus "respectably" escort her to functions, she was very active in social life. She was a regular feature at social gatherings, from "vigil nights" to ballroom dances. She would not miss a traditional marriage ceremony and for that matter a wedding ceremony. And of course, ticket sellers at Patsol Cinema and Independence Cinema knew she would be there at least three days in a week (she enjoyed making alternate visits to the two cinemas). The one remaining day was for Luna Nite Club where *Everybody Loves Saturday Night* was sure to be played by the band. It was one long story of pub crawling and partying from one part of the town to the next. She could not even say whether she was popular or notorious whenever she walked along the streets and several people hailed her. She simply continued for in her opinion, she had no alternative to "life," and as the youth would put it, she had "no future ambition."

Chapter 8

The heady days of the oil boom were just beginning. Nigeria was starting her race toward her high noon. A majority of the citizens were at ease as jobs were available, goods and services were cheap, and business was generally good. There was construction boom as governments at the state and federal levels were sincerely using public funds to provide infrastructure crucial for economic take off. These included roads, bridges, hospitals, schools, and government-sponsored factories. In the cities, however, the age-old culture of hard work was losing currency as a number of people ran after government contracts that promised a windfall for whoever was favored.

Calabar was at its restful best. The thatched houses were still very much there, and the streets were still riddled with potholes. Water was still hard to come by despite the fact that the town is literally submerged in water. Many houses still made do with the hurricane lamp although electricity, supplied by the Electricity Corporation of Nigeria (ECN), was available and in fairly stable supply as the rate of use was low vis-à-vis supply. The military government of Brigadier U. J. Esuene, the pioneer military governor of the Southeastern State of Nigeria, was tackling the developmental shortcomings head-on.

The social scene was as active as the economic scene. With more pounds sterling in the hands of majority of the citizens, men and women, boys and girls attended one ballroom dance after the other, organized private parties for the flimsiest reasons, and watched movies in the cinema halls where John Wayne was the most popular "actor." Frolicking was it.

Violent crimes were by then unheard of in Calabar. Mugging was not in the local dictionary while car snatching was still a decade away, something possibly reserved for Lagos. There was no way one could contemplate assassination. That was reserved for the cinema screen. If there was crime, it was house break-ins of which there must be an insider and those involved would be amateurs. Pickpocketing was accepted as a sacrifice for civilization or development while armed robbery was as a matter of fact not a comprehensible phenomenon. It was not a surprise then that people tramped the streets all night, forced home only by aching feet or drooping eyelids rather than by fear of evil men at night.

Saturday nights were particularly eventful for revelers. A musician had even put it in a song, *Everybody Loves Saturday Night*. The "hot spots" often had the problem of providing enough seats to accommodate the influx of merrymakers. In ones and in twos, men and women trooped into pubs, restaurants or "bars," "joints," cinema houses, and the few night clubs that were available, chief of which was the Luna Nite Club.

It was the day after one of those Saturday night outings that Ekam played hostess to an unexpected visitor. She was reclining in an "easy chair" in the house of her latest boyfriend, Uko, with her legs placed on the center table. It was almost midday, yet she was still snoozing, waking up in starts at every small creak or crack. The bed-sitter had not been swept and dusted, the bed had not been made, and unwashed dishes piled up on one side of the center table where her feet were raised up to ease the ache generated by events of the previous night.

Probably there had been a knock on the door. She faintly heard something like that as she tossed between sleep and wakefulness, struggling to hold on to pleasant dreams. She, however, woke with start when a hand shook her shoulder violently. She sat up and rubbed her eyes that were battling with sun rays that streamed into the room when the door was opened. She was finally able to focus and saw to her consternation, her mother's elder sister, usually called Mmama by the household. She lived in one of the farm villages called Akansoko on the way to the Nigerian border with the Cameroon. It was impossible to know how she found her way to where Ekam was, though the girl knew that news—particularly bad ones—travels faster in the city than the speed of the light that was giving her eyes trouble of focusing.

"You cannot greet us, daughter of a viper," Mmama exploded after waiting a few minutes without a word from the girl. Mmama was feared even by her father who always arranged to travel somewhere whenever she came home, not because she would slap him physically, but because she taxed his integrity and therefore undermined his authority in the house. Mmama's word was law in the house. Of course, Mmama's mother would always say that if the banana stem broke the axe, one should not expect much from a common machete. The woman simply allowed her daughter to pass whichever direction she wanted, also telling surprised onlookers, "When a tree is huge, people leave a sizeable portion of bush around it."

Ekam was paralyzed with fear. She could neither say anything nor run away. Mmama had a most undesirable and repugnant combination—a huge frame with a huge bust, large teeth and bulgy eyes, a monstrous temper, high intellect, and bags of pounds sourced from her numerous farms, most of which she took from people by force.

"Is that child deaf?" Mmama barked. "I don't blame you. You are like your mother—feeble outside, but destructive inside. The baby snake that took in poison while inside its mother."

"Mmama, please calm down. You can see that she is frightened," Mmama's friend Naomi, who accompanied the woman, said gingerly. Mmama turned and faced her friend.

"Calm down you said, eh? Did I hear you well?" Throwing her hands above her head, she screamed in self-pity.

"I thought I had a friend. What is this world turning to? Naomi has children, all good, obedient, and respectful. Naomi's children are often used by parents as reference points, as examples of good children. I brought her here to knock some sense into this useless member of a noble family, only for her to say I should calm down," she paused, adjusted her head tie and loincloth and took in a deep breath.

"But you can see that she is frightened," Naomi pleaded.

"She is not afraid of the men that hop in and out of her life. She carries giants on her tiny belly. How can she be afraid of a fellow woman?" She faced Ekam again.

"What do you think I am struggling for? I have acres and acres of farmland. I own dozens of goats and chicken. I even own five cows! I employ dozens of men, women, and children to work for me. And in these days, how many women own cars? I own a pickup, which carries my produce to the market. I own a three-ton lorry that travels as far as Sokoto in the North, Ijebu Ode in the South, and even to Togo across the Nigerian border.

"The chief of Akansoko has honored me with a chieftaincy title and the clan head of Akpabuyo has sent me words that I am to be honored soon. I am in the village council in Akansoko. I am the chairman of so many functions and committees that I have lost count. But for the bias by the society against women, I would be contesting for the stool of the village head next time around. And I would win! But all that is dust when there is a scandal in my family. I say, if there will ever be a scandal in the family of Uyo-Ekpe it will come from this stupid girl. Whatever I have achieved came through hard work. Should a girl not be proud to have such a big and important woman in her family? Is it not a girl's place to live a life worthy of my good name?" She paused to take in breath.

Ekam was completely tongue-tied. Of all the achievements enumerated, one stood out. She knew Mmama was rich but did not know she owned a car. A car! And even a lorry!

"As I said earlier, what am I struggling for? Of all I have, I can only eat twice a day, sleep on one bed in one room each night, sit on one seat in my pickup van, and wear one set of clothes at a time. If I do more than those, onlookers will say, 'Money has made this woman mad. Whoever puts too much money in the hands of a woman?' And who would lead that discussion? My fellow women of course! Since I am not mad and there is no history of a mad person in my family, I do what ordinary people do—a simple meal, a simple dress, and so on." She paused again. "So, my struggle is for you the new generation, particularly girls. I want our girls to know that good and plenty money is not made by women using the private part. You can dare the world of men and succeed even where they, the men fail. *Ehe*, did I forget to tell you that I have a tipper? Naomi, did I tell you that one?"

"No. You must have bought it after we met at the burial of Mma Nko's mother."

"*Sai*. That means we have not seen each other for over a year. Business is dangerous-o."

"You can say that again. Business is like a forest. When you enter it, there are so many things to harvest if only you keep moving forward. As you keep hunting and harvesting, you get deeper into the belly of the forest till even your family will not see you again."

"Maybe that is why you refused to join me. Your life is simple and it is good."

"Well," she paused. "Meanwhile what do you use the tipper for?"

"What a question. Anyway, men go out there and walk about the stone floor of government offices, wear off their shoes and themselves and hopefully, get contracts. I stay somewhere else and share the money by supplying sand and gravel to them."

"But you could have made more money if you went direct and secured the contracts."

"Not me," she shouted. "How do you expect a whole Adiaha Ekpe to walk in front of people for months begging, begging for everything from the contract document to the payment that may come months after it was due? You beg from the commissioner and permanent secretary—I don't know who made them permanent when they will retire or die one day—to the cashier and even messenger to move your file from table to table. Worst of all, *hmm*," she said and went into convulsive laughter, "the one case I ever tried was very amusing. The accountant that prepares vouchers—ordinary papers!—told me that he wanted his ten percent in cash and in kind! I could not believe my ears. I looked at him and said to myself, so Adiaha will carry this dwarf on my belly just to make money. I told him off and never went back. He came to apologize but, I am like a bone in the body—when you move me out of my natural place, you may never put me back. He brought the check to my house, yet, I never forgave his insult on a whole me." She paused again, and then looked at Ekam. "Probably this one should be hunting for contracts since she can undress for any man—even in the marketplace."

"*A-ha*, Mmama. It is not that bad," Naomi exclaimed.

"You think I am lying or exaggerating? Is the stage in a hotel not a market? This useless thing has opened her legs for a man on a stage in the presence of others just to make money. I heard it."

Ekam who had thought she had been forgotten pulled back further into the seat. She was overwhelmed by the woman's massive physique as she was slight of build. She was overwhelmed by her achievements. She was overwhelmed by the glaring truths told about her indiscretions, acts that she thought were for few ears only. She would have loved to bolt out of the room but could not think of a way as the room, just as other bed-sitters in large compounds, had just one door of which Mmama was standing close to. By now, the woman was breathing in gasps. Ekam believed that blows would descend on her any moment, and that was one thing she could not stand.

Blows. Ekam's father knew that much and used it on her to do his bidding. Just by a mere threat of caning, Ekam would run and carry out any assignment she was asked to. She had lost two potential husbands since her arrival at Calabar just because those men lost their temper and hit her. In one case, the blows kept coming on her till she felt she was coming apart. She ran out of the house half naked and never returned, leaving behind all her clothes and other personal effects. That was three months back before she met Uko, whose bed-sitter she was in when Mmama forced her way in. It was Uko who went to the man's house with policemen, claiming to be her brother, that saw back her belongings.

"I am pleading for this child," Naomi intervened. "You do not get people to change their lives by injecting fear into them. They only cringe and fall in line when you are around. They go haywire once you turn your back. You should know better, Mmama," Naomi said.

"Yes, I should know. That my children are not the best in town does not mean that my approach has failed."

"There are many ways of catching a rat, Mmama. To me, it is easier, less painful, and it lasts longer if someone is made to see reason through discussions and examples."

"That is why I brought you here in the first instance. So talk to her. But before then, let me ask this girl some questions." Ekam withdrew further into the chair, gripping the loincloth wound above her breasts while her breath became heavier.

"Where is the man who owns this pig house?" Mmama inquired. There was silence.

"I say where is this bloke *eh*, a man who has no shame on his face, who goes about spoiling other people's little girls? Can he call himself a man just because he has a worm dangling between his legs? How can he tolerate a girl who has not washed plates for two days, who has not made the bed, and who is sitting on layers and layers of dust? He must be a dirty person, a sissy and a good for nothing." Mmama hissed. She picked up one of the cushions from one chair and hit it on the arm of the chair. A cloud of dust went up into the air. Mmama choked and sneezed.

"You see that, Naomi, don't you? That is where a branch of the Uyo-Ekpe family lives. And you say I should calm down. I should first let my handwork on this bitch so that she will remember where she came from."

"Mmama, manage to sit on the stool. That one is cleaner. Let us talk to this girl first."

"Yes, go ahead. Talk to her. But before then, let me tell her why I brought you." Mmama paused to take a breath, wiped her forehead with a perfumed handkerchief, and then cleared her throat.

"My daughter," she addressed Ekam, "a good parent flogs a child with one hand, then uses the other hand to draw that child to himself or herself. I may bark and howl, I may even bite, but I am a good parent. The Bible says that if we spare the rod, we spoil the child. If you are corrected, then you are loved. Parents that let their children have their way when they are wrong do not love those children.

"Our family has been worried by your lifestyle. Your parents sent a message to me pleading with me to look for you and talk to you after others could not see you. They would like to have you back home if that would save you, and them, from the problems the city is pushing on you. They have heard all you have been doing in Calabar and beyond.

"You were sent here as a househelp, an opportunity for you to learn the basics of modern life for one year before you return to the village to start your secondary education. Now what did you do? Agreed you had a rough stay in the house of Mr. Nduke. Agreed Ekebo abused your innocence and opened up the floodgate. But those are no excuses for this life of prostitution.

"Tell me, how can you change men the way you change your loincloth? In just three months you have lived with three different men, with three or four neighbors of those men having a go at you. Does your womanhood develop itching all the time? Do you think sex is food that must be eaten thrice a day with variety? Don't you know that as you accept one new man, you lose something—your integrity, your pride, and even long life in the process? Before you know what is happening, your name would have changed from Ekam to 'Donatus'! Can't you pronounce the simple word 'no'? You will no longer be your father's mother, for you were named after her. That woman was a pride of the village." She paused and adjusted herself.

124

"You think the world is so large that you can do a lot of things and hide. People used to say that only God sees in the dark. That is changing. We hear there are hidden instruments these days that can record events in a darkroom. So, whatever you do, my daughter, is seen by, not one, not two, but several people.

"I know you think we did not know what you did at Akpabuyo," Mmama said, sitting at the edge of the chair. Ekam withdrew further into the chair despite the fact that there was no more space left behind her. She swallowed spittle so much that her Adam's apple made an upward dance that generated strain in the throat.

"We knew. You left Calabar for a good five months, didn't you? Women noted the way you looked when you disappeared. You told them you were going to work in the farms to earn a living. As if I don't own farms. As if Ekam loves farmwork, and for that matter, any work at all.

"You can deceive your mates, not experienced women. Within one month of getting yourself pregnant, women will know. Probably you will one day tell a prospective husband that you have never had a child. You may succeed, for many men are fools. They look at the face, the chest, the legs, and the buttocks. Some lose their heads when they see a gap between two front teeth. Some start to dance when they see fat mounds on the chest, even if they are sagged and are only held up by a small-sized brassiere. I tell you this, if it were in the olden days, your secret would be bare before your prospective husband's family. Do you know that experienced women can tell which girl has had an abortion, which one has had a child and which one is still intact? That your breasts are still firm does not mean you are still a virgin.

"See Ekam, who barely five years ago could not wash her heels clean. She did not know that one could take one's bath with soap. At best, the sand from the bed of the stream was used as sponge for her feet and heels as well as for brushing her teeth. Now, she piles layers and layers of makeup on her face, looking like a masquerade! All the money she gets from men she uses for cosmetics and clothes! She has forgotten that she has a mother who stayed awake while she had fever, who wept silently while the native doctor mouthed incantations, looking out once in a while, afraid of being seen by a member of her church or even by the reverend. It was your mother who cleaned your ever wet nose. She cleaned your anus each time you passed waste, which was frequent and happened everywhere in the house. That mother is now a distant person, deserving of no concern and care. Sad that girls, who will one day be mothers, ill-treat their mothers."

Mmama paused on her tirade, adjusted her headgear and wrapper, removed her shoes, and settled more comfortably on the hard chair. One did not need to be told that the onslaught was just beginning. What bothered Ekam most was the fact that Mmama knew virtually everything she had ever done, even the ones she considered top secret.

*   *   *

"My daughter," Naomi said after Mmama had apparently burnt herself out, "I came to speak to you. You see, your circumstances have a disturbing resemblance to that of one woman I know of. Her name was, or is, if she is still alive, Imata. You know what Imata means?"

"I do," Ekam said in a barely audible voice.

"Imata was a happy-go-lucky girl like you. She had the world at the base of her feet. You are pretty, but by comparison, Imata should be called a goddess. From head to toe, she was a complete woman. Name it, she had it. Those gifts were however her undoing, for beautiful women are targets of attack—by hungry men, by jealous women, and by an unforgiving society.

"Imata unfortunately did not know that a woman's beauty could be used for anything other than the satisfaction of the appetite of men. It appears that she believed the reason for her creation was to satisfy the sexual desires of men. After all, the

Bible calls woman 'a helpmeet.' Men worked to have her just for a walk on the streets, enjoying the jealous glares of men and women. How many pay packets disappeared into her cosmetics box? Countless. But like sweet dreams, she did not last," Naomi paused and adjusted her sitting position. "You have not yet had your bath. You are yet to eat breakfast. People absorb more when they have a full stomach. I speak better in a clean environment and when I can get my listener's undivided attention. I invite you to clean up this place, have your bath and come over to my place so that I tell you about the life of Imata the Butterfly. I will tell you just the way I know it, for I was close to all the people concerned. I was actually present in some of the occasions, so part of what I shall tell you shall be an eyewitness account. Where I was not present, those who were present told me their experiences in detail. Sometimes, I wish I were a writer like Ama Ata Aidoo, or Buchi Emecheta, or Uche Bialonwu, or Barbara Cartland, or Agatha Christie. I would have loved to publish a book about the lives of Imata, Utibe, and a number of other persons who functioned at different locations but somewhere along the line, their lives came together and merged. I hope you will benefit from their experiences."

*   *   *

After a soothingly warm bath and an objectionable but compulsory cleanup of Uko's bed-sitter at least to please Mmama, Ekam went to meet Naomi at her residence. Naomi welcomed her, gave her a hot plate of well-boiled rice with fresh fish pepper soup sprinkled with fresh okra. It was a great meal.

After the meal, Naomi took Ekam to a place under a tree on the grounds of her residence. The lady went with a sheaf of papers and knitting materials. To wash the good meal down, Naomi offered the girl a cold bottle of Coca-Cola. She politely declined, requesting for a bottle of tonic water or bitter lemon instead. In her circle, these two were regarded as less feminine than Coca-Cola and Fanta orange, that is as the softer alternatives to beer and stout, both of which were staples in her menu since she began to hit the streets. She sipped the tonic water quietly and not a little nervously, for she was apprehensive of what was to come. When Naomi was ready to start, Ekam removed her sandals, threw a piece of loincloth on her legs, and adjusted her sitting position to the most comfortable in readiness for what she speculated would be a long, long story.

BOOK III

Chapter 9

"All over town the name 'Butterfly' was identified as a nickname or simply, another name for the girl called Imata," Naomi started her story by reading the opening lines of a script in her hand.

"The name Butterfly suited her, whether in terms of beauty and color or in terms of flirting from one flower to the next. She was a beauty and she had color—her skin, her smile, her wears, and her ways. She was all bright and beautiful. Sadly, she was a story in flirtation, changing men the way a woman changes her underwear. Her deeds could fill volumes. I would urge you to believe my story, for much of what I shall tell you about Imata in particular are based on personal discussions with her. She has been a friend and probably because I always frowned at her lifestyle when others were afraid to, she trusted me."

Naomi paused to observe Ekam's reaction. Since there was none, she continued, this time off the script. "I had told you early on that I wish I could publish a book about Imata. I have actually started but I have not finished after almost two years of working on it, what with so much to do at home, in the church, and in the office. I guess you know I am now an inspector of education and the head of Guidance and Counselling Unit of the Ministry of Education." Ekam shook her head in the negative. "Anyway, I am with you now because I am on annual leave. Read this." She handed her some handwritten notes. Ekam read the lines, and although some of the words were difficult given her level of education, she enjoyed the flow of thought and the memories that some of the things written in the script evoked in her. After she had read a page, Naomi asked a question.

"I hope you can understand what I have there, I mean, in terms of the English."

"Some words are new, but, I can follow. Our headmaster, Mr. Udofia did not allow any class teacher to play with English language. In fact, from Standard 3, he forced us to attend English and arithmetic lessons after school. This continued even after government changed from standard to elementary."

"I am pleased to hear that. The standard in the 'standard' of those days in our primary schools was far ahead of the standard in the 'elementary' of today. I speak from experience. Anyway, read on but wherever you have difficulty, stop and ask questions." Ekam nodded and continued reading undisturbed for some time while Naomi worked on her needle and wool, looking up once in a while to read the girl's body language.

*   *   *

Imata's formal education ended in standard six. She had started her primary education fairly early because her father had grown up with a reverend father and so knew the benefits of formal education. She, however, discontinued not because her father could not afford it but because she would not have benefited. She failed her First School Leaving Certificate Examination not because she was a dunce but because she had less time for her books and more time for ballroom dances, gossips, and running after her teachers at an age other girls at best play with boys on the way and in the village stream or at night while foraging for snails. Quarrels and once in a while fisticuffs among male teachers in the primary school she attended could most often be traced to Imata. A bloody fight between the muscular Etim, a senior pupil, and Mr. Useme, a schoolteacher, was caused by the girl. Imata seemed to have been made by nature to cause problems among men not only because of her beauty but also because she had grown and matured rather too fast and thus started affairs of the heart early—in her early teens.

After failing her final examinations and indicating her unwillingness to continue with formal education, she was sent off to stay with an uncle at Lagos. It was a disastrous move by her parents. Six months after she left home, the uncle was recalled to the village to answer questions on incest. In the compound where she lived, one couple saw the end of their marriage because of Imata. She also nearly lost a tooth to an irate senior girl who watched helplessly as her dream of at last getting married went up in smoke when her fiancé abandoned his room and spent several nights in a hotel with Imata. It was as a result of too many amorous activities that Imata was forced to leave Lagos.

She spent some time at another swinging city—Port Harcourt. She could not stay too long as news of her exploits seemed to reach home on a daily basis. This was because of the large population of her people at Port Harcourt.

Another attraction of Imata was Kaduna. With stories of Alhaji moneybags beckoning, Imata left for Kaduna. Not much could be said about her "sexploits" at Kaduna as the city is fairly far from home. And in any case, with the religion officially permitting polygamy, Imata did not have to contend with irate and blustering housewives desperate to protect their hard-won turfs. She went back home during the civil war and ended up at Calabar as the war moved from the southeast into the thick of Biafra. Interestingly and to Imata's relief, Calabar had recovered quickly from the effect of the war and life had returned to normal, with the swing that was most important to her coming on strong.

After her long dalliance with the ways of the world, Imata agreed that she had learnt and encountered a lot—several diseases, physical abuse, unwanted pregnancy, loss of dignity, and what have you. She had had her fill of the swing of late pre- and early post-independence Nigeria.

Despite such problems identified after a self-analysis, Imata nevertheless sustained her journey even if at a lower tempo on the path of decadence for she felt that there was no alternative. Her argument was that she had no certificate with which to secure a job. Even cleaners and messengers in both private and public sectors had to have a First School Leaving Certificate. She therefore saw her physique as a certificate and a passport to the good life bestowed on her directly by the all-knowing Creator.

*　　*　　*

Eddie was one of those whom Imata actually fell in love with, after all, love does not go to school even if schooling improves its performance. She was not surprised because she was a woman. She also always believed that one day she would meet her kind of man who would be her nemesis. Probably Eddie was.

Eddie was one of those who was said to have "arrived." He had a Honda Bentley motorcycle, the craze of every young girl in the city of Calabar. The Honda Benly, a smart, sleek, two-wheeled machine with a most appealing sound, was designed for the young generation. Though it was fast, it was not wild. It had grace and beauty. With the handles adjusted by the owners to lie flat rather than at an upturned angle as the makers originally designed, it gave it an air of sophistication and finesse.

The young men on these motorbikes would lean slightly forward, giving even the shortest rider a pose of a tall man. Meanwhile, perched at the rear would be a fine dame with a low-cut, tight-fitting dress, minimum makeup, and of course without brassiere. She either put her hands on her lap while the rider propelled the machine gracefully forward so that when there is a sudden stop, she would inch forward and allow her braless chest to play some games on the rider's back, or she would hold the rider very tightly by the waist, looking seductively at whoever cared to look her way. The only acceptable aspect of these young men was that they rode slowly, not because they were careful or afraid, but because they wanted less lucky colleagues and old folks to admire them or feel jealous, whichever was more appropriate. The slow motion apparently saved the society the pain of witnessing many broken limbs and skulls, if not deaths.

Eddie had taken Imata out on one of those bright Saturdays that the mind finds difficult to forget in a hurry. The day in the month of July when the rains are still doing their bit witnessed sunshine that was neither hot nor cold. The sun seemed to be either shy or undecided on a particular course of action. The sky was blue, though with pockets of wooly clouds. The atmosphere was cool, but not cold; slightly windy, but not wintry. It was a perfect setting that completed the serenity that is Calabar.

Calabar. Imata felt that the name evoked calm and contentment, peace and purity, beauty and ballad. Most cities boast of contrasts in topography and in living conditions. Calabar seemed to have less of such contrasts. Lying flat and sandwiched between rivers, the only major contrast is that potable water did not go round despite the fact that the city was virtually neck-deep in water. When Imata had first arrived, the houses were fairly alike—either the colonial buildings or ones with mud walls and thatched roofs. Whichever one was around accentuated rather than diminished the beauty of the place.

Need one describe the people? Daintily dressed always. The people—both men and women—were like the city itself, never in a hurry! Each gait seemed calculated for the piteously fat or relatively slim. The language sounded melodious and smooth even to a nonspeaker. Whoever has watched the coronation or the burial ceremony of the king, the Ọbọng of the Efiks, would not forget the people in a hurry. Their national contributions to the culinary dictionary hardly needed mention.

On the day in question, Eddie had mounted Imata on his motorbike, and the threesome—motorbike, boy, and girl—had floated round the city. From the Watt Market, which stood at the middle of the city; through Calabar Road where the few banks in the city had their branches; through Eleven-Eleven, a memorial to war heroes; and to Luggard Road where Hope Waddell Training Institute, a nineteenth century post-primary school that trained not idiots, but some of the nation's movers and shakers, including the first president, Dr. Nnamdi Azikiwe, was situated. A further ride took them through the state police headquarters to the Hope Waddell nineteenth century printing press just by Diamond Town. Eddie preferred to pass through this route to the Calabar Cement Company, one of the two industrial wonders of the city, the other being the Calabar Veneer and Plywood Company.

Turning left, Eddie switched off the engine of the motorbike and allowed it to roll down a small gradient that took them through the naval base. A huge embankment built possibly over a century before, hid the "government house'" or where the military governor lived, as well as the city's most prominent health institution, St Margaret's Hospital. One could barely see the hospital's administration building that had walls of enduring wood and concrete ceiling. A further ride up hill after Eddie allowed the bike to jerk itself to a start apparently to elicit a bang from Imata's chest took them to the Wharf, a scene of ceaseless activity. Here the oar-rowed boats, the "engine" boats, the ferries that plied the Oron-Calabar route were either moored or were busy accepting passengers or getting others to disembark. The wharf—where countless items were lost to thieves, where Elder Dempster personnel were virtual tin gods, where fights were the rule rather than the exception, where some people could weep like babies when they missed a ferry, where ubiquitous and itinerant medicine dealers hawked their all-curing drugs with eloquence and oratory—was a study in humanity.

"If you had never traveled through the Calabar wharf, half of your life is gone," people always said.

Up again through a short gradient, Eddie passed through the ageing Lebanese grocery stores that never appeared to change, through Gottschalk building materials shops, shops belonging to GBO, UAC, SCOA, and such other names; the Naval police office; and the Palm Produce Board building to the famed Esuk Nsidung, the first landing point and dwelling place of the Efiks. The market, which sold mainly bulk fish, crayfish, and other seafood, was always a beehive.

By riding through Hawkins Road, famed more for its cemetery than for anything else, Eddie joined Edibe-Edibe Road, one of the longest, broadest, and well-maintained roads in the ancient city. In a few minutes, on reaching the Watt Market, he had completed a full circle.

After a bottle of Coca-Cola, Eddie decided against going left through Egerton Street, but rather through Fosbery Road, linked Target Road, and headed for Old Ikang Road, which finally led him to the aerodrome. Airplanes came once in a while, so there was nothing to see except an abandoned military transport aircraft, a legacy of the just concluded civil war. To the right would have taken him to the ferry point, where dwellers in the hinterland up to the Ikang border with the Cameroon passed through. But Eddie was not going that far.

He turned and rode through Old Ikang Road and linked Marian Road into Big Qua town. A further ride took them through the newly developed area christened "state housing," an emerging reservation for the emerging elite. Finally, he entered the major highway that led out of town to other parts of the state.

By now, the pair was becoming tired. Eddie rode daintily back to town, passing through construction sites where the secretariat buildings, state stadium complex, and cultural center, a bit off to the left, could be seen. The temptation to see the breathtaking view from the old Calabar Sports Club was too much to resist. From there, one could see lush green fields of the government house, the Ministry of Finance headquarters, the Naval office, the Marina, and the waters of the Calabar River, which, though dangerous deep down, moved on unhurried, just as the rest of the city.

To cap the day, Eddie took off to Mbukpa, where the city's second largest market was located. The emerging Kingdom of the Brotherhood of the Cross and Star could be seen along Mbukpa Road, after the first generation Qua Iboe church. Mbukpa Market was thick in the night, when both the dead and the living were believed to buy and sell, with each going its way, unhurried.

Eddie then went down a muddy road toward Esuk Atu, which terminated at the Great Kwa River. There, they bought fresh fish from fishermen that had just docked and then proceeded home for a well-deserved rest.

Calabar—one needed to be there to appreciate its beauty. Some call it a glorified village—with its pothole-filled roads, thatched houses, and banana plants—yet it remained a haven for lovers of peace and serenity. No wonder it was called *Canaan City*. Calabar—Come and Live and Be at Rest—a city that embraced civilization decades before others but still was not in a hurry to be overwhelmed by civilization, which has its own inherent chaos, a trait the people appear to have aversion for.

*   *   *

Imata had apparently fallen in love with Eddie. It was love for real, not passion, which is the wild side of love. Nor was it infatuation, which is a passing phase of a feeling. What she felt was deep and fundamental. It was ecstatic—and in fact esoteric. It was a beautiful, all-consuming, and satisfying feeling—at least so she said.

The problem, however, arises when love is on its way out. True love never dies, but the flame when it burns too hot at a point soon burns itself out. At this stage, participants know they are no longer in love; however, if the feeling was fundamental, the flame may be gone, but the sparks remain.

When a sizzling love affair is ending, hope gives way to despair to the part of the receiving end. That was the way Imata felt when Eddie started seeing her once in two days instead of daily as he used to, then twice a week, then once a week, and, finally, once a fortnight. Imata never got to know where Eddie's love went or why. He never volunteered, for he always had a perfect excuse for his absence and his generally lukewarm attitude.

"What have you seen that makes you think I no longer love you?" he would query.

"I hardly see you these days."

138

"I am busy. Can't you see?"

"I know, but you have always been busy. And you have not changed jobs."

"Have you met another woman in my house or seen me on the street with one?"

"No."

"Then what makes you think I no longer love you?"

Imata never could think up an answer. Somehow, she felt that things were no longer as they used to be. She cast her mind back to when it all started a little over a year before. Eddie had literally sprung on her, suffocating her with more love than she could accommodate. Her varied experiences in love affairs still gave her no clue as to how to handle what she regarded as a monster. His approach was entirely novel, particularly for a girl untutored in the principles of refined love. He had come with songs and solos, ferns and flowers, poems and perfumes. He was gentle, but when she erred, he rebuked her in no uncertain terms. He was her dream of a man—strong, bold, decisive, full of ideas, humorous, caring, and dutiful. He was a brother, a father, and a custodian, but most importantly, a lover. He loved her—she was perfectly convinced of that.

Eddie could not stand two days without seeing Imata. He either called on her on his way to work or on his way back from work. He ensured that she never lacked anything that his resources could accommodate—money, clothes, food, time, and love. He changed the outlook of her hitherto one-room hovel to a mini palace. He took her out not to parties for he felt he would not have enough time to savor her, but to the beach, on moonlight walks, to out-of-town hotels, and such places where extreme privacy was ensured. This was a world of difference from the relationships she was used to, which were basically lustful on the part of the men and material oriented on her part.

Eddie's feelings were most apparent after a journey made by either of them. Imata vividly recalls their meeting after Eddie went on a two-week course north of the Niger. When he came to her house and met her, he held her so tightly she thought all her bones would break. She only managed to breathe. Not that she complained. When he finally relaxed his grip, he was shedding "tears of relief and joy." She wept too. He had surveyed her thoroughly for any sign of weight loss and wanted to know why there was a pimple on her face, why her nails were not filed, and why she forgot to oil her hands after washing, which left them dry.

Then he had held her close, this time gently and kissed her long and deep as if his life depended on it. Imata relived those moments often. She had, however, always felt that it was not right—the depth of the feeling. It was not natural. She was used to the rough-and-ready relationships that she knew in the rough-and-tumble city of Lagos. Time proved her right as Eddie later on stopped seeing her altogether.

*   *   *

It has been said that to get out of a love affair, one has to fall in love again—like the old wives' tale about a hangover. To clear a hangover after a bout of heavy drinking, take a mild dose of another alcoholic beverage. Or like medics would say, to fight a virus, take a mild dose of the virus in what they call vaccine. Imata decided to get into another affair, if for no reason, at least to save her sanity.

This is when she came into contact with Utibe. They met at a public water facility commonly called public pump or tap. For all Imata cared, this was a real man though a closer look showed that he was but a child. Imata was by then a beautiful woman in her early forties though looking very much like one approaching her midtwenties. She was nature's masterpiece, and as masterpieces are wont to be, her beauty was enduring.

Utibe, on the other hand, was just twenty-two years old. His huge frame and manly looks, however, misled people who thought he was older than what he actually was. He could easily pass for a thirty-year-old. As a first son, he was brought up to

140

behave as a man from the first year of his life despite the fact that he was somehow overpampered by his mother.

He, however, actually began to play manly roles from the age of twelve when he went to a fishing village to live with a fisherman for one year. Although he went back to the village to attend secondary school, he was so excited about life at Ine—one of the fishing villages on the coast of the Atlantic Ocean—that he made sure that all his long holidays were spent there. This tour on the high seas invariably affected his outlook on life and possibly his physique. A child that has been doted upon will remain a child even at forty unless seriously jolted somewhere along the line by some event. Thus, some boys in men's clothing end up messing up the society because they were never brought up as men. Those who started playing men from youth, protecting younger ones and running their homes in their own little way, grow up to take their place as men. Utibe was a man from an early age.

The attraction between Utibe and Imata was reciprocal. As he was wont to do, he made the first move. He opted to fetch water for her so as to "save her delicate frame from any ruffian during a fight for water." Which was very possible because public taps were places where young men and women met, not only to exchange platonic glances and, or seal deals, but also to settle scores. It was usually a place for the survival of the fittest where only the strong went home with water on time, irrespective of time of arrival. Brawn rather than brain always ruled. The youths could not appreciate the fact that queuing for water would generate less bile, less broken heads, limbs and pots, consume less time and energy while making everybody a better citizen. Half an hour could go by without anybody fetching water while a fight went on between two people of any gender combination.

Things could possibly have ended if Imata had simply thanked Utibe and left after he had fetched water for her. She stayed back ostensibly to support the man who was by now the subject of jeers and taunts from others.

"Woman wrapper," one girl sneered.

"You have not fetched water for yourself, yet you fight for a woman!"

"Imagine fighting for a piece of meat that you will never eat."

"Who said he will not eat it?"

"This one? How much does he earn that can take care of Imata," a fairly elderly woman said and spat.

"Maybe he did not see a woman in his previous life" and so on. Utibe was completely unruffled. However, a minor scuffle broke out when he tried to fetch water. Utibe was in control. Finally, he left with Imata oblivious of the jeers and taunts.

"I can swear he will only see her underpants when she hangs them out to dry."

"Idiot. Such men never save their salaries."

"I pity his mother. His whole wealth will go to women."

"Stupid son of Eve."

Utibe and Imata did not say much as they went home. As a matter of fact, Utibe only recalled one incident just to break the ice and make him manly. Not being able to make a conversation when a boy is with a girl, Utibe had been told, would appear as if he was afraid of or even overwhelmend by the girl and therefore tongue-tied. So he cleared his throat and said something.

"Did you notice that boy with fat chicks," Utibe asked.

"The one who said somebody should not fill his big bucket so that the water may not finish," Imata responded. They laughed heartily.

"Proper village boy. Meanwhile, his lips are as long as those of a mouse."

"I tell you! Jonny Just Come, alias JJC."

"On second thought, one should not be surprised. The way the tap is constructed with a big cement 'body' gives the impression that water is stored just at the big patch."

"Meanwhile, the boy was dead serious." They laughed again. As neither could think up any other thing to say, they walked on in silence.

When Imata reached her destination, she showed him her residence, thanked him, and left. Utibe went his way. He, however, found it impossible to forget her. He felt a mixture of amorous desire and repulsion that he was unable to explain. Was it her age? Utibe was sure she was a "senior girl" despite her fresh looks. Was she married? Then that would be a disaster. There was this inexplicable approach-avoidance feeling within him that made him decide on the side of caution. Although he later found out that Imata was single and had never married, it was not enough to get him to make up his mind to push his case. Something held him back. A voice always told him, "That woman is dangerous. She is a time bomb. Run." And he ran.

Imata unfortunately saw things differently. Since Utibe did not come out to get her, she was determined to go and get him. The more he avoided her, the more determined she was to get him. The drama of this affair was to become more devastating than the one she had with Eddie and the end more destructive than either of them could have imagined.

*   *   *

As the script in her hand ended at that point, Ekam looked up at Naomi. The lady filled in further details after which she told the girl to go home and come back the following day for a continuation of the story. Ekam left but could not quite determine her feelings. On one hand, she felt she should continue for she loved adventure. On the other hand, she felt the story could strike at the root of her dreams—dreams of a comfortable and carefree life. She, however, went back to Naomi after three days to hear, or if she gave her more scripts, read the story, telling herself that it was prudent to do so if she was to avoid another frightening encounter with her aunt. Naomi was happy to have her back. She gave her more scripts to read. Ekam appeared to relish it despite the numerous diversions, one of which was a flashback on the life of Utibe as told to Naomi by Utibe himself when the encounter with Imata was gradually taking a dangerous toll on him.

Chapter 10

The morning of Saturday, June 13, was like any other morning and like any other Saturday when Utibe woke up from sleep. As with most mornings as far back as his memory could carry him, he had come alive slightly after six o'clock. The time was early enough to enable him catch the first record that wafted from the radio by the head of his bed from the program *Early Morning Melodies*. The only difference that fateful Saturday morning was that he had felt reluctant to leave his bed and could not quite explain why.

Utibe later on remembered when the cobweb of sleep had been brushed away from his eyes and brain that the day was different in a particular way—it was his birthday! He had said to himself in astonishment, "Twenty-two good years on earth!" At twelve months a year, he had spent 264 months already. Not a huge number really. But at 365 days a year on the average, he had spent approximately 8,030 days on earth! At twenty-four hours a day, not less than 192,724 hours had gone by! Minutes? Approximately 11.6 million! He thought of calculating in seconds for life actually ticks in seconds and actually ends in just one second but dropped the pen and paper he was using for it was obvious that the product would run toward a billion. He had used up millions in time but was probably a dozen years away from using up a million in pounds sterling, if ever.

"Just like that!" Utibe had marveled to himself. So much time had gone by since he first hit mother earth. He felt embarrassed by it all.

His embarrassment stemmed from the fact that on reviewing his achievement scorecard to date, he felt he was yet to start. His Ibibio ethnic group had over the years, with some modifications as time went by and circumstances changed, come up with a set of things a man, particularly in his youth, must achieve to be called a *man*. He thought about them—Western education if his family could afford it, a good job, a car or motorcycle, a "zinc" house in the village, a wife and children who must be educated and generally well brought up, and finally proper burial of his parents that would include the man's parents-in-law. Anything after these was regarded as extra, to be applauded but not regarded as compulsory.

If a man occupied an outstanding position in public life, he would be applauded. It was a thing of pride. If he won laurels in sports, academics, the arts, and other such noble professions, he would be received with fanfare. But even a man who had become governor of a state but had no house in his village may not be able to speak in the village with as much boldness and authority, particularly when he was no more in power. Someone was bound to say, "That is not a serious man. He has not put up a roof over his mother's head" and "he has no place where his corpse will be kept for the ceremonies of transition."

Although twenty-two years of age was still small, there was a lot for Utibe to worry about that Saturday morning. He had reviewed his scorecard—West African School Certificate "attempted," a job as a clerical assistant in the civil service, he owned a car only when he paid for a brief ride to and from his various destinations, no house of his own anywhere in the world, no wife, no child, and none in the near future as these formed part of his "five-year development plan." His adoptive father as well as his mother were still alive, and it was obvious that if they dropped dead suddenly, what they would get for all their troubles would be anything but fit and proper burials. What worried Utibe most was the hopelessness of his situation. The future held no promise. If he had been in an institution of higher learning at twenty-two, it would have been just fine, but he was not in one and the probability of being in one was very remote.

This trend of thought was broken by an unwelcome intrusion—Imata. As usual, she rammed into his thoughts so strongly, so poignantly, and so unavoidably. As usual, it was impossible to push her aside. Utibe allowed himself to be carried away by the thoughts of Imata.

A walk by the river holding her hand. Man and woman walk on taking in the motion of the river, admiring the forceful movement as it attacks the bank, a further rebuff and a further retreat, endless attacks and retreats, each time dumping all sorts of waste at the bank. Man and woman plod on, now and then smiling and then drawing up their limbs from what could be quicksand. The odor of live and dead fishes, plant and other animals alive and dead, mixed in a manner that was both repulsive and exciting. Man and woman walk in the forest of greenery by the riverbank with all the folklore of ghosts, water gods, goddesses and lurking snakes, giant salamanders, crocodiles, wolves, and fairies. Man and woman trudge on in mixed excitement and fear at the inexplicable and inexhaustible wonders of nature, wondering what lay in the yet to be fully explored depths of the river and greater still, the seas. Man and woman plod on, contented and comforted at the thought of the fathomlessness of their love for each other, unnatural as it seemed. Utibe and Imata floated on like ghosts known to walk on air, hand in hand, moving toward a land of bright lights afar, oblivious of dangers and threats that lurked everywhere on the ground, in the water, the air—just about everywhere . . .

Utibe floated off to sleep, the last that comes to people just before dawn. The sleep was soothing, smooth, so good, and so heavenly that he felt there was really nothing to worry about in his life. But there was something to worry about at that moment—just outside his door.

*   *   *

146

When Utibe woke up the second time that morning, probably not more than fifteen minutes after his daydream about his rendezvous with Imata, it was with a start. There was no noise, and there was nothing unusual in sight. Daylight had broken with streaks of early-morning light shining through his see-through window covers for the window was not closed. He lay still, straining his ears to pick up sounds. None came, yet his skin crawled. He felt cold despite the heavy cover cloth on him. This surprised him as he had in fact felt hot when he first woke up that morning before he floated back to sleep. He felt numbed all over with fear slowly drifting toward him as if it were physical coming from the yet to be opened doorway. The fear came over him like the icy wave of a cold harmattan night. In his numbed state, he tried to look all over the room to catch a glimpse of anything sinister. Nothing was in sight.

Utibe allowed his eyes to dwell on every item in the scantily furnished room. His mind was quite alert, which dispelled any thought that he was dead. The food cupboard, old but still functional, stood at the right-hand corner of the foot of his bed. His soup pots, pans, cutlery, and metal bucket for storing drinking water were kept there. They were not of the best quality, but he managed to protect them for they provided whatever little comfort he had at that point in time.

To the left of his bed was his makeshift pantry where he stored raw food items—yams, plantains, onions, beans, rice, and the rest. He attended to affairs of the stomach seriously. It was popularly held by his people that it was the stomach that one carried to the land of the dead, not money, cars, furniture, houses, and other items of wealth that cannot be eaten. In fact, it was believed that if a man died on an empty stomach, residents of the land of the dead would reject him. Such a person came back to be a wondering ghost suspended between two worlds and accepted by none, having no rest and being humiliated everywhere. Human beings were quick to call such a person a "stupid ghost" irrespective of that person's standing while alive.

There was a small table close to the head of his bed. It was a typical grammar school student's reading table made of white wood with X-shaped legs that could be separated from the top. In his days at school, owning such a table conferred on the owner some elevated status. For a worker, the story was different. However, Utibe continued to use the table for reading, for writing, and for eating. To his friends who usually laughed at him for retaining the table, Utibe never tired of reminding them that wealth simply meant a new thing meeting an old thing in the house. Besides, he said he was a connoisseur of "endangered species" of everything, which in his room included furniture, books, a hurricane lamp, a radio set, and an enlarged photograph of his mother. Quite much, one would say.

One could not forget the standing hanger by the left side of the bed. Employees of Utibe's caliber generally had "wall hangers" as symbols of high living for people of that class. The hanger bore Utibe's dresses and his shoes, the latter of which were placed on a lower level. It also bore the air freshener that ensured the smells of raw food did not control the room.

The most expensive and eye-catching item of furniture in the room was the bed. Made of fine wood, it bore a spring Vono mattress covered with a clean white sheet. As wood beds were just coming into vogue, Utibe stood out of the crowd. He had often said that the bed was where one spent more than half of one's life, doing a number of things that could be very pleasant. No expense should therefore be spared to get the best of it. What was common then was the spring bed of various dimensions varying from six springs to ten springs with the rich using the elevated type that had long ghostlike poles by the four corners.

Utibe had always looked at each item of furniture in his room with some fondness as each had contributed in one way or the other to make his life worth living. He had acquired them within one year of joining the civil service of Southeastern State of Nigeria. As none of these things could bear mischief, he decided that his feeling of dread must come from other sources. Throwing away the bedcover with so much force that drove away the esoteric numbness from him, he jumped out of the bed and made for the door to take whatever bull was there, nowhere else than by the horns.

*   *   *

Trouble does not blow a whistle as elders would say. What Utibe saw on opening his door left him transfixed and blank. Seated on the bare floor facing his door, and by implication, the transfixed young man, was a woman who could not have been less than sixty years old. She sat with her legs wide apart *in puris naturalibus!* About a foot or two from her stood a black pot ensconced on another that had some firewood and coal burning slowly. No flame was visible. The content of the pot was obviously not visible to the eyes of the uninitiated. It was a female neighbor's screams that brought Utibe back to consciousness. Yet he could neither go back into his room nor move away from the sight before him.

The female neighbor, Ima Ima, came to the scene. She apparently understood what had happened. She went on her knees before the woman, begging her to cover her nakedness.

"Woman, this is not your problem," the visitor intoned dispassionately.

"I agree, our mother. But I have touched the earth. I am holding on to the earth. The person who holds on to mother earth cannot fall," Ima Ima pleaded.

"Woman, this is not your problem," the visitor repeated.

"I agree, our mother. You are a mother. I am a mother. Our son has wronged motherhood. Since the chick cannot be killed when its mother steps on it, we cannot kill our own."

"Woman, this is not your problem," the visitor maintained.

"When two people fight, a person that volunteers to separate them becomes a party to the fight. Our mother, this is my problem." The woman appeared slightly weakened at this stage.

"This boy has disgraced womanhood. He passed through a woman onto the earth. He did not drop from the sky. He did not drop here like the seed of an oil bean fruit," the visitor said gravely.

"I agree, our mother. You have called him a boy. So he is. That means he is a child. You and I know what children are like these days . . ."

"Woman, stop interceding or you may find yourself where you did not bargain for," the visitor warned.

"Our mother, I am still holding on to the ground. A messenger cannot be killed while delivering a message. I beg of you, spare this child."

"A stubborn chicken learns its lesson only when it finds itself in a pot of soup," the visitor continued without blinking.

"I agree, our mother. But where do we keep stubborn children? Where do we throw away wayward children? I remind you, our mother, that there is no forest for dumping bad children."

"In the days of old, we used to sell youths of his group," the visitor said bitterly and spat.

"Gone are the days, our mother. A mother is never tired of a bad child. We, mothers, are stuck with what we bore for nine months, suckled for one or two years after delivery, nursed through sickness and pain to maturity. Nowadays, we beat them with the right hand and then draw them to ourselves with the left. Pardon is what I ask."

"Pardon he will not get," the visitor said with fatal finality.

"Pardon is the word, our mother. Do we not go wrong daily in our words and deeds?"

"Some words and deeds may be forgiven by our cult. But some words, some deeds, some particular words, some particular deeds are never forgiven. You know this as much as I do," the visitor said, spat, and spat again.

"I know, our mother. My request is that for now you should cover up, take this pot away from here, and give us a chance to defend ourselves."

"Woman, is this your son?" the visitor asked.

"He is our son," Ima Ima replied.

"Did he come out of your womanhood?" the visitor asked again.

"Not directly, our mother. Children are owned by everybody. He is your son. He is my son."

"Woman, this is not your problem," the visitor intoned.

"It is our problem, our mother. May I ask, what can we do? There is a quarrel, a disagreement. It can be settled through discussion. As our elders say, no problem is so great that it is beyond dialogue."

"I agree with you," the visitor grudgingly accepted.

"So what do we do to appease the women of the land?"

"Let him bring one hundred and one pounds," the visitor said casually, but determinedly.

"Our mother, only the very rich among our people can produce such money at short notice."

"Short or long notice, if I do not have that money in my hands, I will not leave this place," the visitor declared.

"Our mother, between this boy and his neighbors, we can probably raise fifty pounds."

"Woman, this is not your problem," the visitor said disinterestedly.

"Fifty pounds, our mother, I pledge."

"May I remind you that the one hundred and one pounds is a compulsory fee? If his case is judged and he is found innocent, the accuser will return same amount to him," the visitor said.

"We do not even know his offense, our mother."

"You do not know. Should I tell you, woman?" the visitor asked sarcastically in a threat-laden voice.

"I know, but the boy may not know."

"I will assume he does not know. Let him bring the money. I will tell him," she said.

By now, the tiny compound of thatched roofs and mud walls was filled with inquisitive neighbors, whose mugs bore fear or anger or disgust or glee depending on each person's relationship with Utibe. There was a flurry of activities in the neighborhood.

Utibe was still rooted to the spot throughout the talk session between his neighbor and the sinister visitor. He only managed to whisper to the woman who entered his room to search for money. After what appeared an eternity, the neighbor appeared again, knelt by the side of the woman, and continued her plea.

"Our mother, a search through this entire house had produced sixty pounds. I am aware that the amount is the monthly salary of a university graduate. Our son is very far from that status. In fact, he earns barely twenty-one pounds and ten shillings a month. He pays his monthly rent there from. He maintains a mother with that. He eats and clothes himself with that. He even maintains our kind with that too. Not to forget that he must buy soap to wash his clothes and bathe himself."

"Bathe himself you said?" The woman screamed and became highly excited. "That is why I am here. He said a woman like you smells. He must bathe her. That is why I am here. He must bathe her," the woman said, losing her composure and placidness the more.

"That he will do, our mother, but only when he is found guilty of the charge. For now, please accept this token from him and from concerned neighbors. That we share this burden with him is a testimony to his character. Neighbors do not share a load with bad neighbors."

"You speak well, my child." With this, the woman took the money, picked up the piece of cloth that was by her side, tied it across her waist, did a weird dance facing the four corners of the earth in turn, mumbled a few incantations, then carrying the boiling cauldron and placing same on her head, walked away, swaying her behind in such a way that should have, under normal circumstances, elicited much mirth but now only generated more fear in the hearts of onlookers.

A couple of minutes after the woman had disappeared from sight, the crowd still stood transfixed as if an invisible force held them in one place. When the kind neighbor heaved a sigh of relief, the crowd dispersed.

It must have taken more than a quarter of an hour after the early-morning caller left before Utibe left the doorway he had been standing all through the dawn ordeal. Even without emptying his bladder as he should on waking up, he went right back into his room and crashed heavily on his bed.

For some minutes, he lay staring at the sooty ceiling above him. He was blank. He tried to focus on the drama that had just concluded itself some minutes back. He prayed that it was a bad dream that would vanish when he finally woke up. The spirited discussions outside ensured that his hope that he had just gone through a dream was forlorn. To block his consciousness from the disaster that he was exposed to, he allowed his mind to wonder through his childhood days.

*   *   *

The one pause observed was from Ekam who wanted to know the meaning of the words "in puris naturalibus." Naomi told her it was Latin and meant stark naked. Thereafter, the girl had sustained her reading, with Naomi enjoying the changes in her countenance or body movement as the script progressed. Her body language told its own story, and Naomi believed it would help her review the script before it goes to press.

Chapter 11

It is often possible for people to remember a number of events during their childhood, sometimes as early as when they were two or three years old. The clarity of remembrance depends on the weightiness of a particular event. Utibe could hardly remember his days as a toddler with any level of clarity. All he could remember was that his mother overpampered him. He was her only child. He had been dotted upon, sometimes to a damaging extent, for he had felt a few times in his life that he could probably have turned out a better human being if he had been allowed to see more of the harsh realities that is life.

Utibe had led a sheltered existence. His mother, known to the village as Nya, brought him up in the village of Oboyo. She had returned home one day with a baby boy that people simply described as beautiful. Everybody had been very happy at this welcome development.

Nya had been married for ten good years without a child. As she could no longer stand the harassment and taunts from her in-laws and peers, she had left the village for an undisclosed destination to start life anew. It was therefore to everybody's joy when she returned one day with a baby just three months old to the village. More than a year had gone by since she left the village.

The boy had a semblance of the woman—thin lips, round face, pointed nose, broad forehead, light in complexion, and a bit on the stocky side. Nya's family was overjoyed. There was no need to ask for the child's father. The family's prayer had been answered. That was enough. Her parents had organized a big welcome party by village standards and had named the boy Utibe, which means miracle. This was a miracle baby. Nobody bothered when one wizened man asked, "I did not hear of pregnancy, now I am seeing a baby." To Nya's parents, the accusation by the villagers that they had bewitched their daughter had been debunked. It was jubilation galore.

Better still, Nya's husband had decided to take back his wife as well as adopt the child. The village surprisingly accepted this move and commended the man for his benevolence and maturity.

Utibe had grown fast like a miracle baby. It was as if he was being pulled upward. He overshadowed his peers and even his elders in height. At school, everybody loved him despite the fact that he was stubborn. The headmaster had once told Utibe's mother that the boy was pampered too much, so much that he hardly cared about his future. His mother was prepared to give him all he wanted. So was his adoptive father.

The indulgence was taken quite far. Utibe always had his way. It was no surprise then that on completion of his primary education at the age of twelve, he opted to go to the sea rather than further his education immediately. His mother had protested feebly. His adoptive father, to save face, only said that he had gone through the same training and encouraged the boy to take a plunge.

It was his trip to Ine, one of the fishing villages on the coast of the Atlantic Ocean, which Utibe allowed his mind to dwell on that morning. That trip had some import that he felt could help him take a decision on his present predicament. It had to do with the power of the women folk, particularly those that are from the riverine areas.

*   *   *

He clearly remembered his trip to Idombi, a big fishing village on the Atlantic Coast. He had gone there with other colleagues to watch a ceremony when women were to release crayfish into the ocean. The women had earlier commanded crayfish to disappear for months because one of the fishermen had refused to appease the women after he had told off one of their kind, calling her a stinking daughter of the devil. But before allowing his mind to dwell on that ceremony, Utibe decided to let his mind's eye trace the watery road to the fishing village where he spent some months each year from the age of twelve, including his days in the secondary school which he attended after one fishing season at Ine.

*   *   *

When he took the decision to spend a fishing season at Ine, he did not know what sort of life the people there lived. His decision was a result of a bet at school. One of his classmates, popularly called *Itakafara* (with reference to his developed biceps, which is a hallmark of fishermen who row boats aplenty), had called him a *sissy* and mama's boy. Utibe was miffed. "Can you row a boat single-handedly? Can you face a single wave in an angry ocean? Can you face a crocodile or a shark or even the great snakes that inhabit the creeks?" The questions were endless.

"You cannot call yourself a man until you have gone to the sea. Land is for men and women. The rivers are for men and women. The sea is for he-men." To prove that he is a man, Utibe had decided to go and take the crocodile by the teeth. He was willing to dare the depths of the ocean although he had always dreaded anything that he could not see to the end, particularly running water. He always remembered the words of Nso, his maternal uncle with regard to streams, rivers, and oceans: "Water tastes well only when it is in a cup."

The usual take off month to Ine is October, when the rains are on their way out. Ine is a general name for fishing villages and fishing ports along the coast of the Atlantic Ocean or other large rivers, such as the Calabar River and the Great Kwa River. Each village or town has its own name however. A boy is usually handed over to an owner of a fishing boat or boats. Along with others, the boys would first be taught the art and science of rowing boats, controlling the boats on different temperaments of the sea, collecting drinking water, building dwelling places on water, gathering firewood, determining and deciphering the weather, clouds, currents, colors of water and their implications, rules of survival at sea, and codes of conduct. Then they would be taught the intricacies of fishing and processing of fish, including drying, packaging, and sales. At the end of the fishing season, which lasts from October to about July of the following year when rains disallow much activity and catch is poor, the boys would return to their village with the master, carrying with them some fish and loads of tales plus the sum of ten shillings, which would be paid to their parents.

Utibe did not particularly feel excited when he left home one early morning for the trip to Ine Inua Abasi. He sat in front of a bicycle while his master, Ekong Iba, sat behind. At Uyo, they boarded a lorry for the trip to Oron. At Oron, they joined a waiting boat for the three-day boat trip to Ine Inua Abasi.

It was not a very comfortable situation entering a rather smallish boat with six healthy men. There were containers for water, food, and local gin inside the boat, as well as bundles of fishing nets and other fishing accessories. As the party took off, the edge of the boat and water were about the same level. Utibe doubted the safety of the exercise but could not comment. After all, he was supposed to be a man.

The speed with which the boat moved surprised Utibe. In all, four people rowed the boat, one in front, two at the middle, and one very stout, dark, and fierce looking man sat at the rear. Utibe later on learnt that only very strong men handled the rear of a boat because the major propelling force as well as steering effect came from the rear. He immediately understood the import of the songs that always referred to the men at the rear of boats as being the men that determined the movement of a team or an organization.

From Oron, the team made a brief stopover at Ndito Eka Iba. This was not a fishing port. It was a landmark of sorts. Two trees stood at the middle of the river, giving an impression of twins leading to the name, which means two brothers. It was a crossing point, which led the way to a rather wide body of water with no land in sight. After some further rowing, during which the team mercifully met a number of other fishing boats, they reached Abana, a small fishing port. The team rested there and ate some food. After the meal and some rest, they put to sea again. The boat emptied into an expanse of water called Akpa Usak Edet.

Akpa Usak Edet was quite a sight to behold. This was a large body of fathomless water that moved on directionless, almost without ripples, giving the impression of calm and innocence, beckoning the unwary to take a plunge to a certain death.

The village associated with Akpa Usak Edet looked quite large, the largest Utibe had so far seen. When he had asked to be allowed to call there for sightseeing, the team had laughed at him. The dwellers in the village were reputed to be good at changing form. The fishermen could change into crocodiles, snakes, buffaloes, just anything other than human. Only the strong were said to survive in that village.

Further rowing landed the team at Ufak Inua Abasi, a fishing port cum channel, which lay adjacent to Ine Nung Okon, a large fishing village. On the third day of relentless rowing, the team landed at Ine Inua Abasi, where Utibe's master lived. Utibe and another boy joined their master who took them to a thatched house built on stilts. People visited neighbors by moving in boats. All over the village, there were huge bonfires that were used for smoking fresh fish.

Life in a fishing village is froth with dangers and excitement. No day went by without a remarkable incident—either a disappearance without trace of one of the fishermen or a mass loss of lives following a boat mishap. There could be visits by a water mermaid, or a fisherman could catch a most unusual creature in a net. There was always something to keep someone excited. Life at sea, Utibe thought, would fill volumes and volumes of books if those that bad lived there could sit down and articulate their experiences.

Despite his fear, Utibe, always one to outdo himself and others, had requested his master for permission to go further afield. His target was the tiny African country of Equatorial Guinea with its popular capital, Malabo.

Utibe was granted his wish when one of the teams of smugglers moored at Ine Inua Abasi. He joined the boat, a massive wooden structure that had a depth of over ten feet and a length of over thirty feet. The boat had a number of compartments meant for storage of contraband to escape the prying eyes of Nigerian customs men and the Cameroonian gendarmes.

From Ine Inua Abasi, the boat with two massive Suzuki engines hummed its way into the big waves of the Atlantic, taking the team to Ibuot Efe, a fishing village where Ijaws were very many and where most fishing accessories could be bought. The team leader picked up a number of spare parts and victuals for their trip.

Further on, the boat reached Idombi, a big fishing port. This particular town was later on to host an event that Utibe reminded himself he would have to dwell on.

To Ine Udo, the team pushed, then on to Upenekang, a big town, then to Tiko and then to Ufak Itung. Here it was possible to get nonsalty water as well as local vegetables for food. Ufak Itung boasted of two types of water, salty and nonsalty.

The most exciting port of call was Ọkọ Itiat. This port was noted for two things—a natural gate carved out by nature for passage of water transport and the existence of two colors of water, green and blue. The two colors never mixed. If one attempted to put one color in the other, the quantity so deposited would jump out and return to where it belonged. The crossing point was also important because of frequent boat mishaps. Seafarers must study the weather, currents, and timing

159

before crossing the gate because of the turbulence that was very common as a result of accidental mixing of the two waters. No one was able to explain to Utibe the wonders of Ọkọ Itiat. It was also at Ọkọ Itiat that Utibe could sight the light of Santa Isabel, which was actually the image of the Holy Mary, the mother of Jesus.

On successful crossing of the gate at Ọkọ Itiat, the boat entered the dominantly blue water that led to Santa Isabel. Utibe did not have the privilege of setting foot on Santa Isabel because the boat turned back just after crossing the gate. It was announced that a naval boat apparently from the Equatorial Guinea fleet had been sighted sailing toward the team. As the team leader was in no mood for trouble, he had decided to turn back. Utibe, however, felt grateful for he was not keen on facing the horrors of life at Equatorial Guinea as returnees from the island had often told.

*   *   *

He then allowed his mind to dwell on the drama at Idombi. For three good months, those who specialized in crayfish business had toiled without taking home a single catch. Though the fishermen had heard of a possible reason, they had refused to submit so meekly to what they saw as blackmail, by of all the groups on earth, the women folk.

One of the fishermen, Ekpat, was involved in an affair with an Idombi damsel. Things had gone on well for both parties till on one visit, the lady had met another woman at Ekpat's thatched dwelling. This sort of thing normally did not go down well with the Idombi women who were well bred and strong metaphysically and were thus proud women. The women of Idombi were very well attuned to the sea, both to seen and unseen things. There were lots and lots of folktales woven on the lives and times of Idombi women who were said to live underwater as much as they lived on land.

On the fateful day, Ekpat had come home a very unhappy man. The day had not gone well at sea. His net had broken midstream. Back home, his stock of drinking water, which meant saltless water, was quite low. So was his stock of food. It was therefore a case of one too many aggravations when his Idombi friend confronted him inside his house, seeking to know why another woman should be with him. He simply told her to take her smelling self away from his house. It was a fatal slip of the tongue, the type that comes in an unguarded moment when anger or desperation rules reason and prudence. The genteel lady had quietly stepped out of the house, entered her tiny boat, and rowed back to her village. The lady, Timse, in Ekpat's house, had urged him to immediately inform the village head of his indiscretion.

"These women command the inhabitants of the depths. They obey. They obey because the women pander to their needs. They control fish. They control crayfish. They control everything. Dare them if you will," she had warned. Ekpat had scoffed at such an idea. It was not until two days later, when a group of white-robbed women rowed in a convoy and arrived at the house of the chief of Ine Inua Abasi that Ekpat knew he had made a fatal mistake.

The leader of the delegation, dressed in a long flowing white robe with a red band each on her head, wrists, ankles, and waist, had gone to confer with the village head. She had declared that unless certain rites were performed, the women would seize all the crayfish in the water till further notice.

As they were wont to be, the men, not too exposed to the powers of the women of the seas then, scoffed and refused to play ball. Three months later and with their purses running dry, the men went to beg for pardon and ask for the release of crayfish.

*   *   *

161

Despite the fear of the unknown, which made the eyelids to twitch feverishly as well as generate goose pimples on his skin, Utibe had decided to join the team of "men" who were to go to Idombi to sort things out with the Idombi women.

Prior to the pacification trip, a delegation from Ine Inua Abasi led by the elders had gone to meet the elders of Idombi. The women had been called in for discussions. It turned out that the decisions on the ways and means of resolving the conflict, and by extension, releasing crayfish into the sea, was taken by the women. A number of things were listed to be supplied by the offending party. A date was fixed for the pacification exercise.

On the appointed day, seven boats had been dispatched from Ine Inua Abasi, each filled with men and materials, the materials listed by the Idombi women. An advance party had left the previous day with the more critical items for sacrifice to the territorial water goddess.

Utibe remembered clearly the trip to Idombi. It was not his first. It was not his second. In fact, he had been there so many times that he had lost count. But this trip appeared quite different. He felt quite agitated. The water appeared different. The waves were not very wild, but each mass seemed to come with a being that defied description. The men rowed and rowed, all subdued. Once in a while, a boat would stand still despite strong rowing or spin full circle or shoot forward as if propelled by a jet engine. It was obvious that the water gods and goddesses were on beat.

After what appeared an eternity, the party had arrived Idombi. Utibe could see the coast far off. There were many trees, but the most abundant was the coconut tree.

Prior to the arrival of the team, the women leaders had ordered that all coconut fruits close to the coast should be harvested. The fruits were assembled in a heap close to the waterfront. Men, women, and children lined up the waterfront. Just as they approached the shore, a flag was raised, urging them to hasten up. This was because after a certain hour, nobody must be on the water, for at such an hour, the women society would declare the water closed to traffic. No one dared contravene such order.

Punishment for disobedience was instant disappearance and a watery grave. Such was the power of women in those parts.

After the last boat in the team berthed, a boat carrying only women, all in white robes, left the shores. A little way off the coast, they dropped a short piece of stick that bore a red flag. Ordinarily, the stick should have gone down, taking the flag with it. Or it could have floated along with the flag on top of the water. Rather, the stick stood straight up and still, with the flag fluttering. The hoisting of the red flag was a sign that traffic on all surrounding water was closed until the cessation of the ceremonies.

Two more boats joined the first, all occupied by women that were dressed in white robes, with their faces painted with white chalk. They tied pieces of red cloth around their heads. Despite the butterflies fluttering in his stomach, Utibe could not help but admire the women. They were beautiful, elegant, fearless, and dignified. Women who could hold he-men to ransom could not be expected to have lesser qualities.

To the uninitiated, the ceremony was brief and uneventful. This was because most of what was done was underwater. The chief priestess, at a point on the massive body of water, had dived into the sea. She must have spent over an hour beneath the surface. Meanwhile, the women in the boats drummed, sang, and danced. The drumming could be heard on the shore. The dancing, which involved only the upper torso, was so graceful one could not help but marvel at the flexibility of the human trunk.

The chief priestess emerged from the depths after the long breathtaking period of wait. Her emergence coincided with intense drumming and dancing as she climbed into one of the boats. The party then rowed back to the shore.

On arrival, it could be observed that the chief priestess was not wet at all despite her long sojourn underwater. Utibe could not explain that.

After climbing out of their boats, which were decorated with a mix of white and red cloths, the women proceeded to

163

drum more intensely and dance voluptuously while mouthing incarnations. The scene was beautiful to behold.

To end the ceremony, the chief priestess called on as many men as possible to take the coconut fruits to the sea. As each man cut open a coconut fruit, live crayfish swam away from the belly of the fruits into the sea. Some men were so scared that they abandoned their cutlasses and fled. Others braved it and continued the fearful task of cutting open the fruits, even at the risk of facing an emerging viper.

At the end of the time-consuming exercise, all the coconut fruits on the huge pile had been cut open, each of them letting off streams of live crayfish.

The following day, those involved in fishing for crayfish went home with boats loaded with catch. This ended an unforgettable event that epitomized the power of the women folk in its most exciting, though most exasperating.

*   *   *

Recollecting this incident made Utibe feel very uncomfortable. He tossed over and over again on his bed. How could women, women who must go behind the house or into a bush if they want to ease themselves, women who are just mere clothing and makeup, have so much power even over nature? How could they hold men, men of the sea, real men, to ransom? It was simply impossible to understand. The thought of being subdued by women sent cold shivers down his spine. He instinctively held his manhood to reassure himself that he was still a man.

The revolting thoughts could have helped him make what could possibly have been the most important decision of his life had he not, at that moment, recalled his personal encounter with the sea. He was then fourteen years old and had gone to Ine Inua Abasi during one of the holidays.

*   *   *

It happened during one of those trips by boat hands to collect drinking water and firewood where they were available. Such trips always annoyed Utibe. He never understood why one could be rowing for two days just to source drinking water when one was living on water. He could not fathom why his master did not live at Ufak Itung, for instance, where there was drinking water, firewood, and edible vegetables. Exchanging one's convenience and in fact one's survival with more catch was not his idea of wise decision-making. Economics and common sense should walk side by side.

The team had fetched as much of their supplies as they could. They had made for their base, Ine Inua Abasi, when they discovered that the master's water container had been left behind. Of course, that was sacrilege. They made an about-turn.

On their way, the sea became angry. They fought and fought to no avail. They threw overboard all the things in the boat. Yet sinking was imminent. Then three of the boys, out of fright as one crocodile held on to the side of the boat, jumped into the raging sea. They were never seen again.

Utibe had single-handedly maneuvered the boat through the turbulence. He had rowed and rowed for two days and two nights, not knowing whether he was or where he was headed. He had rowed with all the strength in him, which was renewed from only God knew whence, with the dawn of each new day. It was toward the close of the third day that Utibe sighted a settlement. Tired and numb, he had rowed toward it. Behold, it was Ine Inua Abasi!

There had been jubilation when he arrived. It was difficult to believe that a young man could row a boat on his own without food, water, and sleep for two days and two nights, and most importantly, without a mast called "fadder." Utibe was to learn later that scores of people had lost their lives in the course of that storm. There were songs in his praise, and Utibe was tagged a miracle man. Utibe became an instant hero. His mother was very proud of him when he reached home for the story had preceded him to his village. The women society in the village had composed a song to celebrate the incident, and though it was laced with sarcasm, Utibe still felt good about it. It went thus:

> He left home a gangling boy
> He went to sea as mama's pet
> At sea, he dared the depths
> And fathomed the width.
>
> He left home a fatherless child
> He returned home his own father
> The miracle boy,
> Is now the miracle man.

The remembrance of these buoyed Utibe's psyche. He felt like doing a dance to that song. He was, however, held back by unseen hands. Nonetheless, he felt warm inside. Though he knew that inside him he still dreaded the sea, he still felt comfortable and safe when his mother was about and still felt lost and unsure of himself in the midst of real men, and worse still, young women. He believed he could acquit himself well if occasion demanded. This, most men did and ended up being heroes despite the fact that within them, they were weaklings.

Then a debate raged within me. Two voices demanded to be heard.

"Yes, I dared the sea, what can women do to me?"

"The women of Idombi tamed the men."

"Those were not men."

"They were men. Some of them taught you the basics of survival at sea."

"The thought can become the teacher."

"Women are to be respected—and feared."

"Respected, not feared."

"You cannot dare them."

"I dared the sea. I went, I saw, I conquered. I am the miracle man."

"A woman brought you into the world. She is greater than you."

"Only God gives life and can take life."

"Women bring life. They can take life."

"Though the women of Idombi subdued our men, I can stand up to them."

Utibe felt confused, then another thought struck him.

"This is the city. The city and civilization have dulled the sharp edges of mystery, turning what was possible into mere superstition."

"For fools only. The wise know the limits."

"Ghosts do not roam the cities. Gasoline fumes drive them away. Witches and wizards cannot operate in the city. They dread electricity. Women commit adultery and get away with it. They deliver safely in the brightly lit labor rooms of hospitals."

"Fools believe all those things. What was, is. What is, will be."

With the encouraging thoughts of his abilities and the impact of city life on superstitious beliefs, Utibe jumped out of bed being imbued with a sense of the impregnable. He rushed outside and went to a nearby bush. Holding part of his one-and-a-half-yard loincloth with his right hand while also holding part of his manhood in between two fingers, he proceeded to empty his bloated bladder.

Tilting his head slightly backward, his eyes half closed and mouth agape, he pushed out the waste in him, allowing the cool breeze and sunlight to caress his tall frame. He always enjoyed urinating outside rather than in the bathroom that had a permanent smell of urea. The flow of urine through him, which was a mixture of slight pain and relief he always felt, was a good ordeal. He watched the first spurt of urine come out of him. It was deep yellow in color. He certainly had malaria as it was generally believed. Probably that was what had been the cause of his nightmarish dreams. The flow started to reduce till only drops came.

"Probably that is how life is. It comes in spurts at the beginning, builds up to a torrent in-between then gradually drops off at the end," he mumbled to himself and shrugged. He then proceeded to blow his nose loudly, wipe it with the back of his palm, and then rub the palms together. With all cobwebs encircling him as a result of the scary thoughts that had gone, he strode confidently back to his room to prepare for his twenty second birthday.

Chapter 12

After having convinced himself that he was above *woman* destruction, given the fact that he survived at sea for days all alone in a small boat, he had successfully pushed the unfortunate event of the morning of his birthday to the back of his mind. His neighbors too had within one week for reasons that could not be fathomed ceased discussing the issue, for the generally idle people of the city who relished in such untoward events as sources of escape from the disappointments and frustrations of everyday life spent weeks on end discussing and analyzing every minutiae of such events till a new one came along. As no new event of note had happened within a week other than the normal bickering and brawls of petulant couples, Utibe was pleasantly surprised at the sudden loss of interest in his predicament.

The lack of interest probably helped lay to rest whatever misgivings he might have had. The uninvited caller had invited Utibe to meet with the Esa Iban Isọñ, a women's court where his case would be tried. Though Utibe knew that the court offered an avenue for the fairest judgment any court anywhere could offer, he felt it would be *infra dignitatem* for a he-man like himself to appear before a women's court, more so when it lacked constitutional or legal backing.

Utibe could have forgotten about the whole episode probably to his chagrin had the pastor of his church, Reverend Namsebo, not called on him a few nights after the event. Utibe had been surprised to see him. Reverend Namsebo had told Utibe, to the young man's consternation, to meet the women. The Pastor! How could this man of God tell a member of his flock to bow down to heathen practice? The modus of the Esa Iban Isǫñ was known to all—they use esoteric powers in virtually everything they do, which was uncomfortable, except that it ensured fairness for the practitioners who stood the risk of incurring the wrath of the gods if they dispensed biased judgment. The pastor had said that he was a realist who believed in Jesus' injunction of giving to Caesar what was Caesar's. Since Utibe's faith was not strong enough to enable him fight the case spiritually, the best alternative was to meet the conditions set by the women.

After ruminating into the wee hours of the morning, he reluctantly accepted to meet one of the women to arrange a date for his appearance.

"You are a lucky child," the woman, his mother's close friend, had said. Her name was Mamy.

"How lucky?" Utibe asked with a note of irritation.

"Very lucky. Very lucky," she said, shaking her head slowly in a very grave manner.

"Well?" Utibe asked

"A date had been fixed for a visit by the whole congregation of Esa Iban Isǫñ," she volunteered.

"When?" Utibe asked in obvious alarm. The thought of waking up to face ten or twenty women *in puris naturalibus* at his doorstep was not his idea of manly strength.

"I can see you are agitated," Mamy had said sarcastically.

"How can I be?" Utibe replied, avoiding the piercing and taunting eyes of the woman.

"Well then, we shall see that day," she said and made a move to go away. Utibe held on to her, avoiding pleas with his lips but doing so abundantly with his eyes.

"When . . . are . . . they . . . coming?" Utibe stuttered.

"The morning of tomorrow," the woman said gravely.

Utibe did not collapse to the disappointment of the woman. His stood firm on the ground. He had control of his huge frame, but he could hardly control the internal workings of his body for large beads of sweat crawled along the furrows that had formed on his forehead due to the growing concentration of his thoughts. He wiped the beads off by tracing his forehead with the right index finger and then cleaning the finger on his trousers. He suddenly felt very hot, though the early-morning weather was chilly. In a voice that was barely audible, he mumbled some words that the woman strained her ears to hear.

"I can't hear you," she said.

"I . . . said . . . well . . . well . . . em, can . . . you . . . stop them?" Utibe mumbled.

"It is not my business to stop them. I have no case to answer. You have."

"How can I stop them?" he inquired.

"By being humble. By being less proud. By remembering that women are the source of life. They mold you. They shape you. They make you. They can mar you. That is the way mother nature made them. Neither you nor I can change these," she said.

"You are not helping me, woman. I say, can they be stopped? If yes, how?" Utibe asked, his anger rising above his fear.

"The man once again! If you are that strong, approach them on your own," she said.

"It is not as if they are lions, Mamy, it is just that—" His voice trailed off.

"Just that what? I thought I was discussing with a man," she said with disdain.

"I may be at a position of weakness now. It does not take away my God's given right. Let this be clear—the worst that can happen is death, and I am aware that it is the end for all mortals. I can go a certain distance, not further," Utibe said with his fists clenched and his eyes blazing. To which Mamy cringed and sobered.

"There will be a gathering today, not a full meeting. I can pass on your message, not for your sake, but for your mother's sake. You are an only child."

"Better. Now I am aware that elders are not approached empty-handed."

"Elders! What men can do when they are caught pants down. Yes, the things you must bring include a four-sided bottle of schnapps, a bottle of native gin, a gourd of palm wine, three seeds of kola nut with money to break the nuts, and money for gravy so that the women can sit on the delicacies and wait for you to attend their court." Utibe did not need any prodding to provide those items.

Later in the day, he played back his discussions, actions, and reactions during his encounter with Mamy, his mother's friend. He chided himself for becoming nervous, and worse still, for betraying his nervousness before a woman. He, however, rationalized his actions, telling himself matter-of-factly that the real man is a prudent man, one that is farsighted and can thus recognize danger and wards it off if it is possible. He was aware that not even the police could stop the women for they would not visit someone for the purpose of inflicting physical harm, and in any case, the policeman from the locality would not want to become a party to a metaphysical event they can avoid.

Despite all the rationalizations, Utibe was troubled by his conscience as he fought the voices of reason and pride. Why should he not face the women if they visit him, after all, tradition gives cover to somebody who is attacked in his or her own domain? The women were about to bring war to his doorsteps. Or was it the sight of old women in their birthday suits? Was it the consequences of their actions on his life? The questions were many, but the answers did not come.

"The Pastor," Utibe had announced loudly to an imaginary congregation. "The Pastor caused this. He injected a large dose of fear into me. I could have waved someone else away. But not the Pastor—God's representative on earth! Instead of coming to strengthen me, to assure me of spiritual protection from the worshippers of the forces of darkness, he told me to succumb to their whims. His reason? Realism. Realism my foot! Damn the Pastor."

Utibe was so angry he felt bile rising from his innards and exploding forcefully in his mouth, generating palpable bitterness on his tongue. When a man's source of hope and defense turns out to be his source of despair and capitulation, the product is bitterness and resentment. The only advantage he could think up was that the Pastor provided him a ready excuse for failure, for by and large, with or without the Pastor's intervention, what would be would likely be.

In the end, what settled the internal argument was a small voice that wondered whether the experience he could get would not be worth the trouble. Utibe loved adventure, and this was adventure itself. He had heard so much about this women's court, and since one cannot go there just to watch proceedings as it happens in the white man's court, Utibe now had a rare opportunity not just to watch but to be the principal party in the proceedings—live!

Having been given directions to the location of Esa Iban Isoñ court, Utibe decided to go there alone. He still felt that putting up appearance was unmanly, so he decided not to go there with any of his friends. Besides, he wanted to avoid a situation in which someone would convince him to do what the women wanted if it was against his wish. Before he left therefore, he had somehow made up his mind not to do the women's bidding. This preemptive mental blockade proved rather costly as many preemptive strikes are.

*   *   *

What struck Utibe when he arrived at the venue of the "meeting," as he chose to call it, was the orderliness. He was not used to too much order in women's circles. The *efe* or clearing was a very simple one. The women were arranged in three main groups apparently according to their ages—the ancient, the old, and

173

the modern or very young. The fourth group was a motley of women of different ages wearing assorted, rather loud colors. There were drummers, dancers, stewards, and guards. The old women sat on low stools, looking very intense.

The group that was obviously the center of attraction and center of action was that of the ancient. These were wizened women whose ages were certainly not below three score and ten but likely four scores and above. They sat gracefully, some pulling sedately at their rustic pipes, some contemplating ground tobacco or snuff stacked between their index fingers and their thumbs while others gently chewed kola nuts or bitter kola. One could see that those in the modern group were very excited about the ancient group, staring at the members with a combination of admiration and trepidation. As Utibe learnt later on, a misdeed the young ones commit and thought no one knew because it was executed in the night could be brought up in full glare and instant punishment meted out to the culprit at the *efe*. The most common was a dalliance with someone's husband.

As soon as Utibe arrived, proceedings commenced. The women appeared to have been waiting for him. The session was a special one as men were rarely brought before the court and on a matter as grave and as fundamental as the one Utibe was facing. He was offered a seat, which he politely refused. One never knew what these women held, going by the stories one heard about them, for the stool could decide to develop wings and fly off with its occupant to land somewhere unknown.

A woman, who was gaily dressed, appeared before the group. She announced that she was the prosecutor. She read out the charge.

"That you, Utibe, the beloved and only child of Nya of the village of Oboyo, on a certain date, a certain time, at a certain place of which your brains can fix, announced that mother nature's perfect creation given to you for company smells like a pit latrine, thereby causing great discomfort and humiliation to womanhood and inviting calamity on our people through such abominable indiscretion. Pronounce yourself guilty," the prosecutor said.

"Before he does that or does not do that, let him welcome himself to this gathering of mothers, wives, sisters, and daughters," the woman in the middle of the ancient group said. Utibe had not noticed her until then. The fact was that his mind could not concentrate on any individual for he regarded the entire gathering as a conglomeration of loathsome enemies, out to take all his wealth, his manliness, and ultimately his life. He now noticed that the woman that spoke sat on an elevated stool that was specially designed. Beside her on each side, stood very young and pretty girls whose bare chests bore tiny shoots that announced the onset of puberty.

The prosecutor bowed and moved toward Utibe, stretching her arms. Though he was not prebriefed, he had gone there with a bag containing two bottles of schnapps, one bottle of native gin, kola nuts, and chili. He gave one bottle of schnapps to the prosecutor who placed it on the ground before the person Utibe decided to call Her Lordship.

From another woman, also seated on another carved stool but without bodyguards, came a further demand.

"This son of ours kept his grandmothers and mothers waiting for what was like an eternity. Did he not know that he should be here before us?" she asked.

"Ignorance is no excuse in law, great one," the prosecutor said. "Utibe, you are fined one bottle of native gin, two kola nuts, one fruit of chili, and five shillings for breaking of the kola," she announced.

Utibe rummaged through his bag, sorting and bringing out the items mentioned. Unfortunately, he was not careful enough for he exposed the other bottle of schnapps.

"What is before the temple is for the workers at the temple," the woman whom Utibe decided to call deputy leader said. To which the prosecutor asked Utibe to hand over the drink. Her Lordship cleared her throat and said, "I know my judges are never biased. We cannot, however, close our eyes to the fact that this lad came here prepared. That is manly. Besides, it shows that he respects us. Only son, I salute you."

"That means you are welcome," the prosecutor said. This served a very good purpose for Utibe suddenly became relaxed for the first time.

"Because Ekanyin has declared that you respect your mothers, another fine has been waved," the deputy leader announced.

"What she means is that the fine that could have been imposed for refusing the seat offered by your mothers has been waved," the prosecutor said.

"One up," Utibe said unconsciously in delight.

"Is that so?" the prosecutor queried.

"What did he say?" the deputy leader asked.

"He said one up," the prosecutor replied.

"Who does not rejoice in a moment of triumph?" the deputy leader said.

There were low murmurs among the modern group. Apparently, they were not happy at the early scores recorded by Utibe. These buoyed his spirits, raising his hopes for a fair hearing.

"This outing might not be as objectionable as I thought after all," he muttered to himself.

"Now, young man, pronounce yourself guilty," the prosecutor said sternly.

Utibe bowed to the ancient group, cleared his throat, sucked in a measure of fresh air, which seemed to clear the cobwebs of fear and doubt in his mind and addressed the gathering.

"My mothers, before I present my case, for a man of my age cannot say yes or no in circumstances like this, I would plead with you, having found favor in your eyes, to request that my accuser, the complainant, should be presented to this gathering. Eyeball to eyeball, we will be able to speak such that your fair judges will find it easier to know who is guilty and who is not guilty."

"We do not take orders. We give orders," the prosecutor barked.

"My son, you have spoken well, at least within the limits of your knowledge," the deputy leader said. "However, we have our procedures here. The fact is you have wronged womanhood, not a woman. We are jointly and severally the plaintiffs, the 'we' there including the woman who gave birth to you. The abomination you committed is also against the society, so men too are the plaintiffs. When it is time, and if it is necessary, one person will come out to give evidence. But only when we want her to," she declared.

"I think it is fair to at least let him know the primary plaintiff," Her Lordship said, to which the ancient group nodded their heads vigorously in agreement as Her Lordship's eyes went round the group.

"Her name is Imata," the prosecutor announced. "Are you satisfied?" she asked.

"I am content for now," Utibe said.

"Then tell us your story," the prosecutor ordered.

Utibe cleared his throat, shifted his position from the left leg that had been supporting his whole weight for much of the time to his right leg. With the confidence he had garnered as a result of the concessions already made, he let his eyes take in as many faces as was possible within the few seconds he knew he had before one of the officers screamed at him. His eyes had become very narrow slits staring accusingly at the crowd, particularly the modern group, which had become quite uncomfortable with the developments so far. Apart from the slight confusion with regard to an acceptable mode of greeting the group, Utibe felt generally at ease. He decided to concentrate on the ancient group.

"Ekanyin, my mothers, I salute you," he started. "I stand before you this morning, first and foremost as a son, and secondly though regrettably, as an accused. As an accused, I have to defend myself, but in the process, if I say what is not pleasant to your delicate ears, if I say what offends you, if I move a muscle in a manner that is capable of making your eyes want to pop out of their sockets, I say look at me from the point of view of a son.

In that case, throw away what offends you but draw me to you motherly selves.

"I have my strengths. I have my weaknesses. These make me human. One of my strong points is not equivocation or talking from two sides of my mouth. Rather, the art of equivocation constitutes one of my great weaknesses. I believe that truth is sacred—those in positions of authority may tamper it with it, it may be tampered with by status and by time, and ignorant people may even destroy it. One fact is certain—it will always come to the front. Sooner or later. I love truth, and I am like the stream in our villages. I produce one taste of water, never two." Utibe paused, more for effect than to get a breath of air. He surveyed the congregation that had by now appeared mesmerized and submerged in extremes of emotion—either admiration or loathing. Utibe felt good.

"Though the he-goat may mount its mother, it does not cover the fact that it passed through the same canal it now uses as a football field. The feared man of today was the crying baby of yesterday who depended totally on his mother for survival. That a man can lift his mother with just one hand does not blot out the fact that she once lifted him from his bed or bare floor with just one hand while using the other to do something else for the child's benefit. What more she was around before him and actually brought him into this world.

"Which man can say he can do without women? If you have no daughter, you at least have a niece. If there is no aunt, there is at least a female cousin. Of course, every man has a mother for no man came to the world through an exploded oil bean fruit. And men have grandmothers, who cook the most delicious soups any women anywhere can cook!

"Can a day go by without an encounter with the fairer sex? If one does not cook for you, at least one will ensure you have a warm bath in the morning, and for those who like clean habits, at night too. If one does not have a woman for a good company, one will at least have one that will quarrel with or abuse him. If none is available at one's place of earning the daily bread, at least one will warm the cold harmattan bed for the man during the night." He paused again for effect.

"What will the world be without women?" Utibe again surveyed the quiet crowd.

"But let me not bore you with long stories. I am not a great speaker. I am not so gifted. Great speeches are reserved for Inua Obodom and his gifted friends. Nonetheless, let me stretch your patience a little further by telling you my position on taboos.

"I did attend the white man's schools, but I had a break for one year not because I failed in any class, not because my parents could not pay my school fees or were not willing. I chose a different kind of school for nine months and thereafter went to spend my holidays each year for five good years. I went to the great sea! It is in this school that real men are made. The decision was mine. My mothers, there is nowhere in the world where taboos are more sacred and more observed as on the dwellings along the banks of the great rivers and seas. I spent nine months at *Ine*. I went back several times thereafter because of the excitement and the adventure which the sea offers, for as far as the sea is concerned, life on land is child's play. There, life is heavily regulated and controlled, not particularly by man but by nature and the gods.

"Because of so many unseen gods, goddesses, the elements, and other powers, the dos and don'ts of life on the high seas are a thousand times more than what obtains on land. The wise obey those unwritten rules for disobedience means instant judgment, which may mean a watery grave. When one remembers that any form of land is say three days of hard rowing away, the best thing to do is to fall in line. Need I tell you about the powers of women who live on the banks of the high seas? Those who know it, know it. Aside from the gods and the elements, women reign supreme at *Ine*. They almost control everything.

"Why then would I abuse the custom of my people of which I am fully aware? There is no cause under the sun. And of all things, why would a sane man say something bad about a woman who could be anybody's mother? Mothers are sacred. Wives too are sacred. I never said anything abominable to Imata even when she made the first move. I respect her now as I did the first day we met," he concluded.

* * *

Her Lordship was the first to stir after the gripping presentation by Utibe. She cleared her throat, whispered to her deputy, beckoned on the prosecutor, and conferred with her briefly before she addressed her audience.

"Fellow women, you have heard him, heard his starters that ended up as the main course. For desserts, we better let him answer a few question." Turning to the ancient group, she said,

"I know you have come across the likes of this boy. This is a pure breed of manhood—looks, sugarcoated tongue, and all. I trust that you will not be carried away by his sweet words or his flattery. I trust too that you will not be so angered by his insult of believing that women can always be swayed by volumes of words and flattery, that you will not set him free if he is truly not guilty. Those who ask questions understand a new language."

After a brief silence, one young maiden from the modern group shot out her hand. She was recognized.

"Young man, what is your idea of a woman?" she asked.

"The question is not clear," Utibe replied.

"What I mean is, what must a woman have to attract you?" she asked.

"I am more concerned about the inner person, which is what the eyes cannot see," Utibe replied.

"I say, what would a man want from a woman?" she asked in anger.

"My daughter, put a cap on your cup of anger before you pay a fine," the deputy leader said.

"I am sorry, Akamba Mma. It is just that Imata has all a man would want—a beautiful face, well-proportioned body, straight legs, slim fingers, a gap between her incisors, a long hair, and to crown it all, she is fair. Are those not the things men get crazy about? How can you convince anybody that Imata is trying to destroy you because you rejected her advances?" She paused and sucked in air through her mouth.

"Imata! Imata, on whose feet many a man would sit for seven days without food. Imata, the woman whose smile had made many a man almost run mad! Imata, the damsel who has taken custody of whole pay packets of many men. Our Imata, our beauty queen who is dreaded by housewives but who draws admiration from them in private. I say, how many cars have not been dented by drivers who have lost control of their steering on seeing Imata on the road? Who would believe that a man can turn down Imata's advances, that is, if we are to believe that she can be placed in a position where she makes the first move? Unlikely," she concluded.

"The unlikely things are those most likely to happen, my sister," Utibe said and then looked intensely at the modern group.

"But first, would you regard all the things you have said as very positive and complimentary? Is it a great thing for one to cause problems everywhere all the time? Secondly, beauty is skin-deep. I said early on that it is the inner person that matters more. What is visible is often deceptive, often not real. What is not visible may be the real thing," Utibe deposed.

"The question was, is it true that you rejected the advances of this perfect specimen of womanhood?" the prosecutor asked.

"Yes. But in the first place, is there any perfection in human nature?" Utibe replied. There was a low murmur in the modern group.

"You answer questions. You are not to ask," the prosecutor said sternly.

"The man says he rejected Imata. Can Imata confirm that?" the deputy leader asked. Imata sprang up and walked to the middle of the clearing, standing a little distance away from Utibe. Her dressing, the style apparently borrowed from another tribe, was simple, but extremely provocative. She was using an expensive Dutch wax wrapper. The wrapper stood slightly above the knees while upward, it was wrapped above the breast, revealing partly a deep cleavage on the chest. The upper torso shone as if it had just been polished. With an oval face, slightly pointed nose, a wide mouth, large but sleepy eyes that had the lashes replaced by a wide line "eye pencil" on either side, Imata was a study in beauty. Her legs, straight and smooth, carried a frame that was extremely well proportioned. She stood there obviously agitated, struggling to contain her anger. To those who knew her, it was always difficult to say whether she was not more beautiful when she was angry than when she was gay. Nonetheless, Imata was one of those women people say every man, woman, and child must turn to look at when she passes by, except where one has a severe neck pain.

"Imata, did you try to force yourself on this young man?" the deputy leader asked.

"How would it be said, my mothers, that Imata made a first move? Imata, who has moved the hardest, the most arrogant, and the most proud of men? How would I beg when what I have sells me?"

"Well, it is his word against yours," the deputy leader said.

"It is my word against his," Imata countered.

"It has always been so. And the outcome becomes obvious. Under such circumstance, men face the situation of heads or tails, you lose," Utibe said.

"You have passed a vote of no confidence on this gathering," Her Lordship said gravely. Utibe bowed and touched the ground with his two hands.

"My hands clutch the ground, Ekanyin. The person who holds on to the ground cannot fall. Throw away my words but take me to yourself," he said. The group of the ancients consulted as Utibe stood nervously. Ekanyin spoke after having controlled her rising anger.

"So how did Imata show her intentions that have led to this crisis?" Her Lordship asked.

"How many times did she let her dress 'accidentally' drop on the ground, leaving her standing in front of me naked? How many letters had she sent to me, pleading with me to befriend her? I say, does a man not have the right to reject a woman's advances?"

"Why would you reject a woman, and for that matter, Imata?" the prosecutor inquired.

"An excellent question. My mothers, my sisters, one fact we have all agreed on is that Imata is a very, very beautiful woman. She is the dream of many a man. She is my dream of a woman. But somehow, anytime I think of making any move, something inside me withdraws, leaving me as cold as iced fish," Utibe said.

"How can a person turn you on and turn you off at the same time? Are you a radio set?" the prosecutor asked. This elicited muffled laughter in the modern group.

"Simply put, something inside me tells me that she is very dangerous as far as it concerns me. Something tells me sleeping with her is not right. Something, something tells me I have met this woman before and always, there is this feeling which is difficult to explain," Utibe concluded, shaking his head from side to side and looking very sober. He stood still and quiet, reflecting on the esoteric feeling of *déjà vu* that always left him numbed anytime he felt like making an intimate move toward Imata. There was a brief silence while the ancient group conferred. The deputy leader spoke thereafter.

"You have said many things that one cannot fully understand. But let us continue. Our elders said that for a disagreement or quarrel involving two parties, a potential judge should raise only one shoulder while listening to what is said. For if on hearing one side of a story one raises two shoulders, what happens when the other party tells a different story? It could involve lowering a shoulder, which implies humiliation. Imata, what have you to say? Did you make the first approach and what happened?"

"My mothers, fellow women, I salute you. I have many weaknesses as all humans have. One of them is not telling lies. I shall here tell the truth irrespective of how hearers will react to it. Yes, I made the first approach." There were exclamations in the younger groups.

"You did?" one agitated woman from the old group said.

"Abomination," another said.

"Enough. Interruptions are never tolerated here. I need not remind you of that fact. Imata, please proceed," the prosecutor barked.

"I don't want to bore you with details. It is enough for me to say that I have been thoroughly humiliated. While I sometimes regard him as some kind of punishment from God, I still feel that he should not treat me with so much contempt as he does," Imata said angrily.

"To the issue in question, Imata," the deputy leader interjected. "Did he say to you—Imata, you smell?"

"He did," Imata said bitterly. She felt the bitterness well up within her, making her find it difficult to breathe. She breathed in and out several times. The clean soothing air passed through her system, sweeping her bitterness and anger partially away.

"He did, Akamba Mma," she said again.

"What do you have to say young man?" the prosecutor asked Utibe.

"How did I say it? I clearly remember a case like that. It was one of those moments I was becoming tired after having been disturbed too much by Imata. She then asked me a question," Utibe said.

"And what was the question?" the prosecutor inquired

"Utibe, you have been avoiding me, am I smelling?"

"What was your answer?"

"You said it!"

"Meaning?"

"She said it. Mark my words, all I did was to say, 'You said it. I did not pronounce the words you smell!'" Utibe deposed.

"You are playing with words," the prosecutor observed.

"It is not a clear case as we can see," Her Lordship said.

"In that case, Ekanyin, I should be discharged and acquitted. Where there is uncertainty, the defendant should be given the benefit of doubt," Utibe submitted, feeling good about his decision to go to a magistrate's court with his friend once upon a time.

"It happened on another occasion," Imata interjected, eyes blazing. "This time, it was outside his room. There were neighbors around. I asked him to tell me whether I smelled."

"And what did he say?" the prosecutor asked eagerly.

"Yes, you smell, please go away, leave me alone. I don't like pests."

There was grave silence. Her Lordship broke the silence.

"That one looks like it. Young man, did you utter those words?"

"Again, I will not tell you a lie for I am not given to lying. What happened that day is what happens to any other person whose life has been pestered beyond limit. I lost my temper. I said she smelled, not because she did, but just to see if she would get off my back."

"Did she?" the prosecutor asked.

"Yes, although temporarily, otherwise I would not be here today."

"Young man, summarize your position. The farmer has to tend her crops. The goat herd has to forage for fodder for her goats, a duty made more difficult in the city where houses outnumber bushes and trees. The trader has to take her wares to the market or at least display them at home. Wives have to cook for their husbands and children no matter what they feel about that chore. We shall not be here all day," Her Lordship said impatiently.

"Through the high chair, my mothers, my sisters, I shall be very brief. I stand accused of a crime that even a child will agree, I did not commit. Imata has all it takes to get a man to stand on his head. I could have happily started an affair with her, but for the fact that this bell kept ringing inside my head warning me to keep off. Maybe because she was so determined to get me. I didn't like that. I don't like anybody coming after me like a cat going after a rat. I ended up being so determined to resist her that no matter what she did, I was not moved. Nonetheless, I avoided Imata for some reasons that I feel only God can tell. Probably someday, I will get to know. I wish it will be made known during my lifetime." Utibe paused and took in some air and then continued.

"It is just not possible that I can say that any woman smells. I was well brought up. Besides, my life at sea taught me to respect our traditions, to keep those that should be kept, to avoid like a plague those that are taboos. My encounter with angry Idombi women was enough lesson on the powers of the womenfolk. Women bring life to earth. They maintain life. It therefore follows that they would have it easiest to take life.

"Which man in his right sense would say Imata smells, except in the positive sense? It is interesting what a difference it makes to use one word or not to use it. If I had said to Imata, 'you smell fine,' she would have gone back to her box of cosmetics and standing mirror, spending the whole day plastering her body with assorted perfumes while the world moved on. Imata spends probably eighty percent of her money—and whatever she can get from men—on cosmetics. She spends hours painting her face. Smell is not one word that can be found in her dictionary for she takes her bath at least twice a day, a habit a number of our young girls are yet to embrace. She has creams, pomades, perfumes, and powders, name them, of which she spreads layers and layers on her body. I have always thanked God on her behalf for denying her sweat, for she hardly sweats despite such heavy attack on her skin.

"And who does not know that stale sweat is the basic cause of body odor? So if a woman hardly sweats, yet loves bathing and perfuming, what sort of offensive odor can she give out? None, I say. Imata is a delight to be with, and Utibe is not one person that can insult her.

"I have been abused and blackmailed by Imata and her group. She is looking for something to soothe her hurt pride. I submit that I have been framed. I should be discharged and acquitted."

As it had been anytime Utibe delivered a speech, silence reigned. Again, it was Her Lordship who came to the rescue.

Utibe did not fail to notice a tinge of confusion and indecision on faces around him.

"Imata, please summarize your position," Her Lordship ordered in a rather low tone.

"My mothers, my sisters, I salute you once again. Let it not be said that a guilty son of Adam came to this square, used his sweet tongue to confuse all of us, and went off untouched, only to organize a palm wine party to celebrate another defeat of the womenfolk. This is our ground. No one sits at the foot of the *ekọm* tree to eat its fruits without at least earning a hard knock on the head from another *ekọm* fruit. The facts are as clear as the daylight. Both between us and in the presence of witnesses, this man declared that people should cover their noses or spit anytime I pass by them.

"Yes, it is true I disturbed him. That is not 'natural' in our ancient society. However, the society is changing. We are abandoning old ways, including the good ones and going after new ways, some of which are bad. That is the price we pay to be described as 'civilized.' The city is not helping matters nor is education, film shows, novels, magazines, newspapers, and good old gossip which a lot of spend time doing when there is nothing else to do. And of course, those who have access to television know what it does to those who watch it.

"But most importantly, my mothers, is the fact that a woman can express her feelings and get those things she would have missed had she been the usual soft, quiet, good daughter and mother. Is it not possible that a man can appreciate and even desire a woman but has no courage to make the first move? Most men are very shy and very much afraid of failure, even if they carry their heads in the air to hide their shyness. They are afraid of a 'no.' So what stops a strong woman from letting that man know that he is wanted? Probably we could reduce the number of single girls in our society if girls are allowed to make a move, at least in a manner that is not too open.

"I found out that I love Utibe. I have this attraction to him that I cannot explain. What has he that makes me go mad? He is poor. He is not well educated. He does not have a good job. He does not even have a promising future. But love has a way of its own. It strikes you and takes you to where you should least be. Have we not heard of kings leaving their thrones just to marry common women? Have princesses not eloped with their parents' houseboys or watchmen? How do we explain a madam of the house in the arms of her houseboy? Just that she was lonely and was abandoned by her husband? No. She wanted variety? No, for she could as well get it outside, from men who appear to enjoy affairs with married women. Is it that she was taking a revenge on her husband? Not always, for there are cases of very devoted husbands living with such women. Love, particularly for women, is one thing that can bring someone very low. It presents one source of madness that psychiatrists are yet to study. What has happened to Imata borders on madness."

She paused for a few minutes and wiped off the drops of tears that were slowly crawling like a rivulet caused by water from a low rain. She had not bothered to wipe off the tears, apparently for effect. She blew her nose with a tiny flowered handkerchief, sucked in some air, cleared her throat, and continued,

"Humiliation to one woman anywhere is humiliation to all women everywhere. We have this one avenue of checking the abuses men subject us to, otherwise, we as a group will be a thing to be laughed at and scorned even by madmen—"

"It is not your place to tell us what to do, Imata," Her Lordship said sharply. "We shall now retire and consider our judgment."

While the party of elders moved into a shed that Utibe had not noticed until then, spirited discussions arose among the other women groups. Voices rose to a high pitch, fingers were pointed, and accusations leveled. Utibe, who had moved to a point far enough to enable him take a beeline just in case the women decided to attack him while at the same time being able to hear what was said, was excited to notice that two camps had been formed, those for him and those against him.

Those for him argued that in the main, Utibe had no alternative given the harassment from Imata. Those against were more concerned with the tyranny of men, since men believed that women must be taken for a ride always. The argument had risen to a fever pitch, generating a din that could be heard far off, when the prosecutor emerged from the hut to announce that the elders were ready to deliver judgment. As it started, the voices died suddenly. The group, which can be referred to as the jury, filed out, some walking erect, some bent as far as to the waist, some leaning on sticks, others limping. Despite their infirmities, these wizened women knew that it was their duty to mankind to use their experience and reserve of knowledge to ensure stability and smooth running of the society.

Now seated, the group exchanged further confidences while Utibe and Imata were positioned by the prosecutor for judgment. Her Lordship adjusted herself on her seat gently and deliberately, cleared her throat, and surveyed the expectant faces before speaking.

"As usual, my children, ours is a brief one. We do not need to read through volumes of the printed word before arriving at a decision. We do not need hearings and more hearings, witnesses and more witnesses, and cross examination after cross examination to determine who is guilty and who is not guilty. We do not need hours of long referencing, writing, and reading to make our point," she paused, taking in some air.

"The council of elders, after having heard from both parties, decided that receiving evidence from third parties would not be necessary. We could have called in Utibe's neighbors. We felt it is unnecessary since both of them have accepted their mistakes. Our position is this—" Utibe felt himself stiffening, as if an axe was about to descend on his thick neck. He felt that by tightening his muscles, he could make the axe to bounce off. Her Lordship gave a knowing smile.

"Our position is this. Imata has not done anything wrong by falling in love with a man. Falling in love makes her a woman. Neither can she be condemned for making the first approach. Our society does not like it, but there is no penalty. However, this should be a lesson to our young women. Understand your

189

audience before you speak. If your target is the one that is stretched to the seams with pride, you should watch it. If your target is the one that will cover you, fine." She coughed and cleared her throat.

"Imata did, however, cause problems. That is where she went wrong. She disturbed the young man beyond the limit of endurance. It is clear that he lost his temper during that second encounter. He said what is bad. The council of elders holds that Utibe was provoked. Imata likely wanted him to commit this abomination. She asked a leading question. By provoking him, she knew that she would have an opportunity for revenge so as to make up for her hurt pride. The council of elders is not happy about this forum being used to settle personal scores. We are here to ensure peace, unity, and progress of our society, not to take care of the hurt pride of anybody, man or woman. I am sure you are aware that some men do bring cases here for us to consider and pass judgment.

"For being the cause of Utibe's misbehavior, the council of elders has decided that Imata's court fee of one hundred and one pounds is forfeited. Utibe could have returned it to her had he been found guilty. Also, Imata will pay to Utibe, through this court, the sum of one hundred pounds to cover Utibe's expenses while defending himself." There was a low murmur among the groups of women. Those for Utibe shook hands while those against him beat their chest and swore quietly. No move was made by the prosecutor to quieten them.

"And you, Utibe, miracle man. This place is not the medicine man's shrine or *idioñ* shrine where you must pay something, whether you are guilty or you are not guilty." Utibe shook his head vigorously in agreement.

"Hear me out first. You were clearly provoked, and that is where you went wrong. We are here as your mothers to put you on the right path. If you are allowed to go free, you will go with the impression that you can let loose your temper anytime, anywhere, anyhow, and go free provided you can establish a case of provocation.

"A man is supposed to be unmoved by emotions. Your menfolk say that what the hen sees and screams all over the place is not half as much as what the goat has seen and only grunts. When you hear that a man killed a fellow human being with a knife or gun—find out—the cause was loss of temper when provoked. Men are known to have murdered their children during periods of anger following a slight provocation. And of course, wars are fought because a man was, or a group of men were, provoked, sometimes on reasons as flimsy as the underwear their wives put on.

"It is for that reason that the council of elders hereby pronounces you guilty of uttering an abomination. You will see the prosecutor for further details of what you will do to 'bathe' the woman you declared smelled, in the process of which you declared that all women smell," she concluded.

As the ancient party went back to the hut for refreshments with the drinks presented by the warring parties, another din arose among those left behind. Utibe felt confused. He had thought he was free. Now he stood condemned. And the source of confusion was the judgment itself. Was he expected to be angry with the women or to admire them? It appeared to be a fair judgment, though he still felt that since his case was not established beyond reasonable doubt, he should have been set free. However, he agreed that he lost his temper, an act that should be condemned. As he left the clearing, he could neither read his feelings nor his future.

*   *   *

"You are lucky they did not request for seven cows," Udo-owo said after Utibe had told of his ordeal before the women as well as the list of things he was to present for the cleansing rites—at least the ones he could recall.

"You think the ones they listed are easy to come by even if I can afford them?" Utibe said.

"Certainly not. But consider seven cows, with a cow costing a fortune these days."

"I would not give them. What for?"

"For your life, Utibe. You can't joke with those women."

"What do you think they will do for I will not give them anything?"

"Will not? You must be crazy."

"What do you expect? I think only an insane man would sell his father's land, sell his personal effects, and still borrow to buy seven fowls, one white she-goat without spots, seven bottles of native gin, seven kegs of palm wine, five tubers of yam, seven chili fruits, seven heads of tobacco, seven pods of kola, a piece of white cloth, one comb, seven tablets of toilet soap, one tin of powder, 'nsaŋ' and *iduot*—name them. Then a grandmother basin. Udo-owo, this your brother will do no such thing."

"Even if you had the money?"

"I know what to do with money."

"So what are you going to do?"

"Sit through it. The power of the mind overcomes every negative force."

"Then you should not have gone to the court. Your presence there signified your acceptance of their powers, if not their legitimacy"

"That, I have my Pastor to blame. In the day, they tell you only Jesus saves, don't take any drugs. In the night, they visit the native doctor with their sick and afflicted."

"Judgment will start from the church."

"So be it. But for the Pastor's entreaties, I could have been at the village now."

"But the Pastor was only being realistic. You may deny the existence of supernormal forces. They are however there."

"Because you believe in them."

"Are you saying that you will not comply?"

"Of course, I won't. Is it because I told you? If I have that much money, I will rather buy a radiogram, a standing stove, a solid jean trousers, a tergal shirt, plus a 'surpedo' shoe to match. I would cap it with a Honda Bentley so that I would have access to the prettiest girls in this town and generally be a man about town and on the lips of everybody."

"And you think the money for the ritual would buy all those things?"

"Probably. Seven fowls and a she-goat can buy a Honda Bentley. Seven kegs of palm wine, seven bottles of schnapps, and seven bottles of native gin can buy a radiogram. Need I continue?"

"I hope you heard them well. I have a feeling your list is not correct."

"Maybe. I can tell you that I was so confused after the judgment that when the prosecutor was reading out the items, all I heard was seven, seven, seven."

"Then you should go and confirm."

"Never. Utibe will not be one of their victims."

"You will regret it, that is, if you live long enough."

It was evident that Utibe was determined to face what would come, good or bad. The problem with issues of this nature, Utibe's friend had noted, is that one hardly had precedence to fall back on and not do what should be done as and when due could prove fatal. He hoped Utibe's determination would end in his favor, and that if the women turned out to have the upper hand, there would be a way out before it is too late.

*   *   *

Once again, Ekam could not help but wonder when the detour would end despite the fact that she enjoyed the story. She felt it was time the end came for her system preferred the denouement, the crisis point, the peak rather than the prologue or even the development. But she had no alternative than to keep reading the scripts given to her and listening to explanations and even unwritten details. At a point, she actually asked the woman why the entire script was not given to her to take home and read, arguing that it would make it possible for her to refer to the dictionary for the several difficult words she came across.

"You may not have the time to read it at home. Besides, I cannot afford to let go an original manuscript, which I have no duplicate copy of. If you lose it, I cannot guarantee that I can rewrite. As to the difficult words, although I am not a dictionary or even a compiler of one, I believe I know the meaning of whatever word I wrote down. So you might as well ask me to explain what you are not sure of." There had been a pause apparently because Ekam wanted Naomi to reconsider her proposal.

"But at least you have been able to follow the story," Naomi said.

"Well," the girl replied and shrugged, "if I had not been attending Second Chance Evening School, I am not sure I would have understood anything."

"You did not tell me that all along."

"Well," Ekam only shrugged.

"Is it that school on Ekpo Abasi Street?"

"Yes."

"You see, doing something good is good. Did someone force you to take that decision?"

"It was a personal decision. I guess I wanted to do something—at least one respectable thing. And it was not my first for I had attended Future Scope Evening School before."

"This means you have the capacity to do more. My daughter, a child from a bad home can hardly think of something so worthy and progressive. What this means is that you should do only good things because you were well brought up."

"Auntie, we may not have to talk much on my upbringing."

There was another pause during which Ekam thought of what next to say to convince Naomi to give her the remaining part of the manuscript. She wanted to know how it all ended and would thus have turned to the last page if the script were with her.

She found out she should not have worried for the beginning of the end came surprisingly the next day. What she was given to read was exciting, but Ekam had the feeling that some sections had been kept back apparently because Naomi did not want her to lose interest and concentration.

BOOK IV

Chapter 13

Utibe had felt deeply sad. It was one of those inexplicable feelings that he had once in a while, which often generated spasms of depression in him. For someone who was a teetotaler, he often found it near impossible to get out of what one medical expert called mood swings. Time usually solved this apparently intractable problem.

One way of lifting his spirits, he thought, would be to recall one of the stories his uncle, Nsọ, had told him about the days of yore. Nsọ's tales were usually those of great exploits—hunting, wrestling, war, love affairs that transcended ethnic, cultural, and materialistic confines, among others. Two of them that always excited him came to mind then, forcing a smile on his lips. One was the marriage between a prince and a maid. The other was on the coming of the white man and the resultant clash of cultures. He decided to let his mind dwell on the latter.

*   *   *

"My son," Nsọ had said during one of the storytelling sessions. He had paused. He often did this when narrating a moving story, either for effect or to get back his breath. He was pushing close to eighty, though one might mistake him to be in his sixties. He walked on his own without the support of a walking stick. He had never used spectacles in his life, yet he could read his ancient Bible and sing from the hymnal, ancient and modern. The only evidence that he was one of those that have taken more years from God than the biblical three score and ten was a slight bent of frame, gray beard, hairless head, and disappearing front teeth.

"I was then about the age of this little grandson of mine. About seven years. A magic age, I still remember clearly. All these things were not there by that time—bicycles, cars, zinc houses. Even most of the food items you see, such as beans, groundnuts (my father never saw groundnuts in his lifetime), rice, even *garri*, those that you now regard as staple foods, were not available."

"But Nso, what did the people eat at that time then?" inquired a surprised listener.

"Even *garri*," shrugged an incredulous ten-year-old. Nso paused for some time, looked at each face thoroughly, sighed, shook his head, and then exploded in a guffaw. It was incomprehensible to the little boy that there could be life without *garri*.

"So you don't believe me. You don't. I don't blame you, baby rabbits that grow white tails. Listen to an old man. It was a man from afar that first introduced *garri* into this locality. I was there when it happened. Yes, just a boy of seven. He grated cassava, put the bulk in a bag, tied it with ropes, and placed big stumps on the bag. He kept same for three days and then sieved it. The dust is what he fried in a pot, putting palm oil to make it reddish in color. Then he boiled water, soaked the product, and ate it with soup. I swore I'd never eat it. People thought it would cause dysentery. They regarded it as food for the poor. I later ate it."

"Why, Nso?"

"After my father died, I was no longer shielded as I had been. I started traveling to Ifiayong, carrying goods to sell and then buying crayfish and dried fish for sale back home. Ifiayo ng was the biggest and nearest port those days. Then one day, I went to one of the restaurants we used to call 'bar.' I saw others eating *garri*, which had by now become very popular because it was easier to transport and did not smell like our raw cassava (you need to wash your hands with soap after each meal, otherwise there is a camphor with you everywhere!). It was easier and quicker to prepare, stores longer, and at the end of the day, was cheaper. Then I said to myself, if the others do not die after the meal, why should I? Each person took two cigarette cups, well soaked and hot, with a plate of well-cooked and rich soup. After all that what do you pay?" He paused and looked around for an answer. When none came, he deposed, "One-half penny."

There was no laughter as expected. The little ones could not appreciate the meaning and value of one-half penny. They never saw one. The older ones only sighed, for on comparing a plate of lunch at a 'bar' then and now, one can only curse our gallop into modernization when money has no value and when more pennies bring in fewer goods than half a century previous. Perhaps it was the longing for the good old days that made them pensive. Their faces showed it—a distant look.

"But Nsọ, what were you eating before these foods came?"

"Cassava. Cassava in various forms—raw, boiled, roasted, fermented, sliced. Vegetables. Plantain. Cocoyam. Yams. Sweet yams. Water yams. Fruits. Meat. Periwinkles. Snails. Birds. Palm wine. *Ufọfọp.** We ate those foods in one form or the other. Singly or mixed. Isn't that a long list?" Nsọ inquired. His listeners laughed. Considering the array of food items one could buy in the market or harvest from the fields and from the streams, rivers and seas, that list appeared to be what some people eat during one meal in the present day.

"So how did new foods come and where from?"

"They just came. Maybe across the seas the way the white man came one day. Whether from the skies or from the bowls of the earth or from the seas, we know not. We saw them, rejected them at first as humans do when they see any strange thing, and then we accepted them either with relish and gratefulness or with resignation, but more of the latter."

"Back to the coming of the white man," Utibe had cut in.

"Yes. Let me tell you about the beginning of taxation in our area. It came with the white man. Before this, there never was any form of tax in this area. I mean tax to an alien authority that you call government. There were levies during wars or for festivals. There were donations for the upkeep of the Ọbọng and the poor. But no tax. You knew and you could see what your levy was for. Donation was out of your own free will, and the more you gave, the greater the applause. Not so for tax. When you pay tax, you pay the money whether you like it or not. What it is used for, you cannot put a finger on. If you don't pay, there is a penalty. If you pay, there is no applause."

Nsọ paused at this juncture, fished for his snuffbox from the pocket of his long-tailed shirt, extracted it gingerly, admired it, and then gave two knocks on the rusty box, pressed it open, tilted it left, right, up, and down, contemplated the contents awhile, and then with the index finger, took a measure of the black stuff. After contemplating it, he mashed it with his gnarled thumb and index finger, stuffed some quantity into one nostril, and took a long pull, squeezing his face and then groaning. He repeated the procedure on the other nostril and waited for what seemed an eternity, sniveling and cocking his head to one side as if that angle accentuated appreciation of the snuff. Then he blew out his nose and wiped it with a handkerchief that once saw the white side of life but was now shades of brown, black, and yellow. After blowing on the second nostril, he cleared his throat and completed the snuff consumption exercise by wiping his nostrils with the back of his palm. He then rubbed the hands together and finally reclined on his easy chair. His audience had waited patiently though with slight irritation. One interesting thing was that no matter how long the exercise or other distractions, Nsọ never lost track of his discussion. He would always start from where he had stopped.

"The white man is tricky. He knew that if he forcefully introduced tax, he would not succeed. He spent many years to change the people's mind to accept taxation. He met the chiefs and elders, told them that tax money would be used to build roads. 'Why and what for,' the people asked? 'Because the things I am going to bring will not be able to move through bush paths,' he answered. 'The things will not be able to climb tree stumps, enter and come out of potholes, and generally move through rough ground.'

"The people could not understand, so they refused to pay. The white man went home and thought up something else. 'Pay tax to us. If you do, you will be rewarded. You will be given some presents.' The elders thought this idea was good. They gave it a try.

"By the time they found out that no gifts would be coming, it was too late. Taxation had entered the law books and had come to stay." He paused again, adjusted himself in his chair, held his head in the palm of his hands, jerked it left then right, cleared his throat, and then reclined once more, breathing more evenly. "If you were an adult and you did not pay tax, that meant you had to stay indoors and you could not go to Ifianyọng to sell and buy. Worse still, anytime you heard the sound of a car, you must run into the bush. And that is not how to be a man. Unfortunately, they employed our brothers as tax collectors. They knew where to find us and how to fish us out even when we are in *ndua** tapping palm wine or fishing."

"Nsọ, what about women? Were they also paying tax?" Utibe had inquired.

"No," Nsọ had responded with a low laugh. "Even when a woman was richer than the chief or even an entire village as in the case of Edise of Ntọ Obo village, the white man looked the other way. Why women do not pay tax, they never told us, for we levy our women, only that they pay much less than men."

Listening through a tale by Nsọ was more of a journey, sometimes tedious, sometimes thrilling, and sometimes even irritating. But you had no choice, for what he gave out may not be found in any book anywhere. Utibe had often wondered why our historians delight in copying and modifying the history of the "discovery" of Africa and Asia, the wars and revolutions in Europe, and even the lives and times of kings and queens in foreign countries, without thinking much about documenting the oral traditions of the fast disappearing wizened folks of Africa.

"Nso, how did the white man travel since there were no roads then?" another young listener had asked.

"He did not walk." He paused briefly. "He has no such energy to trek long distances. He tires out very easily. We used to walk for days on end with loads on our heads. Our children were strapped on the backs of our women from here to Ifiayong before we took a boat to Calabar. Three-day walk! Then two days and two nights of endless rowing. Or we trekked to Oron before the boat trip to Calabar.

"The DO (divisional officer) used to travel by *uyihe*, something that was originally used to convey high chiefs and visiting kings. It was made of *ndidi** and looked like a mat made of straw, suspended at the two ends by ropes tied to two poles. Two strong men bore their human burden no matter how long the distance. When the DO arrived at a development area headquarters, he would spend about three to four days, collecting tax money, treating the sick, judging cases, and carrying out such duties as may be necessary. They were jacks of all trades, and to our mind, masters of all. After each visit, any man found, whether he was on a hunting trip or was returning from the stream where he went to fetch water or was returning from an errand or from the bush where he went to gather food for man or grass for goats, would be forced to carry the gifts from the people and elders back to the divisional headquarters at Uyo. And the gifts were usually many!

"When the people started paying tax, roads were built. Big, wide red roads that went on and on, curving to the left then to the right, up the hills, down the valleys, through bushes, forests, and streams. The white man's road, like himself, was no respecter of anything.

"Then the bicycle came. That in itself is a long story. The first man in these parts to own a bicycle was Ikpe Enang Ukwak. It was a great sight. People trooped from the four corners of the world to look at it, of course at a distance. No one knew if it would spring like a cow and kill the nearest person. Children peeped behind elders. The more cautious remained behind trees to marvel at the metal horse from Blackwood Hodge.

"Those were the days before the 'complete set' from Raleigh. These had hand gears that were engaged by turning the pedal about three times backward and engaging the correct gear—one, two, or three, depending on the point on the road. Some came white. Others black. Some had the iron rod for front passengers. The rear carrier was used for loads and as a passenger's seat. All had lights that were operated from the rear tire. They also had bells.

"There were fewer accidents then. Owning one was a big thing. The owner had to know every detail of a borrower's journey. Teachers often owned it, and it made them to be more respected in the villages.

"Cars came much later, the name I cannot tell. But it was reserved for the DO initially. Other whites, such as the missionaries, particularly the Reverend Father of Roman Catholic Mission began to own cars. Before then, motorcycles such as BSA had come. Very noisy and fearful, but a thing of beauty with power, extra power. Only strong men rode on them, sitting curved at the waist and with such pride.

"My children, take me back to those days, and I would gladly give you my age."

*   *   *

The reminiscence on Nsọ's story had taken Utibe's mind temporarily off his predicament. At that time, he was lying prostrate on a bamboo bed, sweating profusely, and feeling feverish, weak, nauseous, and hungry. He had not eaten for almost three days, yet he was increasing in girth with each passing day. His head had puffy eyes and swollen cheeks. His hands and legs were twice their normal sizes. His abdomen protruded like those of sugar daddies who were said to have developed large tummies as a result of drinking too many bottles of lager beer.

*   *   *

Utibe had started feeling sick seven days after his encounter with Iban Isọng. It had started as a slight headache and body pains that graduated into fever and vomiting. Leaves of *dogonyaro* tree had been boiled for him to drink and to bathe himself, after several regimes of malaria tablets and even injections had failed. He had endured the bitter pills of quinine that shook his whole frame after the lighter drugs had failed. His neighbor, Ibiok, even went as far as Akpabuyo to source *ebana* leaves for him to drink. Things simply got worse, more so with him increasing in girth despite the fact that he ate very sparingly.

When the situation became worse, Ibiok and other concerned neighbors decided to take Utibe to St. Margaret's Hospital. This was fairly normal, for self-medication took the first level of attention when people fell sick followed by a native doctor or hospital depending on the level of education and exposure of the person. Prayer houses could be the last resort, but there was no cut-and-dried format, except that self-medication took the priority position. Spending a whole day in the hospital to see a doctor was one reason people preferred to treat themselves first or consult a "chemist" or dispenser before going to the hospital.

Utibe spent two weeks in that hospital, the primary and in fact best equipped and staffed in the city and indeed the whole of southeastern state. When the bills appeared frightening in the face of little improvement, he was taken away against medical advice. He spent another two weeks in two spiritual churches to no avail.

Ibiok had sent his son to call in Udo-owo, Utibe's bosom friend, as Utibe's health nose-dived. Udo-owo had traveled to Ikom to discuss cocoa sales business as he was told the crop would one day become a foreign exchange earner as it was before the days of the crude oil boom. He hurried back, and on assessing the situation, asked questions.

"My brother, if there is anything you are keeping close to your chest, you better say. When a woman has given birth to a baby in a market it is meaningless to tell her to close her legs. There is no shame in the race for life. When one is dead, pride is no more than history. What have you done, or not done?"

"How am I supposed to know?" Utibe answered in a voice barely audible. Staying without food for so many days coupled with the effect of drugs made worse by endless fasting as directed by spiritualists left him dazed.

"Are you sure it has nothing to do with your visit to Esa Iban Isọng?"

"Spare me. I don't believe that."

"You don't have to believe. If an owl hoots in the night and a child has fever the following morning, who would not blame the witch for it?"

"Who do I blame? My mother? My father?" Who?"

"Let's just do something about it before fire reaches the middle of the palm wine tree."

"If you have money to waste, go ahead."

"It would not be a waste. You have wasted money on so many things already—several drugs, hospitals, spiritual churches, try that one too."

"Too many sources of music confuse a masquerade. My system is confused, and I want it to rest."

"Okay, let your people know about it."

"Dare you tell them. I went to *Ine* on my own. I have been taking the big decisions of my life, and I have been right. This is another one."

"Please yourself," Udo-owo had said and left, however, after leaving some money with Ibiok for food and other needs. Probably if he had put his feet down and went to Utibe's people to tell the story or even went to Esa Iban Isọng to ask questions, the story would have been different. Probably there was *nduọhọ* ?* Was there something or somebody somewhere that prevented salvation from getting to Utibe? Some force that ensured that the solution would not be known or accessed by Utibe until it was too late? Sometimes, friends and relations could go the extra mile when they know the right thing that could be done. Could

Imata and her friends in crime have met a juju priest to prepare a potion and send it to Utibe mystically to make his heart to be as hardened as that of the pharaoh of Egypt during his encounter with Moses? Women can do terrible things when their pride is assailed by men. Some would say, "give that man a knock so hard that your knuckle creates a hole in his skull."

Two more days and Utibe's skin became tender and freckled. No one needed to be told that it was time to take the young man home, for if perchance he died, the police would ask the neighbors questions even if for the purpose of extracting some coins from them as "bail bond." The neighbors contributed money and transported Utibe to his village. By this time, he was not in a position to resist or object to anything.

Udo-owo still went to the village three days after Utibe had been taken there by Ibiok and another neighbor. He told the full story of Utibe and Imata. The family brought in juju priest after another to no avail. They all said the same thing—it was too late in the day.

Despite the hopelessness of the situation, Nya, Utibe's mother, held on to the belief that a piece of yam belonging to the child of a pauper cannot be burnt by fire beyond eating. The gods would not take one child away from his mother, for the person that has just one palm fruit cannot be regarded as selfish if he or she refuses to give it out.

Each day increased the pain in the young man and in the hearts of his parents. One night, he reeled out the names of dead ancestors, most of which had died before he was born. This severely frightened onlookers. He sang several telling songs whenever he had some strength.

One cloudy morning, he went into a coma. When he came to, he lay in a daze. His parents had spent nearly an hour pulling his hair and even applying a flame to his toes. In the twilight between consciousness and unconsciousness, Utibe saw portions of his childhood days as a film replayed before him. They were so vivid, yet it was a daydream. He had decided to reminisce, good enough he had an audience that was only too willing to listen for it meant he was still alive. The earliest event he could remember was being extracted from fire by his mother.

*   *   *

It was one of those nights when parents—particularly mothers—returned from the village market fairly late. Sometimes as the popular lore held, ghosts, those beings that felt more comfortable operating in the night being agents of darkness, joined living human beings in the purchase and sale of physical commodities. Where they took their purchases to, and for that matter, where they got the goods they sold from, nobody ever bothered to find out or ever tried to explain.

Utibe's mother, Nya, had returned a little after 8:00 p.m. on the said night, chattering animatedly with a neighbor about the events and nonevents of the market day. Markets being more of a sociological reality than economic fact (for one can always buy what one wants from the sellers whose houses are already known), there was always something to see, hear, feel, and talk about on and after a market day.

On entering her hut, Nya gently lowered the basin that contained her wares and tiptoed around the room. She did not want to wake Utibe that she thought had slept. But Utibe never slept early since he became a toddler. He slept only when he had eaten the last food for the day, sometimes anything up to midnight when it was also held that human beings shared their food with extraterrestrial beings, particularly ghosts.

Since he was not yet asleep, his mother had as usual told him to join her at the hearth. Usually, he would be awake, taking the bits and pieces of fish, crayfish, and whatever else could be eaten before they became part of the soup. Unfortunately for Utibe, he was not as alert as usual, and his mother was deeply involved in the conversation going on.

Utibe had had a hard day from sunrise to sunset, having forced himself to join the early risers to the village stream, some three kilometers away to and from, then playing a lot aside from

209

joining the farming and firewood groups. For a six-year-old, the activities were certainly energy sapping. His brave eyelids struggled to stay apart till the elders returned but started coming together all too often thereafter. Utibe sat close to the fire appearing to be listening to the discussion of the elders. The elders had not noticed that the small human bundle by the fireside was not as alert as usual. It was at the sound of cracking firewood and a scream that their merry laughter died halfway on their lips. Utibe was in the fire!

*   *   *

Utibe also remembered his seventh Christmas in the world. It was one Christmas he had hoped to enjoy fully for many reasons. His closest playmates, Iton and Ita, who had gone to the city to join their parents, were coming home. It was the practice of most citizens of Oboyo to make the pilgrimage home during Christmas not only to reunite with their families, friends, and relations but also to contribute their quota to the various development projects, which unfortunately never seemed to be completed. Thus, the Christmas celebration for the people of Oboyo and environs symbolized not just a celebration of the birth of Jesus Christ but also a period of reunion and rededication to the fraternity and brotherhood of the village. To the young ones and the upstarts, it was a period to display their new material acquisitions, including clothes, motorcycles, or cars, and to negotiate for land to build houses, which may end up never started, or if started, to be completed ten or more Christmases after. Traditional marriage ceremonies and weddings were also common during this season.

Utibe looked forward to this period when he would meet his old friends, admire their clothes, and listen to stories of city life.

Another reason for his high expectation was that for the first time in his life, a pair of trousers or long pants was being assembled for him by the village tailor. It was no mean thing. He had been using shorts or "knickers" (actually, knickerbockers), including the brown "khaki" for school and related activities. Since the announcement of intent by his mother, Utibe had spent the better part of the week preceding the completion of the solemn exercise in the tailor's workshop. The tailor, "Man-made," who always complained of heavy workload, took his time to produce a truly custom-made trousers for Utibe in twenty-one working days! When the job was finished, the product gave Utibe an anticlimactic feeling. He was undecided as to whether the mix of excitement and tension prior to completion was better than having the finished product that was truly his own.

The trousers were derived from a material popular in the forces and schools in those days—the gray khaki. This material had a way about itself. When dexterously starched, properly sunbaked, and professionally ironed, its shiny stiffness which ignored wind and rough usage combined to lend it an allure that momentarily made even the knowledgeable forget that it was one of the cheapest materials available in the market, sometimes sold via the urging of a bell.

The quality was not of import to Utibe. The material thing was that he had a pair of trousers. Whether the city boys came in their "tergal" or "blue navy" was of no consequence. They would all appear in clothes with two long tubes covering right down to the ankle or just a little above it. Utibe so revered the dress that he made up his mind not to try it until the D-day. Whether the waist turned out to be too tight or too loose or it was a "jumped-up" or "keep-the-city-clean," it did not matter to him. After all, was Man-made not the architect of the village's assorted male wears for all age groups? If elders, the school headmaster, teachers, the preachers, and even the councilor could trust their costly "materials" to Man-made, who was Utibe to entertain any fears as to the adroitness of the guru?

Utibe was not too far from being right actually. By village standards, what Man-made had come out with from his aging factory was a perfect fit. The expert would, however, notice that the backside was twisted a little to the right while holes in between the buttons on the flap were rather too prominent such that Utibe's tiny manhood could be seen on a little closer inspection.

Utibe's mother had bought a new shirt for the occasion, this time, a "ready-made," which was unwrapped from a "paper." It was immaterial whether or not a fast bloke in the nearest city had used a Van Heusen wrapper to put in a locally tailored child's shirt. The price tag, however, confirmed that it was "ready-made." It was also immaterial that the color combination of blue shirt, gray trousers, white stockings, and black sandals would result in a color riot. That was for the fashion conscious. To Utibe, that twenty-fifth of December would be a day to remember. And it was.

*   *   *

The day had started well. The sun had risen early, maybe a little too early for others, but to Utibe, just in time to enable him join the early risers to the stream. This day, unlike other days, he did not struggle to stay at the center of the group because of fear of ghosts or wild animals coming from the front or rear or sides. He led the team to the stream, with his excitement acting as the driving force.

"Utibe is a man today," remarked Mma, Utibe's aunt.

"I wonder why he walks so fast as if someone is pushing him by the occiput," Eteka, Utibe's petulant neighbor, concurred.

"When you see an old woman running, it is either something is pursuing her or she is pursuing something," Mma concluded. As he did not react, the team moved on in silence, walking fairly close together, both for protection against imaginary attackers and to exchange much-needed bodily heat to fight the biting early-morning harmattan cold that always left early risers unhappy and discomfited.

The descent of the slippery hill that led to the stream was for once not a problem to the boy. Neither did the ascent initially an exercise that had resulted in many a broken limb or pot and attendant tears. He managed to put his tiny feet in the age-old footholds made at strategic points on the hill, forgetting the ferns and tree trunks that acted as added supports for slipping feet.

The normal thing was that Utibe would dillydally when it was time to bathe and fetch water as the water was always very cold in the morning. He always had to be pushed into the water when persuasion and threats failed. Or an elder person would splash water on him, forcing him to rush into the stream. Taking the plunge was difficult. But so was coming out of the water.

That Christmas day was different. He had undressed as soon as he had reached the stream. In a few seconds, he was naked. With his water container, a small round calabash with a tiny hole at the top, he proceeded into the stream. First, he stepped to the edge of the water then he flung the calabash far toward the middle of the stream. He watched the calabash sail majestically, bobbing with the up and down movement of the stream farther and farther away from him toward the neck of the stream, which led to a darker part where only men went, mostly to set fish traps. Then bending by the waist, he stretched his arms backward, bent his knees, shot his head down and outward, and with a whoop plunged into the stream, splashing the cold water on women washing clothes or processing fermented cassava by the bank. The women screamed and cursed while Utibe swam with powerful strokes toward his calabash, dipping intermittently and coming up for air and blowing squirts of water from his mouth. Not long afterward, he emerged with red eyes and a full calabash, dressed, and got himself ready for the trip home.

"What Christmas can do," remarked Mma.

"My sister, he has hurried into the stream and hurried out, both of which he never does during normal times," Nya mused. "Someone should tell him that the rice and stew would not be ready till midafternoon after the church service."

"Maybe it is the pounded yam and stockfish soup that is pushing him."

"I know children look forward to the rice and stew which is a once-a-year special food."

"Rice and stew, Christmas food."

"There is something you all have forgotten," Mma said.

"What is that?"

"The trousers!"

"You are right. My son will wear his first trousers today," Nya said and laughed.

"Might as well, it will hide these tiny legs of his, though his wasplike waist will be seen more than before." The laughter of the women made him feel very shy and uncomfortable. He blew his nose forcefully, making a sound that reminded one of air being blown through the hollow of the stem of a pawpaw leaf.

After what seemed like an eternity, the elders were ready to go home. Utibe could hardly conceal his impatience and irritation. He yanked the small calabash onto the folded piece of cloth on his head and made for the hill. He refused to heed the shouts of the elders to exercise caution.

Despite the slippery nature of the hill, he had made a quick and successful climb to the top and could have reached the peak with triumph if not for the sudden emergence of a rabbit from the bush. He screamed, lost control, and slipped. The two—boy and calabash—made a descent, rolling as if they were twins. It was difficult to know which was faster, the child or the calabash. At the end of the tumble, calabash and child lay alongside each other, the calabash crushed and the child in a heap. With a broken forelimb, swollen head, and several wounds on his body, he was taken home piggybacked. His much-anticipated Christmas celebration ended with wails at the home of the bone mender.

Recalling those events made him smile, a wry smile. He had looked at the faces around him, most with fixed smiles that belied the fear, pain, and uncertainty they felt. They had undoubtedly forced themselves to enjoy Utibe's reminiscences. He sighed.

"I seem to have been falling all my life, always rolling down just when I think I have almost made it to the top of the hill," he had said to no one in particular. "Probably it is because I am always in a hurry. I leap before looking, but this time around I did look. And I did not even leap! Probably if I had leaped, things would be different. Probably." Utibe had sighed, so did the others.

*   *   *

The script ended, but Ekam was reluctant to leave. She looked at Naomi and actually requested for the pages that follow. The story had at that point got the girl fairly nervous. She wanted to know how it all ended. Naomi understood but told her that she had to cook for her family. Ekam left reluctantly, only to appear the next day earlier than usual for what she felt would be the end of a tense story. She continued, however, to marvel at Naomi's storytelling ability that made a third party narration sound like a personal experience. She looked forward to the following day, incidentally a Saturday, when the final episode may come her way.

Chapter 14

The moon had just climbed to the center of the sky. It shone with all its glory and majesty, a perfect roundness, stainless, and dazzling with a yellowish hallow about it. The sky was midway betwixt blue and gray. Stars dotted the blue parts of the sky. It was one of those nights adults loved to sit around and tell folktales to children while elders pulled sedately at their rustic pipes. It was one of those nights children would rather be on their own, the innocent playing, singing, and dancing while the not-so innocent preferred the game of hide and seek in pairs of the opposite sex.

Imata was one of those who relished this glory of the universe. She had come home to see her parents after a long absence. She had postponed her trip to the village several times despite several messages from home regarding the poor state of her mother's health. Although she met her mother in fairly good health, she did not regret her decision to visit home as it gave her an opportunity to have some rest.

That night, she had pondered on city life briefly, how city dwellers hardly and in fact did not notice the birth, maturity, and death of each moon; and how they missed the purity of nature as evidenced by the clean night air, the caressing moon rays, the rustling of leaves by the gentle movement of breeze, the singing of the birds, each at a different time of day, culminating in the hooting of the owl at night and the crow of the cock early in the morning as folks struggle to catch the last of blessed sleep before the rough and tumble of day. She contemplated the pure water from the village stream, the paths kept clean by human feet, the well-kept compounds, and most importantly, the simple nature of the people whose needs and desires where simple thus making their pursuits of the mundane things of life simple. The simplicity of life and the serenity of the environment apparently contributed to the longevity of rural people, she concluded.

The sound of the *ntakrok*, a small wooden instrument for public announcements in the villages, unfortunately truncated her reverie. It took her back to the world of reality. *Kpoi, kpoi, kpoi, kpoi* went the instrument intermittently. The voice that came in-between was hardly audible, but in the still night air, was still discernible. It was that of a woman. As it drew nearer, it could be heard more as a wail and then a supplication. Imata listened intently, her whole body surprisingly tensed up. Something was amiss. *Kpoi, kpoi, kpoi, kpoi,* the sound continued.

"Hear, my people," the shrill voice announced.

"I say hear me everybody." *Kpoi, kpoi, kpoi, kpoi.* The air of suspense is not lost on village people on such errands.

"Children, elders, strangers, and indigenes, pagans and churchgoers, witches and wizards, the good and the bad, the dead and the living, gods and goddesses, I say give me your ears." *Kpoi, kpoi, kpoi, kpoi.*

"Wake up, everybody. Men on their women please climb down and listen first. You may continue thereafter if you still have the appetite to do so."

By now, the voice was very distinct. It seemed to have stopped in front of Imata's family house. Imata was tensed up the more.

"Wake up those that are asleep for we cannot sleep when there is fire on our roof. We cannot sleep when a cobra is at our doorstep. We cannot sleep when nature uses its ugly spoon to churn our stomachs. Sleep flees when death stands before us in blood and in flesh." *Kpoi, kpoi, kpoi.*

217

"I say hear me, people of Oboyo, village of the seven cobras, village of the cotton tree that walks on its crown at night, village of warriors and brave men, the village that women deliver four children at a go and live to tell the tale. Oboyo, where visitors trot rather than walk while passing through, I say wake up and hear my tale of woe." *Kpoi, kpoi, kpoi, kpoi.*

"One who has just one palm nut cannot be said to be stingy if he or she refuses to give it out. He who plants cocoyam expects to get seeds there from. He who marries a woman does so because he wants children. Listen to me, for as the tombstone said, 'Today I stand here, tomorrow it might well be your turn.'" *Kpoi, kpoi, kpoi, kpoi.*

"I have but one child. His name is Utibe." At the mention of the name, Imata screamed. Could this be the Utibe she knew? Could Utibe also be an indigene of Oboyo? Unbelievable! What an unfortunate coincidence that would be! Meanwhile, Nya continued while Imata hoped the Utibe she knew had nothing to do with the one Nya was talking about.

"It is no secret how I got the child. If children were bought with money, I would never have one. Who does not know the poverty that is Nya? God gave him to me. At my old age, he put milk in my breasts to feed him with.

"What do we want children for? I say why do we suffer to bring up children—so that they can give us a key to heaven? I say no. Can they accompany us on our journey to the land of the dead? I say no. They come on their own when their time is due. Is it just to ensure that they care for us during old age? Not necessarily. Many of them, particularly the men, continue to take from us till we die. Probably their bones will be used for our burial? I say no.

"Our children are there to give us respect at old age and happiness by their achievements, some of which we longed for but could not achieve. They also give us a decent burial, for the burial of the childless is worse than that of the penniless. Most importantly, we have children so that people can say, so-so-and-so once walked this earth. Our children outlive us. They bear children and sustain the family name. That is why we always pray that we must never inherit our children's property because it is a curse. Our children must inherit our property." *Kpoi, kpoi, kpoi, kpoi.*

"But my people, someone is about to make me childless. Someone is about to make me inherit things from my son. Someone is about to make my old age a curse. Someone is about to make me die unsung, without mourners, and finally dumped in a grave like the carcass of a cat or a diseased cow. I am saying that if you don't wake up, my son will soon be a name whispered secretly and I, a thing to be avoided and mocked at in the name of consolation." Then in frenzy she continued.

"I say—that Imata is about to kill my son to satisfy her sexual desire for him. A woman has a right to reject the advances of a man without suffering for it. I say—has a man no such right? Must my son's life be sacrificed to placate the hurt pride of a vagabond who has never tasted the pains of childbirth or spent a sleepless night to see a child through a combination of fever, cough, frequent stooling, and stomachache?

"Here is a woman who has never trembled before a preacher because of fear of a revelation to the effect that on one of those sticky nights, she did run to the juju priest to help remove evil spirits from her child when all medicines failed. Has she ever found herself tongue-tied when caught while delivering a pack of lies to a medical doctor, asking questions on self-medication? Does she know what it takes to satisfy a hungry and sexy husband while ensuring that the demands of the children are not given a second place?"

Nya paused for breath, blew her nose, and continued beating the *ntakrok*. Imata had not noticed that her brother, Ikafia, had left the house with a knife and made toward Nya. Nya was also too occupied with her emotions to notice the approaching shadow. She continued her tirade.

"My people, that is Imata, the ageless butterfly with straight breasts that never fall, who perches on every new flower, sucking the nectar till the flower wilts, only to fly away younger and more beautiful to the next unfortunate flower. I say—will you sleep while . . ." She was cut short by Imata's brother who violently pushed her away, threatening to cut off her head with the gleaming knife in his hand if she continued.

"You should not have done that," Imata managed to say when she recovered a bit after Nya had left and her brother had come back to the house.

"Why not?" fumed her brother. "How can you sit at the foot of the *ekom* tree to eat the fruits thereof? She can do what she wants to do but not in front of my father's house. I won't live to witness such insult."

Nya had taken off, now in a trot, screaming her head off. "Help! Help! Help!" she screamed, beating the ntakrok as she ran. "Imata has killed my son. Now her brother wants to kill me. I say help. The father of the village, our forefathers, men and women, boys and girls, strangers and visitors, man and animal, gods and goddesses, stop sleeping. Come and help a lone flame about to be put off. Help! Help! Help!" The voice sounded distant till it tapered and finally died off.

Once again, there was stillness. The insects resumed their chirping as if nothing had happened. There was a fierce struggle in the room close to Imata, a death fight between a cat and a rat. The struggle soon ceased, with the squeals dying off slowly and the cat emerging and walking victoriously with the prey in its mouth. Imata's flesh crawled at the sight. "Another victim," she thought.

Outside, the air became chilly. Dark clouds gathered, rushing past the moon that seemed to struggle to regain control of the sky. The gentle breeze became a shade harsher and harsher and then almost violent, gathering dust particles, leaves, and broken branches in its wake. The sound of thunder was the last straw. Everyone went indoors, closed their doors, and checked the windows to ensure that the bolts were in place. Those with makeshift windows or doors felt once more the strength of the supporting sticks that wedge the windows or doors or both. Women placed pots and pans at strategic places outside while those with leaking roofs placed the same at the leaking points. It was surprising that everyone seemed to have forgotten that this was the peak of the dry season and that rains were not expected for at least two months hence.

*   *   *

The night following Nya's disturbing announcement, Imata was reclining on her father's "easy chair" in the family living room after a good night's meal of *fofo* and bitter leaf soup, laced with bonga fish and a lot of pepper. Her dessert was sliced cassava chips sprinkled with salt, which she ate with salted fish called *ekpumo*. It was her favorite dish. Imata felt at peace with the world for once. The cares of life, which had been telling on her, seemed to have receded. The discovery that Utibe could be her blood brother had weighed her down all day, but the tension appeared to be receding. Still as the end of the ordeal could not be determined, her mind went back to it frequently, and each time, she experienced violent palpitations. She was all regrets, but like most regrets, it came too late. She did not know how to assist. However, she decided to relax and wait, hoping for the best.

Meanwhile, Ikafia went and sat by his sister. He was quiet for some time, to Imata's serious discomfort.

"Can I ask a question?" Ikafia ventured.

"That is strange," Imata replied. "You are not known to ask people for their opinion before you speak or act."

"Maybe."

"Please speak," Imata urged.

"This Utibe business, does it resemble you?"

"Why do you ask?"

"You have always said, and for all I know, you have kept your words that no man from Oboyo will ever see the color of your underwear, except when you hang them out to dry. How could you have been involved in a relationship of a fatal nature with Utibe?"

"It is difficult to explain."

221

"Are you sure it is not another Utibe that you were involved with?"

"It could not have been. With the story I have heard so far, the Utibe that is dying, God forbid, is the one I met at Calabar."

"How did you meet him?"

"That is a question for the gods. When you meet people in the city, you don't start a relationship by asking them where they come from or whether their grandmas still have teeth to chew stockfish. You ask them what they do for a living, where they live, and for us ladies, whether the men are married or single. What is of interest is what you can get from them, not where they come from. Such questions only come if marriage becomes an issue."

"So you mean you did not know that Utibe is from Oboyo?"

"Absolutely not. I would not have touched him with a foot-long pole. I have never had an affair with a man from Oboyo or the neighboring villages, well until this fatal one. The reason for my apparent discrimination is that I just don't want any man to come here and brag—*that one I have finished with her-o.* Let it be from a stranger, not an indigene, which to me include men from the neighboring villages of Obo Atai, Mbiakọt, Ukat, and Ikọt Ofiọk."

Ikafia apparently had more questions, but he did not feel like asking. He thought for a while and sighed deeply.

"All the same, nothing really happened," she said when she observed his reluctance to leave or to ask further questions, even when it was obvious he had more questions.

"What does that mean?"

"That he did not sleep with me, well because he refused to."

"How then would things have gone this way?"

"The fault was mine really," she said and paused as her voice cracked. "I took him to Esa Iban Isọñ."

"Disaster! But why?"

"He said I smelled."

"Did he actually use those words?"

"You appear to doubt me."

222

"It is not like that. But Utibe—he is an Ibibio man, more so he had lived at Ine. He should know better."

"How many people really know things better? How many people live by their experiences? Anyway, as I had said, only God knows why this has happened and how this will end," she paused and wiped tears from her eyes and cheeks. She blew her nose too. "What can pride not do, *eh*? My hurt pride pushed me to take a simple case to a complex place. His pride made him decide not to do what the women decided. Now it is 'had I known' for the two of us."

"If I know anything about those women, it is simply too late to do anything," Ikafia said and sighed.

"Too late for him, too late for me. The most painful thing is that he is largely innocent. He spoke those words, but I put them in his mouth. I made sure he spoke those words. How can an innocent person die? Why can't the gods be flexible? They know the truth, but they never shift ancient boundaries. The arithmetic is simple, if this, then that. Anything in-between is not recognized. What kind of world is this? If an innocent person dies just as a guilty person dies, should people not just go ahead and do what is bad? Why should people take all the trouble to do what is good—or at least avoid what is bad?" Ikafia had no answer. He sighed, sat for quite some time with this mysterious kith of his that he had always wished he could be close to or at least understand. Probably her family's distance from her had contributed to the way she turned out. For all her waywardness, Ikafia knew he loved her like he loved his mother. This was his blood that had gone sour, and like the elders would say, the blood in a person's mouth presents a terrible dilemma—one is unable to swallow it and unable to spit it out. As she continued to cry and he always felt extremely uncomfortable wherever people are crying, he reluctantly left her, although he knew she needed his presence.

After Ikafia left, Imata dozed off. She floated between sleep and wakefulness, dreaming, or she thought she did, of a glittering world of a monarch with Utibe as the king and herself as the queen, walking hand in hand in all majesty with an unworldly music floating afar. There was a full complement of court attendants, jesters, lords, ladies, and all, a scene she had seen a number of times in cinema houses.

Suddenly, something she could not explain jerked her out of her dream. She listened intently to pick up any faint sounds in the still night air of Oboyo village. Her skin crawled, and she started looking all about her for signs of intruders. She wished her mother were around. She looked more intently. Nothing was in sight. Her heartbeat increased at a violent pace. Then she *heard* it. It was the sound of a cockcrow!

Her eyes darted to the grandfather clock on the wall. It was thirteen minutes past the hour of ten. Thirteen minutes past ten o'clock! And a cockcrow!

She decided to push it to the back of her mind. But it came up forcefully particularly when she remembered that a vulture had perched on the roof of her family house earlier in the day. The raven also crowed all day. "Go to where there are many spoons and many plates," she had intoned, smiling at such superstition. And now!

She struggled to come up with something that could explain away the cockcrow and so calm her fears. Probably the clock was not working well. But that was far-fetched for the 1925 clock was known to have justified whatever was spent on acquiring it. It was called Big Ben after the eternal clock on the Tower of London. She dared to look at her wristwatch. The difference was just two minutes on the faster side, likely hers being the wrong one. Had she not slept off a long while before?

"Maybe it was not a cockcrow after all," she thought to herself. That thought was yet to die in her mind when another and more distinct crow pierced the stillness of the night. She was visibly agitated by now. Her mother rushed into the room. Imata felt grateful and less jittery. They looked at each other briefly. The eyes said it all.

"It is not a good sign," Imata's mother remarked. No response came from her daughter.

"That cock should be killed immediately," the woman said again, a command to no one in particular. Imata only licked her lips. The cock might have been killed already, but the message had been conveyed. All they could do was to sit and wait, an almost endless wait for eight hours before daybreak. The slow movement of information to someone in need of immediate news can be an agonizing experience. In a village and in particular in the night, information moves slower than the speed of a snail.

Imata and her mother did not have too long to wait however. Sleep had not come actually as Imata had been in a state of suspended animation for the period. She found herself unable to think at all, to which she was grateful.

Then it happened. At exactly thirteen minutes past the hour of midnight, a wail issued from the direction of Utibe's house. It was long, but soon ended abruptly—as abrupt as it had started—the wail of a woman in an agony that will be perpetual. A wail proclaiming a transition, a wail proclaiming death.

Chapter 15

The night had been that of extremes of emotions for Utibe's household. At sunset, he had seemed to be in very high spirits, singing his favorite songs and even simulating a dance with any part of his swollen body that could permit such. The happiness pervaded the entire household.

It had to be so. The day before, the witch doctor from Afia Nsit Udua Nkọ village had performed the last ritual that was supposed to free Utibe from the clutches of the evil forces that bound him in a clasp of death. The old man was famed for his magical feats, having delivered hundreds of people miraculously from the mouth of the grave. He did express doubts, for as he said, fighting the magical powers of womanhood is like fighting the supreme being directly. Women bear life, he had said, and since they bear life, they can also take life with greater ease than men, who have to rely on physical means more often for those of them that believe taking life is fun. Yet he was prevailed upon and he accepted, for the singular reason that "a chicken cannot die when trampled upon by its mother," a proverb that listeners found impossible to decode or relate to the present context. Yet they held their peace, grateful enough that he had agreed in the first instance to try something.

There was happiness despite the juju priest's parting words to the effect that "only God is all-powerful." The happiness was accentuated by Utibe's lightness of heart and the fact that he requested for his favorite meal of soaked and salted garri with fried groundnuts. Only his father winced at the request.

At about eight o'clock that night, he suddenly relapsed. He was intensely feverish, becoming incoherent, and even foaming from his mouth and nostrils. This alternated with bouts of intense coldness and spasms, which on each occasion made the heartbeats of onlookers temporally cease. This sudden change from signs of recovery to near death was not strange to Utibe's father. He had known that the end was near when Utibe asked for his favorite food.

"I am afraid," he addressed nobody in particular. "The upper eyelid of my left eye has been dancing these last two days. I am afraid."

At a point, Utibe started speaking in tongues and then discussing with people long dead, the names of whom he mentioned. These included his grandfather, his uncle, his mother's closest friend, and his first girlfriend, which he kept saying, "The cock and hen will never be separated again."

*   *   *

The little crowd around Utibe had also heard the crow of the cock. It was not in their house for there was none in the henhouse. There was subdued weeping when this was heard. Nya clung to her son so tightly the skin depressed on those parts as if her hands would sink in. No one had the courage to pull her away. The cock crowed two more times before the fourth was stopped halfway, apparently by the owners who must have killed it.

Everything remained still till one minute past midnight when Utibe's breath started coming in gasps. The crowd had been waiting in expectancy, just waiting, helpless, but with strong hopes, which is only human even in the face of complete hopelessness. Utibe's mother in particular could never bring herself to believe that Utibe could be anything but her lively son.

227

At twelve minutes past midnight, Utibe opened his eyes for the first time in many hours, surveyed the sympathetic faces around him, and smiled weakly. Then he fixed his face on his mother for a long time. He sighed, jerked forcefully upward as if struggling to escape from a strangling rope, collapsed in a heap, and gave out one long sigh. He was gone!

There was a minute of general indecision. Everything stood still. Utibe's father held Utibe's pressure point at the wrist. There was no movement. He knelt down and listened to his heartbeat. There was none. He touched his feet. They were cold. He stood up, straightened, held his hips, sighed, and declared, "He has gone to our forefathers." To which Nya gave out one long scream as she was wont to and which was heard all over the village and beyond. Then she lapsed into quiet discourse with herself.

*   *   *

"My god, if you are and if you really exist, what did I do? What crime did I commit in this life or the life before? Is it my sin or the sins of my forefathers? Why did you not forgive? We were taught that you are the all-forgiving father. Did I not go for confession before your representatives on earth or were those not genuine enough and acceptable to you? Or you did not just listen to my confessions? But it is you who gave me this child. Years I prayed for one. None came. Then you led me in a dream to where I could get a child. It was a dream child, good, obedient, hardworking, handsome, pleasing, and promising. You answered my prayers. I went to church regularly. I ensured that he always went to church too. I pay tithe. I even attend Sunday school that many Christians find boring or believe is for children that require more spiritual food. I have always been a good member of the church." She wept silently, cleared her throat, and continued.

"Where did I go wrong? What did I not do or did wrongly? What is a woman without a child? Who is she without a son, at least a son-in-law? Sons do not give their mothers their used clothing. But they give their mothers pride, boldness, and respect.

It is they who can face a lioness that attacks their mothers even when they, the sons, are powerless before it. Enemies think twice before they invade a woman's home when they remember that her son is there." She stopped, coughed, spat on the ground, and beat her chest repeatedly. "It is one's son who buries one. Who has not witnessed the burial of the childless? Can there be much noise and color? People will drink, dance, and chew but will always remember to remark *she was childless*, or worse still, *she was barren*. Who has forgotten the song that followed the burial of Nne Nko? The burial was grand to the surprise of everybody. Everyone came, saw, ate, drank, chewed, danced, and made merry. But it was her only daughter's boyfriend that paid the bills. The day after, Iban Isǫŋ came out with a song:

> Who said loving is not good
> Who said a lover is not good
> We all thought, yes we thought
> That Nne Nko will go unsung
> But she went like a princess
> Who by? We all saw
> Her daughter's friend
> Yes, her daughter's boyfriend.

"It was a song of praise but pregnant with meaning." She fell silent for a while then wailed again and continued her monologue.

"The gods of our fathers, why have you abandoned your child? Probably because I did not pour libation, I did not offer sacrifices. But I am only a woman. Women do not approach the gods, except if they are ordained to do so. I am not a chosen one. Did our elders not say that parents should not inherit wealth from their children? Did they not say that it is only the parents that can leave debts to the children, not the other way round? Why must Nya be different always? Why must my traps fall on their backs rather than on their bellies? Why must Nya inherit things from her son? Why must I outlive my son?

"Am I going to dance at my son's burial? It could have been my son who would dance during my burial with a one piece loincloth hugging his huge waist, a feather in his hair, and powder on his face, his body glistening with sweat, his left hand bearing a bottle of *kai kai* while hidden within his armpits would be a bottle of expensive four-sided schnapps and White Horse whisky. These would be crowned with a grandfather clock in his right hand, dancing proudly, surrounded by his friends and admiring young girls and women. And I would be lying there, surrounded by mourning women who would sing my praises while also appealing to our forefathers to accept my spirit into their fold peacefully. They would be drinking *kai kai* and eating roasted meat or fish as they sing, knowing that I may hear but I would see nothing, as it is held that the dead has lost its sense of sight but not its sense of hearing. I would float peacefully and join my dear grandmother, who loved me so much she denied me my greatest desire. I would join my grandfather and my auntie, both of them leaders of song and dance groups in Oboyo. I would be gone a happy woman. Now where do I go? To whom do I turn? My son, my great son, my only reason for living, is gone, dispatched, of all reasons, by the anger of a daughter of the devil that no man has ever been able to satisfy. My proud son sent packing by a woman, my god, a woman that is only clothes."

She lapsed again into silence. Then she jumped up, walked as if in a trance, moving from one onlooker to the next, staring into their vacant faces.

"What will you write on my tombstone?" she asked each in turn. As no answer came, she swiveled, did a weird dance, and stopped abruptly. She then went to her husband, looked at him closely, and asked again.

"What will the world read on my tombstone? What will the writer put down on the cement block of remembrance? 'A child is honor,' 'a child is wealth.' What will you write on mine? 'Nya was childless.' Tell me, tell me-e-e," she screamed. "Won't someone help me? Is the world asleep? *Iya-mio, Iya-o.*'

Chapter 16

For a society that hardly believes that anybody can die of natural causes, it was routine business that a group of men, comprising representatives of Utibe's immediate and extended families, representatives of Imata's immediate and extended families, and representatives of the village council as impartial team members, be dispatched to find out the cause of Utibe's "untimely" death. The team left as early as five o'clock in the morning and headed for a location in Annang land where diviners abound. With Utibe's loincloth as company, the story was told which sent the group back, not in anger as it should be, but in deep sadness.

Seven days after Utibe was buried, the team set out with Ukpotiot as the leader. Ukpotiot was widely known as one young man who waged a relentless war against witches and wizards that were fond of cutting down young people in their prime. The expectation was that whoever was said to be responsible for Utibe's death would see hell right here on earth, especially with Ukpotiot as the head of the team.

The village council met as soon as it was common knowledge that a solution had been found to the knotty issue of "the mother hen and her baby." Many had thought that Utibe's mother had given her son to the witches as was sometimes rumored of other women. At the meeting were Utibe's mother and father and their extended family members; Imata, her mother, elder brother, and their extended family members; the village council members; and a select group of elders and leaders of thought. It was a solemn occasion.

"My people, I salute you, the chief of the village had said as the proceedings commenced. "We need not spend much time here. We are not here as a court in session to take statements and listen to witnesses. We are here to listen to the result of an inquiry. As is our practice, we shall accept the verdict of the spirits and base our action on it. I have already listened to them, but as our elders say, a chief hears a story twice. Let the leader of the team speak."

"The Village Head, elders, my people, I salute you," Ukpọtiọt had said solemnly. "Today is a sad day for me, as it is for my team. We went out with anger. We came back sober. I will tell you, not only our findings, but also the suggestions from my team on a possible course of action.

"We went to three—not two, not one—diviners. We wanted to be sure. It costed us money. It was trouble, what with our car breaking down often. Yet all the oracles said the same thing. It could not have been a coincidence." He cleared his throat, shook his head, and stamped his left foot.

"It is indeed the mother hen. Yet in this case, the diviners say, there are two mother hens."

"No human being has two mothers," one man interjected.

"Quiet. Let him put his words in the house," the chief barked.

"Who is a mother, who was your mother when you were a baby, a toddler, a child?" Ukpotiot asked. "It is the woman that wiped mucus from your wet nose, the woman who cleaned your anus after you defecated, who cuddled you when you were cold and wept over you when you were sick, who fed you when you were hungry and clothed you even when she was going about virtually naked, the one who cared and continued to care is your mother. So also, though to a lesser extent, is the one who carried you for nine or ten months depending on how stubborn you were and then screamed while you shot yourself into the trouble spot called the world. Utibe had two mothers, and both of them are probably here."

There was a low murmur in the gathering. People cast furtive glances at the two women whose lives intimately touched Utibe's.

"You speak in parables, my son," the chief said. "He that understands, understands. He that does not understand, does not understand."

"Before I end my speech, Chief, let me say this. My team passionately appeals to this council to tamper justice with mercy. Whatever was done was done in ignorance. Let the woman's conscience punish her. It will amount to double punishment to inflict any other punishment. I plead that you accept this suggestion, particularly coming from me since you know my position on matters like this," Ukpọtiọt concluded.

"We shall respect your views only to the extent that doing so does not negatively affect the welfare of our village. There is an abomination, I believe. If the guilty party is ready to do what should be done, of course, we shall leave her to her conscience. Otherwise, justice must take its course, which may include banishment. Meanwhile, Mama Utibe, what do you have to say?"

"Our dear Chief, elders, men, and women," Nya said heavily, "do not stare at me expecting tears. I have exhausted whatever I had in my stock for the rest of my life. No more weeping. It brings nothing. King David realized that thousands of years ago," she cleared her throat and blew her nose.

"I will not cry even if my voice shakes." She paused and looked around. "I thank God, yes, God, for I said something about my father in heaven when my son died—God is good. Now the world will know I did not kill my son. I know witches are heartless, but I don't think the worst of them would eat his dream." Again she paused, turned, and looked at her husband who nodded. "Yes, the story is true. Utibe was my son. But I did not carry him in my womb. He did not pass through my womanhood into this world." She paused again while a low murmur went through the gathering.

"I had said it again and again. Those who listened carefully might have understood. My grandmother loved me so much that she denied me my greatest desire, which I believe is the greatest desire of every woman, having a child. My grandmother was a witch. It was common knowledge. She sucked all the seeds that could bear children in me. She ensured that I had every other thing—material wealth, good health, a caring husband, love, and respect from all. Name them. Witches are capable of so many things, terrible ones at that reason. In the entire Bible, people are officially allowed to kill witches. 'Suffer not a witch to live,' so says the Holy Book.

"Why did she deal with me that way? It was because I refused to join her in a club that only very few eyes can point to where meetings are held and only few mouths can say what is done during meetings. I once said to her, grandmother, when the community says all weavers of mats should raise their hands, you do because you are one. All members of Iban Isọñ should raise their hands, you do so proudly. But when someone says witches should raise their hands, you don't and no woman does, why? She would simply change the topic of discussion. Meanwhile, she decided to deny me my greatest desire—children.

"We may recall that I came home one day with a baby. The day I arrived, my grandmother died. She was heartbroken! She did not know the secret despite her secret powers.

"It was at Akpabuyo that I picked up a beautiful boy, just one-day-old in the bush. I had just arrived and felt like easing myself in the bush. Behold, I met an abandoned child! I believed it was God's gift to a barren woman. I gave him my breast. He sucked it till milk came out. I nursed it, loved it, and when he became a real human being, gave him all I had. It was not possible for people to know because I had just come to Akpabuyo from Santa Isabel where I had gone to work to hide my shame after my husband married another woman who gave him children. I headed back to the village to announce that I had come home with a baby. Gladly enough, my husband accepted the baby and me and allowed me back into his house. He played a dutiful father to the boy. Three parties only—my husband, my god, and I—knew the secret. And between the three of us, the secret has been kept for over twenty-two years! But now, it is an open secret. Chief, that is my story."

There was silence for a rather long time. The chief finally cleared his throat and spoke.

"Imata, what have you to say?" Imata walked gently to Nya and held her in an embrace.

"My tears too have since dried up," Imata said solemnly. "In the city, I have heard people talk of the law of karma, nemesis, or whatever. Big, big words, which I know simply means you pay for your sins or your sins find you out later. I have always been told that for severe cases such as this, it is a punishment for an offense in one's past life. That may be true for Utibe, for he never did anything with or to me that could make him die young and in the way he did." Imata, on the other hand, is paying for her offenses in this very life.

"It so happened. I became pregnant at Lagos. I was about eighteen years old. I said to myself, how would this be heard? Imata who educated young arrivals on the art of birth control to be caught with an unwanted pregnancy? Impossible. Meanwhile, the fool who was responsible was a very poor man. He was a houseboy. I gave myself to him to spite his master who had used me and dumped me like a used thing called condom. The boy could not afford a decent abortion, so I decided to carry my shame to where I thought I could hide. I was delivered of the baby at Akpabuyo on my own. I refused to look at it. I did not even know it was a boy. I left it in the bush, praying that it will be another Moses to be found by a rich princess. You can see that God heard my prayer. A rich woman that wanted a child to love and to care for picked up the child.

"Now I know better. I now know why Utibe always said that something inside him told him that I am dangerous. I now understand why he kept saying that he gave him a feeling that we had met somewhere. Poor boy. Each time I tried to touch the secret part of him, it was as if a live wire had touched him.

He would jump out of the bed, which is why I kept asking him whether I smelled. Blood is too strong. His spirit revolted against what could have been a clear case of incest." She shuddered and said, "Imagine Utibe finding out that he had slept with his mother!" She then addressed Nya.

"Mama, Utibe is my son, your son. Probably it is good he died. Can you imagine the eternal shame on him, on you, and on your husband if he had made love to me only to find out later that I was the woman that bore him? Of course, by our tradition, the story would have come out, sooner or later, whether the deed was done inside the deepest well or at the market square. Utibe was my son, your son. We have both lost him. But I lost more. The Almighty God will comfort you. It will not be said that you died childless for you had one as Ukptiọt rightly said. I will die childless, for though I bore and delivered a child, I never gave a child suck. My breasts have rather been sucked by faceless men, whose only interest has been to suck them flat and drop them like an orange fruit without liquid. I never cared or loved a child. I can never claim to have been a mother.

"I have not ceased to wonder at all the events that led to this event. Why did I visit that particular tap that day rather than the one that was near to my residence? Why did Utibe go to fetch water when he did? Why did he not fight for water for himself but rather decided to fight for me? I did not ask him to. Why was I not attending the village association meeting at Calabar? Probably I could have met him there if he too was attending, and immediately, I could have lost interest in him. So many "Ys," no "Zs," for Z would mean the end or the answer.

"My position is that there is power somewhere outside of us all that controls every action of man and woman. That power is like the masquerade handler who holds the big rope tied to the waist of the big masquerade. The handler directs the movements and actions of the masquerade.

"Am I looking for excuses for what I have made of my life? Maybe. Maybe not. Maybe each of us can review our lives, for although we have what our pastor calls free will, there are too many things outside us that often force us to act against our wishes and even our decisions. At the end of the day, the thing that takes place, which we call our decision, may well be what was to happen, which made us take a particular decision rather than another likely better one." She paused to clear her throat and take a breath. She did not cry.

"My people, tell your daughters my story. The butterfly perches on every flower in search of nectar. What did it get instead? Drops of concentrated poison! People thought I was enjoying myself. One cannot call endless dancing and drinking enjoyment, what with hangover and blows from jealous men and women! And for God's sake, never abandon a child. Rear it, for it might be the turning point of your life. Tell those of them that live in the cities to visit the village often and get to know their relations and other villagers. Tell them to ask proper questions before getting into relationships. Ours is a small world." She stopped and remained very still, staring blankly into space.

"Imata, your case will be decided at the next meeting of the council," the chief declared.

"There is no need, my Chief. The gods have decreed my fate. I shall go where no one knows, and no one should stop me. I curse whoever tries to trace me. My mother, my brothers and sisters, forgive me. My father in the land of the dead, forgive me. If I join you soon, accept me as the daughter you always loved. Nya, please forgive me. My people, forgive me. As for me, I shall carry my load—alone."

She walked out of the court hall, her head held high with the same measured steps that always attracted comments. One year after, no one had seen or heard anything about her.

*   *   *

Ekam dropped the script on her lap and looked away. She could not tell whether it was the end of the story or another script would be produced—another day. Naomi appeared to study her emotions for some time.

"My daughter, that is my story, our story, the story of one young woman who led a bad life. It is a story that can be any other person's. It is not a new story, yet it is as gripping as any one that is stranger than fiction. One wishes it were possible to make Imata's case the last," Naomi said to Ekam who was by now looking tired. She wiped her eyes, which were glistening with tears.

"*Em*, auntie, well, is that the end of the story?" Ekam inquired.

"What do you think?" Ekam did not answer, making Naomi wonder whether her question had to do with the desire to read more or the desire to end the story.

"But if Imata has not been seen since, who told you the final part of this story since you are not from Oboyo and Utibe is dead?

"You can carry out what is called research, that is, you go out of your way to find out things. You dig deep, deeper, and deepest for as long and as far as your interest and resources take you."

"But why would you take so much trouble? What do you think you will achieve?"

"If someone reads this work, learns a lesson, changes, and becomes good, I would have achieved something great. Stories of the past are meant to act as signposts, either for readers to walk toward or away from."

"I understand."

*　　*　　*

Ekam breathed out heavily, adjusted herself on the seat she was sitting, and reclined backward with her eyes half closed. She allowed her mind to drift back to her days at the village of Oboyo as a little girl. She clearly remembered the moonlight nights. The emergence of the moon always generated much excitement in the village. Though its hues could cause increased heartbeat, its illumination in a most soothing way was a thing to be relished. It is a far cry from the punishing rays of her half sister, the sun.

238

Ekam remembered that the emergence of the moon always attracted boos from children in particular. At least, so she thought, the sound *uwuu* was specifically for boos. Even at her present age, level of exposure, and intellectual development, she could not understand the rationale for the boos when the people were excited and grateful to mother nature for another fortnight of reduced darkness. Probably *uwuu* signifies hooting in excitement.

Moonlight nights were periods to be remembered. Sated adults and well-fed children would sit around to tell and listen to tales, mostly those that had to do with ghosts. It was difficult to understand why the people relished spooky stories at night when every shadow, every movement of a leaf or an animal would give one an impression that a wondering waif was lurking somewhere, ready to spring on the defenseless.

She remembered that on such nights, while the innocent and good kids listened to tales, the not-so-innocent preferred the game of hide and seek, oblivious of or deliberately discounting the hazards of the bush, such as reptiles, spikes, and holes, because the rewards of the game were worth the risk. It was common to see the children disappear in pairs of the opposite sex, only to emerge later with the girls looking down—as if the eyes could be seen—while the boys carried their heads high in triumph, meeting later to compare notes.

A mischievous smile played on Ekam's lips when she remembered those heady nights. It occurred to her that moonlight nights in the village as well as encounters while searching for *afaŋ* vegetable, snails, and firewood, fetching water from the stream, and even on the way back from choir practice that was deliberately delayed by the choirmaster for less than noble motives, not forgetting burial eve ceremonies tagged vigil night, contributed to the decadence of youths in the villages.

"My daughter," Naomi broke into Ekam's reverie, "I hope I have not wasted my salt on the entrails of the porcupine. This one that you smile like a baby having her dream of breast-feeding, I wonder what is on your mind."

"Nothing, Ma," Ekam replied.

"There sure is something. I hope you will learn from the mistakes and misfortune of Imata, someone who, like you, walked on a perilous path."

"I have learnt a lot, Ma. A whole lot, in fact a frightening lot, enough to last me a lifetime. I shall try my best not to fall into the same ditch. I promise to straighten my ways."

Ekam wondered how such a coincidence could exist—same village, same start, same way of life, same place of delivery, abandoned child, and so on. She shuddered.

"Forgive my curiosity, but why did you choose this dangerous path in the first instance?"

"I would not know. All I know is that it was a personal decision. Our world has changed so fast and so much that someone with a good First School Leaving Certificate can't even have the hope of getting a job as a cleaner in an office. Yet that qualification fetched people big jobs ten or more years ago. Standard Six Certificate was a ticket to a teaching job with all the food and respect that used to be given to the village schoolteacher.

"Ma, I believe that to whom much has been given, much should be expected as our teacher taught us. Our fathers are struggling to shrug off that belief and that women's education is a waste of money since they, the women, will end up as mothers, wives, and cooks! Why would a father spend money to train someone that will be a househelp or a cook? So girls are told to wait while the boys complete their education. By the time boys have spent two to three years at school and the girl is still waiting, along comes pregnancy! She ends up the way her mother ended up—an article to be used and abused, never complaining, always grateful for the honor of being a wife and mother given the army of spinsters that roam the streets and churches praying for husbands. I did not want to be just a Mrs. This and Mama That. I believe I can live my life in a different way. I like my freedom."

"Freedom or license?" Naomi asked.

"Either. After all, the Almighty Creator has given us freedom to choose our paths. Because wives are more or less house girls, I think it is better to be on one's own."

"Will you consider marriage?" Naomi asked in consternation.

"If I must, I must. If I must not, I won't. I do not regard marriage as compulsory. What to me is a woman's debt to society is to have children so that the world will continue. That assignment can be carried out even outside marriage. And I have done so already."

"Those are sad words, my daughter."

"It is unfortunate, Ma."

"Meanwhile, where is the product of your debt to humanity which was a gift from God, a blessing that, like rain showers, does not reach every roof?"

"I don't know. I don't want to think about it. I can only ensure that I avoid like a disease, any male that is younger than me."

"But can't you decide to change for the better?"

"I am what I found myself. Too many things have happened in my short life that I never wished should happen. I had no control of them—they just happened. The only thing I had to do was to adjust myself to be able to live and continue living. Tell me, Ma, what did I do to Mrs. Nduke? Her husband did not even touch me in passing one day. He never showed interest in me, and I never saw him as anything other than my father.

"Now did I tell Ekebo to force himself on me? I trusted him because he is my brother. Auntie, that one pains anytime I remember, and I will never forgive him. See the flower I thought I was keeping for my husband or at least a responsible man that I can always be proud of. My mates had opened their eyes long before me. I told myself that no dirty village boy will boast that he opened me up. See an irresponsible man that has no conscious and no feelings took away my pride." She struggled with tears, brought it under control but spat as if the memory was a venom as bitter as the intestine of a porcupine. Having regained her composure, she continued her tirade.

"Then of course, why did my fellow traders in the market group deceive me so that my young business failed? And why did Enọmma refuse to see that I did not make the business to fail just to make her lose her money? Must I continue?

"Can you imagine an innocent girl going to government work and a man that should be his father in the office decides to force himself on her, and when she fought him, he beat her up. Then the innocent girl is sacked while the guilty big man goes overseas at government expense for treatment. Auntie, is that the world's idea of the thing they call justice? You are guilty because you are poor. You are innocent because you are rich. *E-he*!

"Even the child came—I don't know how. Look at that, just look at that. There are dozens of girls I know who change men the way they change loincloth. Some cannot spend one night alone without a man. Yet they never become pregnant. Why me, *eh*, why me?" Her voice cracked, and she struggled with tears and evidently swallowed quite some quantity.

"Ma, consider all the things that have happened to me since I came to this town, and particularly all that people I trusted put on my path against my wish. I doubt whether anybody could have done better," she paused and fell silent. "In any case, why did I have to come into the world in the family I came into? Why not the family of one of those rich people? Was I part of the decision to come to this world when, where, and how I did?"

"What is your plan now?" Naomi managed to ask for she did not quite like the things the girl had said. There was no doubt that the young girl, totally ill equipped to handle the difficulties and complex situations that came her way, was traumatized by not just one but a string of difficult events and circumstances. Her way of managing was to rationalize decadence as a means of survival.

"What I can assure you is that I have accepted that there is need for a good name and a good image. Ma, although I have read your script to the end and our meeting on this matter ends today, I want to assure you that I have accepted what you have said in the scripts and what you have spoken. I have put them in my knees."

"Before you go, permit me to ask you one question. How many times have you gone home since you came to Calabar?"

"For what?"

"At least for your family to know what is going on. Maybe they would have helped you."

"They might have made matters worse."

"How?"

"They have heard what is going on. In fact, they have sent messages to me to come home. But I cannot go because I am afraid they may force me to stay back in the village. Imagine your father saying, 'If you go back to that hell, you are no longer my daughter and spitting on the ground.' Worst of all, imagine your mother beating her breast and saying, 'If you go back, you are cursed!' Auntie, I don't want that to happen. I love my family. I don't want to lose them, but I also don't want to lose what I am enjoying here." She paused and contemplated and then added solemnly, "I will go back one day. We all go back. And when I go back, they will take me back. If they refuse, my extended family will remind my father and my mother that there is no forest where bad children are thrown into, and that to own a child, the parents must follow up and never give up."

"That is sad. People go home only when they are in trouble and when the rest of the world rejects them." Ekam appeared to lose her cool at this stage and blurted out.

"Auntie, I am not the first. I will not be the last. Parents know this kind of things happen, yet every year as children finish Elementary Six examination, they announce that they have 'finished school.' What next? The few that are rich send their children to secondary school. The majority that are poor say, 'Go to the town and learn the ways of the white man, after one year, come back and start secondary school.' How many ever go back home and start secondary school? For the girls in particular, they are more likely to become pregnant, and if they are lucky, they get a husband from among those that were sent to the city to 'learn the ways of the white man.' They end up in one room in a dirty compound, produce several children that may also end up as househelps and bricklayers and truck pushers and small traders and even pickpockets!

"What does the government do? Nothing. I say nothing. Have the big men finished taking ten percent? Have the men finished with innocent new faces as it happened with the shameless permanent secretary who attacked me? Auntie, you are in the Ministry of Education as you have said. What have you people done to take care of fresh school leavers whether at the primary school or at the secondary school level? You provide a few jobs to the Elementary Six holders as cleaners and messengers. Then you promote them every three years till they become chief messenger or chief cleaner and retire! They live false lives telling themselves that they are big men.

"Those of them with school cert* become clerks and rise to chief clerk or at best chief executive officer. They ride Honda Bentley, get married, have numerous children, and suffer till death.

"Meanwhile, the big men continue to be big. Their children go to Nsukka* or Ekpo Abasi* and return to be big men and women. Auntie, you are different, but our rulers and big men do not care for those of us from the villages and poor families." She stopped abruptly, lapsed into silence, and sighed deeply.

"But you should still go home," Naomi added more to keep the conversation alive and to minimize the discomfort at the home truths from this rustic girl that has evidently been severely traumatized by a faceless society.

"Whoever goes home, except during Christmas? We of the city go home once a year not to give our parents a little of what we made for the city. It leaves you with nothing after taking what it gave you. You pay rent, buy cosmetics and provision, eat, go to cinema, drop a few coins in the tray on Sunday. What do you have left? Remember it is said that what you make in Calabar you spend in Calabar. You just save enough to buy clothes that you will use for one week, walk up and down the streets of the village in the style that cinema people do, laugh even when there is nothing to laugh at or about then take money from your parents and return to continue from where you stopped. When you are there, you tell your mates big stories that will force them to force their parents to look for a family for them to attach to as househelps."

"Finally?"

"When you retire or you are about to die, you go back and die. That is all."

"Have you ever gone to the village since you came to Calabar?"

"I went there once. I told the most beautiful stories and my hopes and plans. If I had told my father about Mrs. Nduke, how she beat me up, or about Ekebo and how he forced me, not only would he have gone to the village head and send *eyei** to those people, he would have stopped me from returning. Meanwhile, I had nothing to give to anybody. Rather when I left, my mother gave me *garri*, assorted vegetables, and fish for soup. My uncle gave me a bunch of plantains. I was ashamed."

"So we are still where we were?"

"No, Auntie. I think I am a better person now."

"Thank you, my daughter, and God bless you," Naomi said finally, not very convinced that her efforts had registered any impact. Naomi asked Ekam to kneel down for a prayer. After the solemn prayer, Ekam thanked her again. They embraced and parted at sundown.

Epilogue

On leaving Naomi's residence, Ekam walked in silence down the streets of Calabar, still ruminating on the lives of Imata and Utibe, the events that led them to a fatal meeting point, and the way their stories ended. She felt frightened at the coincidences, and she was exceedingly worried about the need for her to start a new life so that her life may not be a notorious one to be used to teach children that are not growing up the way society expects. She wondered how she would start a new life, a life of all work so as to support herself and a life of drabness since she would no longer visit the cinemas, the nightclubs, and bars. She knew it was possible to live an upright life, but she was not too sure she would fit in. She was, however, determined to turn a new leaf, for who knows the child she abandoned at Akpabuyo could have been a boy, could grow up like *nkokot** only to end up being his mother's bedmate. She shuddered at the thought. She swore there and then not to have an affair with anybody that was younger than her, and in fact to go for those that were old enough to be her father if she must have carnal relationships at all. The only problem was that love, she knew, was one emotion that one could hardly control when it pays one, particularly a girl, even an unscheduled visit. There was always madness in the whole thing, and it was that same madness that pushed Imata into what she did not bargain for.

Along Inyang Street, she decided to sit on the lawn of the primary school and reminisce on the day she heard she was to leave home for Calabar.

*   *   *

Calabar! Ekam could not believe her ears then. Calabar, the city of contrasts. The city famous for matters of the heart and matters of the stomach. The town where tons of things happened every second, yet on the surface, nothing seemed to happen. Life was so relaxed, so unhurried. Even cars moved at the speed of the buxom maidens, despite the fact that the roads were almost never congested. The city that cleaned itself and its inhabitants. The city of peace and the good life!

Ekam had read and heard so much about this lovely city. Her colleagues and friends had woven dozens of tales around it, some tall, some true. The elders who spent their early lives at Calabar either as pupils or apprentices or househelps also told many tales, some seamy, some inspirational, from the fantastic to the ludicrous. Of course, the transistor radio her father owned started and ended every news broadcast with the word "Calabar." Newspaper articles also idolized the town.

Ekam had dreamed of the moment she would step into the city. A real life city! Her expectations actually went beyond Calabar *per se*. She thought less of the culinary delights, such as *edikaŋ ikọñ, ọtọñ, afia efere ebot, ukwọhọ* for which the culinary engineering ingenuity of the Efik women was internationally known and acclaimed. The musical way of speaking of the Efiks, the arresting and calculating gait of the womenfolk, the elaborate cultural displays, burial ceremonies, and near worship of the king, were not uppermost on her mind. What she thought of were the bright lights, the water from the pipes flowing right inside the house which would eliminate the boredom and tedium of going to the stream, the nightclubs and cinema houses her colleagues talked about, the fanciful dresses, the flashy cars, the amorous and blunt men with their myriad methods of approaching the opposite sex, the perfumed air, the big beds with linen sheets, the inexhaustible flow of hard cash, drinks, and food, and of course, the opportunities to become something. Name it and the city held it as she was told.

Face-to-face with reality, Ekam now knew that only very few citizens can dream of perfumed air while the majority must develop special apparatuses to strain pure oxygen from the stench and staleness of the city. Fewer still slept on big beds. The majority sleep on mats on the hard cold floor with heat and stale air oozing from several nostrils that share one room. Yet fewer are those that own great things, such as cars and surplus cash.

Ekam got back to reality when a car stopped forcefully close to the lawn. She got up and continued her walk. As she walked through Inyang Street, through the narrow Ephraim Street, then left through Abua Street, she burst into the wider Edgerly Road and thereafter into Chamley Street where nightlife was very thick. She quickened her pace as if she wanted to provide herself with an ultimate test somewhere ahead. But then she became quite agitated as she tried to explain to herself why her life had gone sour. And she started talking loudly despite the fact that she was aware people might think she had gone mad or the process was beginning.

"I believe this is how the Creator planned it all. Yes. The Creator wanted me to live this kind of life. If not, why was I not born into a rich family? I should have attended a secondary school, finished, got a job, married a rich young man, and everything would be perfect. Which kind of Creator is this that would give me so much brain but no means to develop it? Which Creator is this that would give me so much beauty without placing me where it can be used outside making idle men happy? Why would the world blame me, *eh*?

"Ekaete was like me—a girl from a poor family. Her parents sent her to Lagos, not just Calabar, for one year to learn more about life and return home to start secondary school. It was as if it was planned. She has even finished from Calabar Polytechnic, is married, and has three children. Why was my case different?

Why did Ekaete's madam be a mother to her? Till today, Ekaete still visits that family at Lagos. But Ekam? She was beaten black and blue as my English teacher said, except that my skin color did not change after Mrs. Nduke beat me up.

"I remember the case of Eno. And Nnene. And *em*—many others. Everything worked out. It was only Useme who ended up in a hotel as a full-time prostitute. Probably the Creator has a quarrel with the two of us. I wish I know why." She shed hot tears even as she walked down the busy road. Few things in life are as frustrating as not being able to come up with answers to questions that are tearing an individual to pieces.

"Maybe I should run home to my uncle? But I have nothing to show for all these years away from home. And my story has already reached home. Would my uncle embrace me or smoke his pipe while looking at something else even while I stood before him? Sometimes, I am afraid to go home because I cannot say how he will receive me. I now understand why Ededem has not seen his mother for twenty years. He has been living in Lagos, and once came as far as Ikot Ekpene, just thirty minutes road journey to Uyo where his mother lives. He turned back after the burial ceremony he attended, reason? Nothing to present to his mother. He will attend her burial ceremony anyway. One wishes village people would expect less from city dwellers. If one or two people have been able to go to the village and give something to their families, has anybody asked how that person or those persons made the money?

"Why would the world blame me?," she asked an elderly man who was passing by. The man looked at her in surprise, but with pity on his face. She moved on and continued to speak to herself.

"Why would a loving Father in heaven send me to Ekebo? He has the power to stop everything. He could even have made Ekobo to be a perfect gentleman, a good Christian. Why was my only friend allowed to push me into a merciless world? Where was my auntie when things were slowly but surely going wrong? Like the mother goat said, why would her owner wait till a lion came, entered the goat house because there was no door and go away with her husband? Then he came and built a strong door after her husband was gone. Why would people not invite the rainmaker before rain begins to fall?

"I reject any suggestion that I can fight the battles in my life. How can a man with ordinary hands fight a hungry Biafran* soldier who has a loaded riffle with a sharp knife at the end of the gun? I have nothing, yet the enemies lined up to fight me are so well armed with the worst weapons. Oh God, like one elder in Oboyo said, "You are up there and you cover yourself with clouds, both black and white. You threw down Satan when even you could not manage him. Then you said the good and the bad should live together. Have you not seen how the bad are eating up the good?"" She sat down at the entrance of Manila Hotel, pulled up her knees high, and tucked her head in between.

"God, I am not behaving like an ostrich that hides its head in the sand while the big body is left for the enemy to feed on. I am ashamed of what I have been saying about you. Well, I am sure you are used to it anyway. When the human beings you created fail, they blame you. When things go as planned, they may not even remember to thank you. For me, I would like to pay tithe, but your Holy Book says people should not pay tithe with the kind of money I make and money from sale of dog meat. Can you imagine that? Sellers of dog meat don't mind that anyway. Me, I mind, it is just that I have no alternative—no certificate, no godfather, nothing other than a fine face and fine shape, which you know what those ones can be used for.

"I have since stopped going to church because I am afraid you will not accept my money even as offering. But is that why you have abandoned me? I am not even a woman, for women may not have muscle but they can fight battles using their experiences. Which is why I failed in business—lack of *expi*, as it is called. I am but a weak sex, in fact, the weakest sex, young, no education, no experience, and no elder to lead me. Rather, the older ones I know are out to finish me by showing me the way to hell. My teacher would call them twats!

"Maybe you can give me another chance, yes, second chance, just like the evening school I attend. May be then, I shall change. But let me tell you-o, if you decide to give me a second chance without giving me the things I need, don't blame me if I fall back. Church people call it backsliding. So if you have agreed to give me another chance, give me things. In my village, if you give someone a farmland, you provide a hoe and a machete, otherwise should the person scratch the hard soil with nails or cut the thick bush with the teeth?" Then she cocked her head to one side as if listening to something. Presently she jumped up and resumed her walk, now quiet and composed. Nothing soothes like talking to a source you believe has the willingness and ability to take a load off your back.

Once on Chamley Street, she noticed a group of revelers having a party outside one of the houses. She paused to watch them. Women wriggled their bodies so vigorously it was as if their lives depended on it. The men jumped and kicked. Some danced with bottles of assorted alcoholic beverages held firmly in their hands or bottles of spirits under their armpits. "I will miss all this fun," she said to herself. She walked away from the scene. In her confused state, she did not look left, right, and left again before crossing the road as her schoolteacher taught in class. She heard the screeching of tires of a car as the brakes were applied forcefully. Onlookers shouted and rained abuses at her. She moved on as if she was not in the least affected by the close brush with death. She wanted to reach the epicenter of nightlife so as to test her resolve to stay off parties, movies, alcohol, and nightlife.

Her movement inevitably took her through Bassey Duke Street toward Fosbery Road. Patsol Cinema was way behind while Independence Cinema off Calabar Road was far off, but Luna Nite Club was close by and beckoned on her. She felt extremely nervous and had a sudden urge to empty her bladder but kept on walking down the road toward Luna Nite Club.

The screeching of the tires of the car generated in Ekam a trend of thought which put the final nail on the coffin. She remembered her trips from one part of the South Eastern State to another, including the one through Akamkpa, Ikom (Four Corners), Ogoja to Obudu. She remembered that reckless drivers, on seeing a vehicle mangled beyond repairs as a result of an accident, would rationalize their recklessness by saying, "That was the destiny of the occupants."

Destiny. She told herself that she believed in destiny. Inside her, a battle ensued. Two voices talked to her simultaneously. One reminded her of her dream of being the ultimate city girl and the fact that she was not suited for hard work again. The other reminded her that she hails from a noble family and that her auntie is but a shouting distance away. The first voice reminded her that her situation was forced on her by circumstance, and therefore, she could not be blamed for her misdeeds. The second reminded her of the story of Imata and the closing words of Naomi said in Latin, "*Vox populi, vox dei*," which means the voice of man is the voice of God. She had been shown the right path only recently, and if God will be willing to understand her past that she claimed innocence, the same God who had sent an angel in the form of Naomi may not be ready to understand a future of decadence. Ekam had no further excuse. She was confused but then stopped suddenly and said aloud, "Destiny is it. That was Imata's destiny. My destiny will certainly be different." People standing close by who were witnesses to her brush with death a short while earlier wondered aloud about her sanity. She ignored them.

She quickened her pace and emptied herself onto Fosbery Road, turned right, and walked slowly, very slowly down the declivity toward the junction of Target Road and Fosbery Road. Luna Nite Club was in full view, and the sounds of strings, pipes, and drums as they were being primed for action could be heard clearly outside. Revelers stood in pairs, buying Tom Tom, Hacks, chewing gum, cigarettes, kola nuts, and and related consumables for the night.

One more look at the pairs holding hands and moving into the club and the rationalization that Imata's destiny did not have to be Ekam's destiny, the young woman carried her head up and walked confidently toward the residence of Uko, her latest boyfriend, to prepare herself for another Saturday night.

Glossary of Some Vernacular and Related Words

isadok (p. 18)

Lowest quality of clothing material, but loud in color and rough in texture; it produces a lot of sound when it rubs on another cloth or as the wearer walks; used derogatorily to mean a person who talks more and boasts a lot but achieves little

fadder (pp. 18; 165)

The sail used in boats

oga (pp. 26; 54; 71)

Big man or important person

ajasco (pp. 36; 42; 81)

A dance style

dogonyaro (pp. 36; 206)

Leaves from a tropical tree believed to have medicinal properties

garri (pp. 37; 46; 200; 227; 245)

Processed cassava roots (ground, fermented, washed, and fried) eaten with soup

mbakara (p. 39)	White person (Caucasian)
odudu (p. 41)	A brownish low-flying bird, common in secondary forests or bushes
shit (p. 44)	Pidgin for feces
Ikọt Obio Ọffọng (p. 45)	A village in Akwa Ibom State known for the work of a man who molds human beings, animals, and other shapes with cement
440 (p. 45)	A competitive race of 440 yards in length
kai kai (pp. 45; 230)	Native gin distilled from palm wine
mononias (p. 45)	Pidgin for millionaire
editan (p. 75)	Local vegetable that has a mild bitter taste
fofo (pp. 97; 221)	Processed cassava (not fried) eaten with soup
osusu (p. 105)	Thrift savings
ufọfọp (p. 201)	Same as *kai kai*
ndua (p. 203)	Marshland close to a stream
ndidi (p. 204)	Highly tensile stem material used for making ropes
nduọhọ (p. 207)	A belief that lethargy or indecision can be induced in a person by

supernatural means by another person or being such that the victim is unable to take preemptive or timely action to solve a potentially fatal problem

School Cert. (p. 244)   West African School Certificate, qualification obtained on completion of high school in many West African countries; administered by the West African Examinations Council (WAEC)

Nsukka (p. 244)   Host city of Nigeria's first indigenous university; name at a time synonymous with higher education or grandiose words and phrases

Ekpo Abasi (p. 244)   Name of a street in Calabar Municipality where one of Nigeria's oldest polytechnics was located; use of street's name often understood to mean the institution

eyei (p. 245)   Yellow shoot of the palm frond; generally signifies danger or warning sign where used

nkokot (p. 247)   Green plant with a soft stem that grows very fast

Biafran soldier (p. 251)   A soldier that fought for Biafra during the Nigeria-Biafra Civil War (1967-1970)

Lightning Source UK Ltd.
Milton Keynes UK
UKOW02n1334271014

240695UK00002BA/6/P